OH
DEAR
ME

GEORGE EDMONDS-BROWN

Michael Terence
Publishing

First published in paperback by
Michael Terence Publishing in 2020
www.mtp.agency

Copyright © 2020 George Edmonds-Brown

George Edmonds-Brown has asserted his right to be identified
as the author of this work in accordance with the
Copyright, Designs and Patents Act 1988

ISBN 9781913289805

All rights reserved. No part of this publication may be reproduced,
stored in a retrieval system, or transmitted,
in any form or by any means, electronic, mechanical,
photocopying, recording or otherwise,
without the prior permission of the publisher

Cover image
Copyright © Sergey Nivens

Cover design
Copyright © 2020 Michael Terence Publishing

I dedicate this book in loving memory of Everild Edmonds-Brown, née Hardman (1941-1988).

Chapter 1

Peter Parker pressed the blade of his knife into the edge of the omelette on the thick white porcelain plate in front of him. To call it an omelette was, perhaps, too great a compliment to its creator. It was certainly made of eggs, as was clearly demonstrated by the streaks of pale yellow and patches of congealed egg white that punctuated its surface. Peter found that, by employing a gentle sawing movement, his knife made some impression on the rubbery substance. That, however, dealt with only half of the problem. On transferring a piece to his mouth, he discovered that his teeth were even less inclined than his knife to deal with the cold undercooked surface and overcooked base of the omelette. Peter turned his attention to the pickled cabbage and the mamaliga, a mushy ground maize that made up the rest of his meal.

'Tastes like shit, doesn't it?'

'Well...' Peter looked up at his dining companion. 'Well it's OK, perhaps a bit cold.'

'Look,' Stefan smiled, 'you don't need to observe your diplomatic niceties with me. It tastes like shit. I know it and you know it. If the Government wants to encourage tourism it has to knock these hotels into shape. Our beloved Ceaușescu talks about building a modern Romania, but these damn bureaucrats don't tell him how things really are.'

'Well,' said Peter, carefully 'I have to admit you are right. Western tourists will not come to these new seaside resorts if the hotels don't provide a basic standard.'

'I'm afraid that it goes a bit further than the tourist industry,' said Stefan. 'The whole system needs a big shake up. Do you know Ceaușescu visited a new factory last month to see how the agricultural machinery plant was progressing. The management were so behind in their Plan targets that they constructed the façades of some of the warehouses, to make it look like they would be able to begin production on time. What's worse, the local party officials knew it and, it wouldn't surprise me, if Ceaușescu knew it too. All that really mattered was that the President was able to say that the Plan was on target and that the newspapers could report it the next day.'

Peter was mildly surprised that Stefan was being so open about the deficiencies in the system. As the Second Secretary (Commercial) at the British Embassy in Bucharest, Peter was well aware that the claims of the Romanian government on the progress of the economy were not solidly based. Romanians were, however, very careful about what they said to foreigners and it was rare for them to criticise the regime in their presence. It was true that Stefan was employed by the Embassy as a Commercial Officer, but in some ways that meant that he had to be even more careful. There was little doubt that some members of the Embassy local staff had contacts in the Securitate. Most were probably required to file routine reports on their work in the Embassy and on Embassy staff. Many were loyal to the Embassy and, if they did file reports, it could be assumed that they were sanitised and not intended to be damaging. Others were less scrupulous and either through fear or benefit were prepared to pass on, to the Romanian security services, anything they found out. Peter wondered if he should encourage Stefan to be even more indiscreet. Certainly, any inside information on the workings of the regime would be helpful to him in carrying out his job. He decided to probe a little further.

'Do you think Romania can achieve a reasonable rate of development, even if it doesn't meet the Five Year Plan targets?' he asked.

'Who knows,' replied Stefan, with a slight smile. 'Anyway, to get back to more serious matters, I suggest you forget the main course and have some more tuiça.' He leant forward and topped Peter's glass up with some more Romanian plum-brandy.

'Thanks,' said Peter gratefully. He picked up the glass and took three or four large sips, blotting out the foul taste of the omelette with the more acceptable oily sharpness of the alcoholic liquid.

'I suggest we have some cake and coffee and call it a day,' said Stefan. 'Tomorrow we have to make an early start for our meeting with the Town Councillors.'

Peter nodded his agreement. He and Stefan were on a trade promotion visit to the eastern Black Sea coast of Romania concentrating mainly on the principal port of Constanța, but also visiting the tourist developments in Mamaia and the small coastal spa town of Mangalia. They discussed the programme for the next day, and the points that Peter should try and make to the local officials. Peter downed two or three more glasses of tuiça before Stefan stood up.

'Well if you'll excuse me, I think I'll get some sleep,' he said.

'Fine,' replied Peter. 'I shall just stay a bit longer and read through the papers for tomorrow's meetings. Goodnight.'

'Goodnight. The bill is settled so we can sort it out later from our subsistence.' Stefan turned to walk away and then stopped and added, 'Feel free to finish off the tuiça. It's already paid for.'

Peter lingered for another half an hour, topping up his glass three times in the process. He looked at his watch, ten minutes past eleven. He really didn't feel tired. The idea of going up to a cold bare room, which didn't even have a television, just did not appeal to him. On the spur of the moment, he decided to take a stroll before turning in. A waiter was removing the red table-clothes from the tables and stacking the chairs. Peter asked him if the front door would still be open if he took a short stroll. The waiter promised to ensure that it was kept open until his return, and Peter handed him a packet of Kent cigarettes, which he knew would serve as a much greater incentive to the waiter's memory than tipping him in lei, the local currency.

Peter slipped up to his room to get his coat, hat and gloves, taking care to make as little noise as possible so as not to alert Stefan, who had the room next door, of his intentions. Not that it really mattered if Stefan knew that he was going out, but one of the consequences of living in a police state was that one did not advertise one's movements. In Bucharest, it was scarcely possible to breathe without the Securitate knowing what one was doing. They seemed to take a perverse pleasure in letting foreign diplomats know that they were being watched. Here in Mangalia he had a feeling that he was off the leash although, if pressed, he would have admitted that he was probably under as much, if not more, scrutiny when travelling outside the capital.

Peter walked out of the hotel and down the road towards the sea. The night was silent. It was early February and the ground was covered with two or three inches of fresh snow. A few snowflakes were falling out of the sky onto his fur hat and thick leather coat. Peter pulled up his collar and lowered his head to reduce the area of his skin open to the elements. He had no idea where he was going, but somehow, he felt the need to explore any new environment, however desolate and uninspiring it might be.

As he trudged slowly onwards, he became aware of a figure ahead of him moving in the same direction. At first, he paid little attention to what was no more than an anonymous mass moving through the silence. Something was, however, clicking in his mind. By instinct or observation, he became conscious that the shape belonged to a woman. He quickened his pace slightly, so that he found himself gradually gaining. Yes, he decided, as he got a little closer, the figure certainly did belong to a woman. It was not the shape itself that confirmed this, but rather the way it moved. Peter was twenty-nine and had not yet found a partner to share his life. Most of his thoughts and energies revolved around his work. He had joined the Diplomatic Service a little later than his contemporaries and knew that he would have to work hard if he was to end his career with a Post of his own. He was ambitious and was more than happy to make the effort. There was, however, a part of him that vied with work for his attention. This was an almost uncontrollable desire for female companionship. Bucharest was very much a closed community; social activity had to be directed at, and solely at, members of the foreign community. This was mainly comprised of diplomats and their families. Single women were at a premium and Peter's successes had been limited to a brief relationship with the Head of Chancery's nanny and a short liaison with a secretary from the French Embassy. In the case of the nanny, the Head of Chancery had very quickly warned him off. He explained, not without some sympathy, that his wife, Pricilla, felt that the relationship was interfering with the girl's work and he would be very grateful if Peter could direct his efforts in some other direction. Peter obliged. The French Secretary posed no such perils, but the girl herself had met a Counsellor from the Italian Embassy who outshone Peter in both looks and money.

Peter did not, of course, contemplate for one moment establishing contact with the female shape ahead of him. That would be little short of madness. But he did allow himself the harmless fantasy of wondering what kind of woman was encased in the heavy winter clothes belonging to the shape. Her figure was upright and, by the rhythm of her movements, he surmised that she was young, probably his age or less.

Peter moved steadily forward keeping the distance between himself and the girl to some ten to fifteen meters. It is difficult to say for how long the pseudo chase would have continued, before Peter would have realised that following strangers in the snow was not such a good idea. Perhaps, it would have dawned on him sooner rather than later had not the girl suddenly turned left into a side street. This was the moment when, by all laws of common sense, Peter should have kept walking in a straight line. For some inexplicable reason he did not. He found himself turning left in quiet pursuit. It seemed darker in the side street and Peter had to strain his eyes to make out the figure ahead. Some thirty meters further on she turned again this time to the right. Peter, now committed, followed. On turning the corner, he was jerked out of what had almost become a hypnotic trance. The girl had disappeared.

Stefan Teduscu lay on his bed, silent and listening for the sound he knew would come. Eventually he heard it. The sound of a key turning in the door next door. Gently he eased himself off the bed and moved quietly towards the door. Listening intently, he waited. After a few moments he heard the door open again and footsteps move towards the stairs. With a gentle sigh, which registered his mild irritation at having his rest interrupted, he quickly slipped on his coat, boots, gloves and hat. Before buttoning his coat, he moved to his suitcase, opened it and unzipped a side pocket. With professional ease he slipped the revolver into a holster under his armpit. Still listening intently, he left his room, went down the stairs and slipped out of the front door of the hotel.

Peter looked around in surprise, but there was no sign of the girl. Suddenly he heard a movement to his right. Flinching and turning he saw a figure move out of a doorway beside him.

'Why are you following me?' the girl hissed in Romanian.

'I... I... I'm sorry, I mean I wasn't... I was not following you.' Peter's Romanian was good. He had studied for three months in London under one of the Foreign Office's teachers and had followed this up by working hard with the Embassy teachers in Bucharest. The need to respond in Romanian did add to his confusion and hesitation and he was aware that his accent still had a heavy Anglo-Saxon tinge to it.

'*Strain,*' said the girl. 'You're a foreigner... what are you doing here... what do you want?'

'I'm sorry... yes... I am a foreigner... I'm very sorry' he mumbled, not sure what to say.

'What are you? Russian? German?'

'No, English,' Peter replied, instantly regretting having proffered the information.

'Ah English,' said the girl leaning forward to look at him more closely in the dim light. 'And what does this Englishmen look for? A woman perhaps?' The girl chuckled softly.

'No... No, of course not,' protested Peter, trying hard to add conviction to his voice. 'Look, I'm sorry. I really must be going.'

'OK,' she replied. 'But you really should be more careful... Wait' she hissed her tone changing sharply. 'Someone's coming. I mustn't be seen with you.' The girl grabbed him firmly by the arm and dragged him forcefully through the doorway.

'Look...' protested Peter, but the girl firmly clapped her hand over his mouth.

'Shhhh,' she said. They waited side by side in the dark room. Outside they heard footsteps pass the door, stop and return and then move on again. They stayed silent, straining their ears for a further sound. Peter became aware of the presence of the girl, her faint fresh scent, the gentle pressure of her body beside him. They waited in silence, one minute, two then five. Finally, she spoke. 'Good, I think they have gone, but you'd better wait a while before leaving. Just to be safe in case they come back.' She turned and switched on the light.

Peter blinked at the brightness, even though the room was only lit by a single low wattage bulb. He looked around him rapidly taking in his surroundings. The room was small, apart from the front door two other doors led from it. The furniture was simple, but traditionally made of solid wood. A fire was smouldering in the grate and above it was a rather fine icon. A bookcase in the corner was well stocked with books and on two of the walls were Grigorescu prints. Finally, he turned to look at the girl who had removed her hat and was in the process of taking off her coat. Peter gave an involuntary gasp. She was beautiful. Her long dark hair and well-sculptured Latin features were well complimented by a slender but curvaceous body. Peter found himself looking straight into her eyes, which were brown, or rather, amber.

'Perhaps, Mr Englishman, you would like a cup of coffee?'

'Yes please,' he said, without hesitation.

'Do you take milk and sugar?' she asked in English.

'You speak English?' asked Peter raising his eyebrows in surprise.

'Yes,' she replied simply.

'But... how?' queried Peter, still hardly able to contain his astonishment.

'The English are not the only people in the world who can speak English you know,' she replied sweetly.

'Yes, but...'

'But what? You mean you didn't expect a poor Romanian girl, who you'd tried to pick up off the street to have an education.'

'No... well... that is,' Peter found himself blushing crimson. 'Look, you are right, but Mangalia is a small town and it is a long way from Bucharest. Not many people here do speak English. Where did you learn it? You speak very well.'

'Thank you. You see, although I live in Mangalia, I do spend most of my time working in Constanţa and Mamaia. Most of the time I act as a tourist guide, but sometimes I do interpretation for business meetings for the Foreign Trade Enterprises. So, do you take milk and sugar or not?'

'Yes please.'

'Which? Milk, sugar or both?'

'Both... err three teaspoonfuls of sugar.'

'You do like living dangerously don't you?' she said with a smile. 'By the time you are forty you will be as fat as a pig or dead of a heart attack.'

'You sound like my mother.'

'I hope I don't look like her too.'

'God no. You are really beautiful… I mean. Well you know what I mean.'

'I think so,' she said turning and opening one of the doors, which led into a small kitchen.

Whilst she was preparing the coffee Peter wandered around the room taking a closer look at its contents. The icon was really rather fine. The face of the Madonna was delicately painted in dark colours and coated with varnish. It was surrounded by silver leaf, which covered almost half the surface area of the piece. The Grigorescus were only prints but were of reasonable quality and mounted in heavy gilt frames. Peter had become enamoured with Grigorescu very early on in his tour. Romania's main Impressionist painter deserved international recognition; but was unknown to the general public outside Romania. One of the pictures was of a peasant girl making yarn on a traditional stick, the second was a rural scene and the third an excellent drawing of a donkey.

'Do you like paintings?' she asked, coming back into the room with two steaming cups of coffee.

'Yes, very much. Especially Grigorescu.'

'Me too,' she replied. 'Unfortunately, Romanian artists today are oppressed. They are only allowed to paint what the State wants them to, and that is usually portraits of Nicolae and Elena Ceaușescu.'

They sipped their coffee quietly for a few moments and then both opened their mouths to speak. Their laughter broke the ice and they soon found themselves deep in conversation telling each other of their life and dreams. Peter refrained from saying where he worked concentrating mainly on his early life, his family and his time at University. She told how she wanted to travel, how her big ambition was to leave Romania and start a new life in Europe or the United States.

After what must have been nearly an hour Peter stood up. 'Look it's getting late. I'd really better go.'

'You don't have to,' she said, standing up and moving closer to him.

Deep down Peter knew that this was the moment when he should politely give his thanks and say goodnight, but it was not to be. Overtaken by some inner irresistible force he took a step towards her and took her in his arms. From that moment the die was cast, there was no turning back. In what seemed like seconds, but was probably several minutes, their clothes were scattered across the floor and they were lying on the bed in the small bedroom, which was on the other side of the second door. She disappeared briefly into the bathroom, paused to close the bedroom door and was soon lying on top of him. Ten minutes later he entered her with a gasp.

Chapter 2

Peter was suddenly alert as he heard the front door open and bang to. He turned to the girl who was lying peaceably by his side. 'What was that?' Silently and swiftly the girl slipped off the bed, picked up a white cotton robe off the chair and covered her nakedness. She went to the bedroom door, opened it and looked out.

'Oh, it's you Nicu. What are you doing here?' At this point she entered the main room and closed the bedroom door behind her. Peter heard two voices arguing in rapid Romanian. Straining his ears, he tried to make out what was being said on the other side of the door, but the combination of the speed of the conversation and the thickness of the door meant that he could only make out a few words. He heard the man's voice repeat the word foreigner several times, each time accompanied by an adjectival expletive. Finally, he heard the girl's voice raised telling the man to mind his own business and get out.

The girl came back into the room and sat on the bed. 'My younger brother,' she said. 'He's always causing problems. Anyway, he'll be gone in a few minutes. He lives with my mother but keeps some of his things here.'

'Had I better go?' said Peter; suddenly conscious of the grave risks he had been taking.

'You'd better wait until he's gone and give him a little while to get home. It's better that you don't meet him. Nicu doesn't like me talking to foreigners. He's a keen party member and thinks we should keep away from Western capitalist influences. He strongly disapproves of my wish to go to the West.'

Peter looked at her. She still looked beautiful and wholesome. He noticed her robe had fallen open revealing lightly bronzed well-formed breasts. His eyes drifted down to her crossed legs and the patch of soft dark hair just visible at the bottom of the gap in her robe. He felt his lust rising again and leant forward and very gently kissed her on the lips.

'I'll stay another half hour, then I'd better get back to the hotel,' he said swaying slowly away from her. 'Will your brother report us?'

'No,' she said. 'He is my brother and he would never do anything to hurt me.' She smiled, 'and what do you want to do while we wait half an hour? Would you like some more coffee? It might be a good idea.'

'Well,' he replied. 'Coffee would be nice, but I know what would be nicer.' Peter pushed her gently back down on the bed and pulled open her robe. Her breasts were perfect; her nipples erect. Peter's mouth found one of the sensitive brown tips and began to suck.

'OK,' she murmured. 'You win.'

Nicu was angry. He loved his sister, but sometimes she was unbelievably stupid. There were plenty of decent Romanian men around, but all she wanted was foreigners. She lived for her dream that one day a Westerner would come, fall in love with her, marry her and whisk her off to live in the West. Nicu knew better. They were pigs all of them, capitalists throwing their money around and abusing the workers. What they wanted from his sister was sex not marriage, but she just couldn't see it. Even if a decent one did come along, the Party would never let them marry and she would not be allowed to leave the country. Nicu would happily have beaten up the foreigners who preyed on his sister, but she was older than he was, and he had always found it hard to challenge her. He also depended on her for much of his income, as she had a well-paid job and he was in his final year at school.

He picked up the packet of cigarettes from the stock he kept hidden at his sister's house. His mother still believed that he did not smoke, so he dared not keep them at home. He looked around the room and frowned as he saw the foreigner's and his sister's clothes strewn around the floor. 'They couldn't even wait until they got into the bedroom' he thought, his anger rising again. The foreigner's trousers were lying on the floor at his feet. Looking down he noticed a strip of black leather poking out of the back pocket; a small revenge perhaps, but now was his chance to make the foreigner pay for using his sister. He removed the wallet from the pocket and glanced inside. To his amazement a diplomatic identity card was prominently displayed held in by a cellophane cover. This could indeed be useful. Nicu removed it and slid it into the back of the cigarette packet. Putting the wallet in his coat pocket, he went to the front door, opened it and went outside.

Stefan was cold. He had had little difficulty following Peter's footsteps in the fresh snow and had arrived outside the girl's house just after Peter. He had walked backwards and forwards two or three times, making no effort to hide his presence by walking quietly. He had then moved on and waited several minutes before returning. This time he used all his skill and training to make sure that he was not heard. Several more minutes passed, and a light went on inside the house. The heavy curtains on the two windows looking out onto the street were drawn, but one revealed a chink, sufficiently large for him to view quite a large area of the small room inside. He watched as Peter and the girl sat on the settee and talked. He watched as Peter took the girl in his arms and he watched as the two threw off their clothes and disappeared through the door into the bedroom. 'Silly bugger,' he murmured to himself. Stefan never ceased to be amazed by the recklessness of human beings. He marvelled that Western countries could send out diplomatic officers so totally lacking in discipline and common sense. Fortunately for him human frailties were not so rare; much of his successful career had been achieved through exploiting such frailties. In his early days he had worked mainly on compromising Russian Embassy staff, but such was his effectiveness that the KGB were beginning to take a very close interest in him. The job at the British Embassy came at a perfect time to avoid unpleasantness and he was now a useful asset to the Securitate and, when it suited him and his masters, to the KGB as well.

On seeing that the couple were safely installed in the bedroom, for the time being at least, Stefan walked some distance away from the house and used his radio to call up a colleague in the local Securitate office. He had noted down the street name and the number of the house and asked for an immediate profile on its occupants. The house was occupied by Suzana Cuza, a tourist guide and translator. She did not have any strong affiliations with the party, but her brother Nicu was a keen member of the youth section and had already been marked down as a possible future party official. Nothing was known against the girl although, as her work brought her into regular contact with foreigners, she was kept under routine, but partial, surveillance. Stefan was satisfied from the information he had obtained that Peter had not been the victim of a Securitate honey trap but had merely been acting foolishly on impulse. Stefan returned to the house to wait in the cold until his Embassy colleague reappeared.

Fifteen minutes passed and Stefan was beginning to feel irritated by the thought that Peter's pleasure was leaving him both freezing and without his full quota of sleep. Still, he reassured himself, the information gleaned from the evening's activities may well prove to be extremely useful to him in the future. Suddenly Stefan was totally alert again. Someone was coming. He moved quickly and silently into the shadows of the doorway of the house next door, hoping that that was not the destination of the new arrival. Stefan was able to get a glimpse of the individual as he opened the door of Suzana's house and went inside. He made a rapid assessment concluding that the figure was that of a man and probably little more than a schoolboy. Given the way the boy went into the house, confidently and without knocking, Stefan surmised that he must be Suzana's brother, Nicu. Stefan returned to his chink in the curtain and, from the confrontation he witnessed between the boy and the girl, was satisfied that his conclusion was correct. He watched as the girl returned to the bedroom and then watched the boy remove something from the trousers on the floor. Unfortunately, the boy had his back to the window and Stefan could not see precisely what he was doing.

Nicu walked briskly along the street, keen to get home and examine the contents of the wallet more closely. More from instinct than from his physical senses, he felt a presence behind him. He turned quickly, but not quickly enough. Before he could react, he was thrown forcibly against a wall and a strong arm was pressed horizontally against his throat. An instant later his body was swung around so that his face was pressed against the ice-cold roughness of the wall. He felt a touch of cold steel pressing against the side of his neck. His knees turned to jelly, and he felt a sudden pressure in his bowels. He waited, hardly able to breathe, for the gun to explode and blow his head off.

'You are Nicu Cuza?' the voice was quiet, but was as cold and hard as the gun at his neck.

'Yes… s,' he stuttered. 'What do you want with me? I have no money.' How did the man know his name? It had to be the Securitate, only they would dare to behave in such a way and only they would know who he was. 'Look,' he pleaded. 'I am a loyal member of the party. I have done nothing.'

'Perhaps,' said the voice. 'Answer my questions and you will come to no harm.'

'Yes, anything you want to know,' said Nicu, beginning to hope that he was not in real danger.

'Where have you been tonight?'

'Just out with my friends. We went for a drink.'

'Did you go anywhere after you left your friends?'

'No,' Nicu was already wondering whether the interrogation was connected with Suzana and her foreign boyfriends. He felt it better to distance himself from her, both for her and his own safety.

The man's reply was swift and Nicu felt a searing pain in his kidneys as the punch landed. Bile rose into his mouth and he wanted to vomit.

'Did you go anywhere after you left your friends?' the question was asked in the same quiet, cold tone, as it had been the first time.

'Just… just to my sister's house to get some cigarettes.'

'Was she alone?'

'Yes,' Nicu knew almost before he spoke that it was the wrong answer. This time the pain was even greater; this time the vomit came.

'Was she alone?' the man repeated.

'No,' Nicu knew it was useless to lie. The man already knew all the answers; there was no point in holding out. 'She was with a man.'

'A foreigner?'

'I didn't see him… yes I think so,' Nicu added hastily before the man decided to punch him again.

'OK,' said the man. 'Now give me the wallet.'

'Yes… here it is… take it. I just wanted to teach him a lesson for messing with my sister.'

'Did you take anything else?'

Nicu hesitated briefly. He thought of the diplomatic identity card inside the cigarette packet. If that were discovered Suzana would be in great danger. To go with a foreigner was one thing, but a foreign diplomat was another thing altogether. Nicu was a courageous young man. He dreaded being punched again and knew that persistent kidney punches could cause permanent damage. But he had to protect his sister. 'No,' he replied with as much conviction as he could muster.

The man did not hit him, so clearly he knew nothing of the card. Nicu felt the man's hands frisk him rapidly. They seized on his keys and loose change and dropped them in the snow at his feet. He felt the man's hand clasp the cigarette packet and withdraw it from his pocket. He waited, trying hard not to tremble. It was several seconds, each of which seemed like an hour, before he heard the cigarette packet drop to the ground to join his other possessions. He suppressed a sigh of relief, as the man appeared satisfied with his search.

'Now listen carefully,' said the voice. 'I think you have understood which public-spirited organisation I belong to, and if you haven't then you will very quickly discover it if you fail to follow my instructions to the letter. If there is any further contact between your sister and the foreigner, I want to know immediately. Contact includes anything, visits, telephone calls, even a postcard. Is that understood?'

Nicu nodded. 'I'll try,' he said. 'How do I contact you?'

'There is a card in your coat pocket. Any information you have, telephone that number and ask for Colonel Babu. Do not speak to anyone else, only Colonel Babu. He will pass the information on to me. Is that understood?'

'Yes,' said Nicu.

'I am going to leave you now. Stay exactly as you are. Don't turn round and don't try to follow me. If you do you will regret it for the rest of your life. Understood?'

'Yes,' Nicu had absolutely no desire to follow the man. He waited, pressing his forehead against the wall. He was shaking, he felt his eyes watering and cold tears running down his cheeks. Still he was still alive, and the man seemed to have gone. Gradually he turned round; nobody was in sight. He bent down to pick up his belongings and recoiled in disgust as he discovered that they had landed in the pool of vomit at his feet. Cleaning them in the snow, as best he could, he put the items in his pocket and made his way home. He wondered whether he should go first to Suzana to warn her; but decided against in case the man had returned to watch the house. He would speak to her tomorrow; perhaps she would see sense once she heard about what had happened to him.

Peter got dressed and put on his coat in preparation for the cold night outside. As he was preparing himself to leave, the diplomat in him started to take over. He began to take stock. He felt a small pang of shame at his recklessness. Such behaviour, if it ever became known, was more than sufficient to get him put on the next plane home in disgrace. It was not the moral question of picking up a strange girl off the street that mattered, but the fact that he was now a security risk. Who was this girl? Had she been planted on him by the Romanian Security Service? No, he decided, that would have been impossible. Nobody could have known that he was going to leave the hotel and take a walk. The Securitate often seemed to know everything, but even they were not that good. This did not mean that he was safe, however. The girl might still tell the authorities about him. She may even be a member of the Securitate, trained to lure foreign businessmen into her bed to find out the trade secrets Romania craved so much. But she had not asked him anything. Perhaps she was a prostitute. Peter suddenly remembered how he had entered her, no protection at all. Christ, perhaps he had caught something. What could he do? He could hardly go and visit an Embassy panel doctor. Another thought struck him. Should he offer her money? He looked at her. She was standing, her robe now discretely covering her body, watching him. It was as though she was tracking his thoughts.

'How much do I owe you?' he said, moving his hand towards his pocket.

'*No*,' she almost spat the word at him, with a ferocity which belied her earlier tenderness. 'What do you think I am, a prostitute?'

'No, no… of course not… it's just…'

'Well for your information, I'm not. I do not make a habit of going with strange men. You seemed different, but you're just like the rest. You'd better go. Now... Get out.'

'Look I'm sorry. That was crass of me. It's just that you are so beautiful. I couldn't see why a lovely girl like you would want to be with me. I don't even know your name.'

'It's Suzana,' she said her voice softening a little. 'But you had better go. I am tired. I have to work tomorrow.'

'I'm Peter,' he said, suppressing the thought that even giving his first name might be dangerous. 'Will I see you again? I'd like to.'

'No,' she said. 'I don't think so.'

'It was nice,' he said.

'Yes, it was nice,' her face broke into a smile. She went to the bookcase and picked up a card. 'Here,' she said. 'Take this. If you come back this way you can take me out to dinner.'

'Suzana Cuza, Intertourist' was printed on the card. 'Thanks, I will.' He moved towards her to kiss her, but she gently pushed him away and ushered him out of the front door.

Peter walked back to the hotel. He still felt some remorse at his recklessness, but far more powerful was the elation he felt at what had been the most exciting, and sensual experience of his life. He arrived back at the hotel and crept in quietly. His elation stayed with him until he was safely back in his room and until he made a shattering discovery. His wallet was no longer in his back pocket.

Peter did not sleep well. He tried to remember what was in his wallet. Money, two credit cards and - he winced with horror at the realisation - his diplomatic identity card. What should he do? Perhaps he should go back, but what purpose would that serve. If the girl had taken the wallet, she would deny everything, maybe that was why she had reacted so strongly when he had offered her money. Could it have fallen out of his pocket on to the floor? He decided not, the wallet had fitted into his pocket tightly and he was sure he would have seen it on the floor. Anyway, if he went back what might await him? Even now the Securitate might be waiting to arrest him. No, better to stay where he was. Perhaps he could say the wallet was stolen in the hotel? How could he be held responsible if it turned up somewhere else? What alternative did he have? Only one, and that was to go to the Head of Chancery when he got back to Bucharest and confess all. They would send him home of course but maybe, after two or three years in Records Department, he could get another posting. He wondered if he could ask Stefan for help, but could he trust him? He decided to tell Stefan at breakfast that his wallet was missing from his room. Perhaps, if he left his door open whilst they had breakfast, he could then discover the theft on his return. Should he try and prevent Stefan calling the police? If he did, then his story would lose its credibility. Eventually he fell asleep, but that gave no relief. He dreamt he was strung up on a rack in a dungeon. Suzana was there, dressed in black. She threw her head back and laughed as she waved his wallet in his face. She moved towards him thrusting her face towards his own but, as it got closer, the face changed into that of a man in a black military uniform. The man raised his fist to strike him and Peter heard himself let out a scream. He sat up in bed, sweat running down his brow. Peter got out of bed and looked at his watch. It was 5am; he had slept for nearly two hours. He took the papers for the day's meetings out of his briefcase and began to read. He could not face his dreams again.

'Good morning Peter,' Stefan put down his newspaper and picked up the jug of coffee. 'Coffee?'

'Morning. Yes, thanks.' Peter sat down. His head was throbbing and every bone in his body seemed to ache.

Stefan looked at him. 'Are you alright,' he asked. 'You look exhausted.'

'I'm fine,' said Peter trying to smile. 'Just didn't sleep too well. The bed was a bit hard and the radiator was making a noise.'

'Would you like a brandy with your coffee? That will get the blood flowing again.'

'No, I'm fine thanks really. I'll just stick to the coffee.'

'Probably wise, I don't doubt we'll get our share of tuiça at the meetings.' Stefan picked up a paper off the table. 'Do you want to go through the programme again?'

'Yes,' replied Peter. 'Good idea.' He felt that he already knew the programme backwards, but work was probably the best thing to take his mind off his head and his wallet. Peter wondered whether to mention the wallet now or wait until they got back upstairs, when he could use the excuse of having left his door open.

They talked about the day's events for about half an hour. Then Peter stood up. 'I expect we had better get going,' he said. 'I'll just go upstairs and get my coat and case.' He touched his pocket and added. 'Oh, and my wallet. I think I must have left it by the bed.'

'Ah,' said Stefan. 'I nearly forgot. When I came down this morning the waiter gave me this.' Stefan handed him the wallet. 'He found it under the table where we had dinner last night. Better check it's all there.'

Peter took it, suppressing his astonishment. How could this be? Did he really lose it in the dining room? He opened it and quickly checked the contents. All his money seemed to be intact, Romanian lei, some dollars and five pounds sterling. Driving licence and Embassy gate pass. All in order then, his heart missed a beat, his Diplomatic Identity card was missing. 'Yes, I think so,' he said. 'No, wait a minute. My Diplomatic carnet is missing.'

Stefan swore silently to himself; the bloody kid had kept the card. Well he would live to regret it. 'Are you sure it was in there? I don't think the waiter would have taken it. Being caught with a foreigner's diplomatic pass would get him in deep trouble, and it would not be much use to him. If he had been tempted to take anything it would have been the dollars.'

'Well I think so,' said Peter. 'But of course, I can't be absolutely sure.' He was absolutely sure, but he thought it better not to admit as much to Stefan. 'Anyway, no real problem. I'll get Admin to replace it when we get back to Bucharest. Which waiter was it? I'd better give him something for his honesty.'

'Oh, don't worry, he's gone off duty. I gave him a packet of Kent and he was well satisfied.'

'Thanks, I'll let you have a packet when we get back.' Peter was convinced that the waiter story was made up, but how could Stefan possibly have got the wallet? Maybe the girl brought it to the hotel and Stefan did not want to embarrass him. He was glad to get his wallet back, but he was not out of the wood yet. It would be many months before Peter could relax and feel reasonably secure that some stranger would not approach him using the missing identity card as proof of his impropriety.

Chapter 3

Peter lay on his bed in his flat in Bucharest. It was about time they repainted the ceiling, but he dismissed the thought almost as soon as it entered his head. The flat, like those of most of his colleagues, belonged to the State, and was part of Bucharest's diplomatic ghetto. It was convenient for the authorities to have all the diplomats together. This made it easier to keep them under surveillance and, perhaps more important, prevented them from getting too close to Romanians. The flat was spacious enough, but it was rather gloomy and shabby. He was fairly sure that there would be eavesdropping devices planted in the walls, although the last time it had been swept by technicians from London, they had found nothing. He imagined that the Romanians knew when the technicians were around and had somehow temporarily removed the offending instruments. It was, of course, possible that the Securitate relied on the bugs they planted in the telephone system. When he first arrived, he had found it odd when Romanian telephone engineers arrived at the flat, without notice, to repair telephones that were not broken. Now Peter just accepted it as a fact of life.

His thoughts moved on from the ceiling, his landlord and the routine bugging to his recent trip to Mangalia. This was not the first time that he had gone over in his head his meeting with Suzana and the possible consequences. In fact, it would be fair to say that he had thought of little else. When he drove his car along the dimly lit streets of the capital, he found himself constantly looking in his mirror for a mysterious black car, full of nondescript strangers in dark suits. Frequently, he saw such vehicles and his heart would miss a beat. Sometimes they would seem to be following him but, so far, none had kept up the chase. It was no better when he was walking along the uneven pavements. Every stranger walking towards him looked sinister, and his surreptitious glances over his shoulder often produced someone who just had to be a tail. Even in the Embassy, he did not feel safe. A routine call asking him to pop in and see the Ambassador or the Head of Chancery turned his knees to jelly, in case they wanted to tell him that he had been found out.

To add to his misery there was Mavis. Mavis had arrived two weeks ago to take up the post of PA to the Commercial Counsellor. Mavis was tall and plump. She had dark frizzy hair and a complexion that had defeated the efforts of the various proprietary cleansing products that she had brought with her in her baggage. In short, Mavis represented just about everything that Peter found unattractive in members of the opposite sex. Peter had been asked by the Commercial Counsellor to meet her at the airport and to look after her until she found her feet. In itself, this did not pose much of a problem as Peter did not have a current girlfriend, and Mavis could prove to be an important ally in his day to day working environment. Peter showed Mavis around the city; he took her to the fish restaurant by the lake, where you could eat fresh sole, and to the Doui Cocos. It had been the Doui Cocos that had been his downfall. The restaurant, as its name implies, served up large portions of roast chicken, washed down with generous quantities of Romanian red wine. Gypsy violinists serenaded diners with expert renderings of Giorgiu Enescu's Romanian Rhapsody and, by the end of the evening, both Mavis and Peter were mildly intoxicated by the combined effect of the wine and the music. Of the two, Mavis was by far the more affected. Mavis had become bubbly, if such a word could ever be used to describe a young woman of such dour looks and personality. As they left the brightness of the restaurant into the darkness of the night, Peter felt Mavis' hand clasp his own. He felt her body press up against his and he heard her let out a deep-throated chuckle. Later on, he could never understand why he did it, but he did, Peter took Mavis in his arms and kissed her firmly on the lips. Mavis' reaction was immediate and unequivocal; she returned the kiss with a forceful passion, which almost knocked Peter off his feet. Mavis moaned and muttered his name. She took his hand and pressed it against her ample bosom. 'Oh Peter,' she groaned. 'I'm so glad you feel as I do.'

From that moment there was no retreat. He had driven her home and accepted the offer of coffee. She had sat on the sofa allowing her short skirt to rise so high that every inch of her solid thighs was in view. Peter had responded. Whatever she looked like in the office, in the dim light of the flat her exposed thighs looked inviting. It was only the next day, when he awoke with a splitting headache and staggered into the office that he began to realise what he had done. Mavis, for her part, was not going to let him forget it. When he arrived in the Counsellor Commercial, Jack French's, office for his morning meeting, she greeted him with a conspiratorial smile. For the rest of the day, every time they passed in the corridor, she stared him straight in the eye with a knowing smile on her lips. At 6.30pm, Peter packed up his papers for the day. He placed his trays in the combination cabinet and twiddled the knob. He turned and there, just behind him, was Mavis.

'Would you like to come round tonight for a bite of supper, Peter?' she said.

'Err,' Peter thought quickly. 'That's kind of you Mavis but I really must prepare the draft Quarterly Economic Report for Jack.'

'But that's not due until next week.'

'Yes, but it is quite a big task you know. I'll have to translate a chunk of the Five Year Plan from the paper, so I must at least make a start.'

'Oh, come on Peter, don't be such a workaholic.' She moved closer until he found himself pressed up against the cabinet. 'We could do it again if you like,' she said.

'Do what?' he asked, knowing only too well what she had in mind.

'Oh, you silly boy, you don't have to be shy with me. You know what.' Her expression suddenly changed and her face saddened. 'You did like it, didn't you?'

'Yes, of course I did,' he insisted. 'It's just that I really do have a lot of work and I'm a bit tired.'

'Well I shall tell Jack that he is working you too hard,' said Mavis, her lips moving forward to form a huge pout.

'Perhaps I could come for a little while?' The very last thing Peter wanted was Mavis pleading on his behalf to Jack French. She would probably end up telling Jack that he had slept with her and then abandoned her.

'Yes, just for a little while.' Peter could see from the self-satisfied expression on her face, as she uttered the words, that not only had she got her way but that his chances of sleeping in his own bed that night were very slim indeed.

Stefan picked up the phone and dialled slowly. He waited as it rang several times. There was a click as someone picked it up at the other end.

'Hello.'

'Giorgiu, is that you? It's me Stefan.'

'Stefan, how are you? It's good to hear from you. You were down this way the other week, why didn't you drop in for a drink.' Colonel Giorgiu Babu sounded genuinely pleased to hear from him. This was not surprising, as they had been friends since they had met on their first day at the Securitate training school.

'I would have liked to, but I had one of the Embassy people in tow.'

'That would be Parker, the Commercial Secretary?'

'Yes Giorgiu. On the ball as usual. You don't miss much.'

'Just doing my job old friend. What can I do for you?'

'Yes, I do need your help. Do you know a Suzana and Nicu Cuza?'

There was a moment's silence as Giorgiu considered the question. 'Yes, I think so. Brother and sister; live in Mangalia. He is up and coming in the Party's youth branch. She… she… yes, works for the Tourist Board. Quite a looker if I remember rightly.'

'Spot on,' Stefan never ceased to be amazed at Giorgiu's ability to remember the personal profiles of hundreds of seemingly unimportant people living in his bailiwick.

'So, what do you want to know about them?' asked Giorgiu.

'I just wondered if you could keep an eye on them for me. Nothing too intense just regular reports on anything out of the ordinary. The boy Nicu might possibly contact you to pass me some information.'

'May I ask why?' Giorgiu's tone was still friendly, but there was just a hint of an edge to it. 'Not enough for you to do in Bucharest, eh? To what do this pair from the humble provinces owe the attention of headquarters.'

'Giorgiu, I know I can trust you. This must be strictly between us. Do you agree?'

'Yes, fine. What have you been up to?'

'Well, my companion on my recent trip ended up in bed with the girl, and the boy saw them.'

'Ah, that could be useful. Does the Directorate have anything in mind for him?'

'Well, not exactly,' Stefan chose his words carefully. 'Look Giorgiu, old friend, this is one I need to keep in my own hands. This one is likely to go quite high in the British Diplomatic Service. Now he's worth very little, but in ten years' time who knows how useful he could be to us. I don't want any of those idiots at the Centre messing it up by putting pressure on too early.'

'Are you telling me that you haven't reported it?'

'Not yet, but I will when the right time comes.'

'Are you sure you haven't gone native? Working with all those cricket lovers can get to people.'

'No,' Stefan laughed heartily, trying his best to sound convincing. 'I know where my interests and loyalties lie. Have no fear of that.'

'Well I certainly hope you do,' Giorgiu did not sound fully convinced. 'And what is more important to me is that you want to involve me in your irregularities.'

'Listen Giorgiu, you know I wouldn't do anything to put you at risk. We go too far back for that. Anyway, my telling you this puts me completely at your mercy. If you wanted to you could destroy me.'

'Yes,' Giorgiu replied thoughtfully. 'That occurred to me too. Anyway,' his tone lightened somewhat. 'What do you want me to do? Just keep an eye and report to you anything of interest?'

'Yes, that's all.'

'OK, and how is the lovely Rodica? Come to think of it now that I have you at my mercy, I might have another go at taking her from you.'

'Rodica is fine and very pregnant,' replied Stefan with a laugh. 'If you do, I shall tell Elena and it will be you who is at my mercy.' Rodica was Stefan's wife. She had been on the same Securitate training course with them and he and Giorgiu had battled over her affections. Giorgiu had lost, but he and Rodica were still close friends. Giorgiu had been his best man and Stefan had reciprocated the favour when Giorgiu married Elena three years later.

'Ah you have me there. Congratulations on the forthcoming baby. Does little Stefan junior want a brother or a sister?'

'He wants a brother to play football with, but Rodica and I are determined to have a girl.'

'Then a girl it will be. I'd better be getting on Stefan old friend, there never seems enough time in the day.'

'Goodbye Giorgiu. Give my love to Elena.'

'And mine to Rodica. Goodbye Stefan and take care.'

Stefan returned the telephone slowly to its cradle.

Suzana entered her front door and went straight into the bathroom. She had had a heavy day interpreting for a group of businessmen and felt exhausted. She pulled down her tights and pants and sat on the toilet. Carefully she removed the pad and examined it. Still no sign. She was late, very late. Normally her periods came almost exactly on the day they were due, but not this time. She slid her hands up her jumper and touched her breasts. Did they feel sore? She thought not, but maybe it was too soon for that. Could she be pregnant? She thought back to the night with the young Englishman. Why had she not taken precautions? How could she have been so stupid? First, she had to find out if it was true; she would go and see Doctor Vlad tomorrow. If she was pregnant, should she ask him to end it? She knew he could and would if she asked him to. She had been a patient of Dr Vlad since her early teens and he had made his first move on her not long after her first visit. At the time she knew what he was doing was wrong, but she had not realised until much later the power it gave her over him. When she was eighteen, she told him that if he touched her just one more time, she would report him. Since that day he never had, but she knew he would still help her if she asked. But did she want an abortion? She shuddered at the thought. But what was the alternative? Then she thought of Tom, the gangly young English businessman who could not keep his eyes off her. He was very shy and easily became embarrassed when she spoke to him. But if her instincts were anything to go by, he only needed a little encouragement and he would be eating out of her hand. What was even better was that he would be on another sales visit next week. Yes… if she really was pregnant then perhaps Tom was the answer.

'Morning Peter.'

'Morning Stefan,' replied Peter, looking up as Stefan entered his office.

'How are you this morning? It looks as if spring has arrived at last.'

'Yes,' said Peter indicating to Stefan to sit down on the chair in front of his desk. 'I can't say I'm sorry, I find the winters here a bit hard. What can I do for you?'

'I thought you might like to cast an eye over the replies we've had to the export opportunities we sent back after our trip to the East Coast.'

'Yes please, any of them any use?'

'Well,' replied Stefan, with a wry smile. 'Nothing exciting, six replies in all. Two of those are not even for the products requested. Of the other four, only one looks to me to have the sort of capacity to be able to do business here.'

Peter took the bunch of papers proffered by Stefan and began to look through them. After a few minutes he looked up. 'Yes, I agree. It's a bit disappointing, all that effort and this is all British industry has to offer.'

'Still the trip was useful, I think,' said Stefan. 'We built up some good contacts with the local authorities and it gave you the opportunity to get out of Bucharest and see a bit of the country.'

'Yes, I certainly appreciated that. It's difficult to write economic reports and brief businessmen, if all you have seen is Bucharest and the diplomatic ghetto.'

'Next time,' said Stefan in a slow almost conspiratorial voice. 'We will have to go there in the summer.'

'The summer, why is that?'

'The girls,' Stefan laughed. 'They have some lovely girls down there, but in the winter, they are all wrapped up and you can hardly see them. Unless, of course you go into their homes, but you diplomats can't do that can you?'

'Certainly not,' Peter let out a hollow laugh. 'It would be more than my job's worth.'

'Yes,' Stefan looked hard at Peter. 'Yes, but what is life about if you can't live dangerously. Anyway, you've got Mavis so there wouldn't be much point would there.'

'No, I suppose not,' Peter was beginning to feel distinctly uncomfortable by the way the conversation was developing. He had always had a good relationship with Stefan and a little irreverent office banter between them was not unknown. But this was getting a bit too close for comfort. He did not like the reference to Mavis either. As far as he was concerned Mavis was not his girlfriend, but quite clearly that was not the way it was seen by others. He was sure Mavis did everything she could to make sure everyone saw them as a couple. 'Look, Stefan, I had better be getting on. Perhaps you could leave those replies with me and I will let you have my comments.'

'Fine,' replied Stefan. 'Take care, and don't do anything I wouldn't do.'

'That leaves me plenty of scope then,' said Peter, with a light chuckle, which did not reflect the way he felt. Did Stefan know something? Was he sending a coded message, warning him that he had been found out? Peter shuddered and picked up one of the letters Stefan had given him. He began to read without enthusiasm.

'Tom,' Suzana gave him her most alluring smile. 'How nice to see you again. I was really hoping you would come.'

'Bad pennies always turn up,' said Tom with a nervous chuckle. 'I mean… that is… it's wonderful to see you too Suzana.'

'What is this bad pennies?' asked Suzana crinkling her forehead.

'Oh,' Tom blushed a deep red. He had always found Suzana maddeningly attractive, by far the prettiest of the Romanian interpreters. She had always treated him in a friendly if somewhat hands-off way, but her greeting on this occasion had been positively warm. 'It's just an English expression, it means…' Tom thought hard, what exactly did it mean and how do you explain it to a foreigner? 'It means… well it's just a joke actually.'

'Oh, I see, a joke,' Suzana giggled enchantingly. 'Just a joke. Oh, I do like you English you are so amusing. Well this bad penny has turned up too and she is pleased to see you.'

'Ha ha,' said Tom, not quite sure whether to laugh at what he took to be Suzana's joke. 'You are funny too… I mean funny ha ha not funny peculiar…' Tom blushed again. He was making a terrible hash of this. He asked himself for the hundredth time, why it was that he could negotiate confidently with the toughest business opponent, but when faced with a slip of a girl he came out with the most inane gibberish imaginable. Perhaps, he should just come straight out with it. She had never been quite so friendly before, perhaps now was the time. 'Look Suzana, will you have dinner with me?' That was it, he had said it. He had blurted it out a bit, but he had done it.

'Tom,' she looked at him with a serious little frown. 'Tom, you know I can't. I'd love to, but it would get me into terrible trouble. I might even lose my job.'

'I'm sorry Suzana, I didn't want to put you in a difficult position. Forget I asked.'

'But I am glad you asked… perhaps… perhaps if we are very careful and keep it secret. Perhaps then I could have dinner with you.'

'But,' Tom could feel his heart pumping in his chest. 'We would be noticed in any restaurant around here. How could we keep it secret?'

'You could come to my house for dinner.' She looked around anxiously. 'But we would have to be very, very careful.'

'Could I? You mean… yes that would be great… but I don't want to get you into trouble.'

'Don't worry,' she said smiling sweetly. 'Come tonight at eight o'clock. Here is your official programme for today. Inside is a piece of paper with my address and directions. Don't look at it now, my supervisor over there is beginning to notice how long we have been talking. I will see you later and be careful.'

'I will.' Tom took the file off her and said in a slightly louder voice. 'Thank you, Miss Cuza. These arrangements sound fine.'

It was only later that Tom began to wonder whether she had planned it that way. Why was her address already in his folder? How did she know that he would ask her out? Well, what the hell did it matter? He was going to have dinner with the most beautiful girl in the world.

It was Mike's first night alone on the job. He had only recently joined the Foreign Office as a Security Officer, after serving fifteen years as a prison officer. Bucharest was his first posting and he was full of enthusiasm. He had arrived two weeks ago and felt that he was settling down well. He missed some aspects of the prison service: certainly, he felt that he had had more status. The prisoners had, at least to his face, shown him respect. He was recognised as a hard man, a screw who would stand no nonsense. In the Foreign Office he found himself at the bottom of the tree, at least among the UK based staff. The older and more senior officers showed him respect; they saw in him a man experienced in life who had already had a successful career elsewhere. It was among some of the younger ones, that he encountered an attitude of superiority. They saw themselves as budding young diplomats; they saw him as a glorified doorman. Some of his Security Officer colleagues openly resented this attitude and compensated by being gruff and uncooperative to the main offenders. As far as Mike was concerned, he was glad of the job and glad to be working abroad; his cheerful, helpful attitude was already winning him friends. He began his rounds trying carefully to remember all the instructions the Chief Security Officer had given him. He checked that the doors to the secure area were shut and spun the combinations to make sure. He checked that officers had locked their cabinets and went through their wastepaper baskets to make sure that they had not thrown away any classified documents. At last, well satisfied, he returned to his desk and sat down. He put his hand in his pocket and took out a packet of cigarettes. A sudden noise made him sit up sharply, just as he struck a match to light his cigarette. He swore silently as the flame burnt his fingers. He blew out the match and put the cigarettes back in his pocket. The alarm was now ringing loudly, and Mike went quickly up the stairs to the first floor to investigate. Suddenly another alarm started up and then another. Mike ran downstairs again and picked up the telephone. He had to speak to the Chief Security Officer and quickly: something was wrong, seriously wrong. He heard the phone ringing at the other end, and then he felt the floor beneath his feet begin to move.

Peter knocked on the door. The door moved slightly inwards and he realised that it was off the catch. Tonight, was the bar night at the Dip Inn, a little piece of England in the Embassy compound. He had agreed to pick Mavis up, as she still did not have her car. He looked at his watch: it was just after half-past eight. Mavis had said that she would be ready and waiting. He knocked again and pushed the door a little further open.

'Peter, is that you?' Mavis's voice echoed through the flat. 'Come in, I am in the bedroom.'

'OK,' Peter pushed the door open and walked into the lounge. The flat was quite large, much larger than a secretary would expect in most postings. The system in Romania, however, was inflexible. Embassies were issued with apartments by the State and there was no guarantee that family circumstances were reflected in the allocation. Peter stood in the centre of the lounge. Mavis' possessions were still quite few, as she had not yet got her heavy baggage. She had bought one or two local trinkets and dolls dressed in Romanian costumes, but these tended to accentuate rather than alleviate the bareness of the dark, wooden furniture. Peter decided to remain standing, he was determined to keep his relationship with Mavis as formal as possible, although he knew that he had probably already passed the point of no return.

'Peter, I'm in here. You know you don't have to stand on ceremony. Come in and chat, whilst I finish getting ready.'

Peter cursed under his breath. He really did not want to go into her bedroom again, but there seemed little he could do to prevent it. Perhaps he could hurry her up if he went in. He walked along the short corridor into her bedroom. Mavis was there and his worst fears were quickly realised. She was wearing a pink bra and pants and some matching pink stockings.

'Nearly ready,' she said brightly. 'Have a seat on the bed.'

Peter sat down. 'We'd better hurry Mavis,' he said. 'They are having a quiz night tonight and I promised to be on the Commercial Section team.'

'Oh, don't fuss so, Peter, dear. I'm sure they can manage without you for a few minutes. We can still be there by nine.' Mavis walked towards him and gently placed her hand on the front of his trousers. 'That is unless you would like to play a little bit first.'

'I think we should go Mavis,' said Peter conscious that, in spite of himself, his penis was being more responsive than he would have liked. 'A promise is a promise and I hate to let them down.'

Mavis's hand had begun to move up and down, alternately stroking and pressing. She giggled. 'I do believe you are going hard you naughty, naughty boy.'

Peter winced. Going hard, what the hell did the silly cow expect? Of course, he was going hard, she was virtually masturbating him. 'Mavis,' he pleaded. 'We really ought to go.'

'Don't you like it?' she asked.

'Yes... but...'

'But what?' she said, unzipping him.

Peter sighed 'But nothing.'

'Shall I lick it?'

'Mmmm.'

'Does that mean yes?'

'Yes... Yes... YES.'

Peter lay back and groaned. How could he handle it? Did he want to handle it? Oh, what the hell... what will be will be...'Yes,' he said aloud. 'Yes, there, just there.'

They lay naked, side by side, on the bed. Peter looked at his watch, nearly quarter past nine. 'We really should go,' he said.

'Put it in me first.'

'I can't, I don't have a johnny.'

'Go on, just slip it in for a moment. Then we can go.' Mavis, with great agility for her size, jumped on top of him and lowered herself down.

Peter felt himself slide in, it felt warm and nice. But he knew he had to be careful, a pregnant Mavis would be the end, the end of his career, the end of everything. It was time to come out, but he couldn't. Suddenly he felt her moving above him; then the bed began to move… everything began to shake… she screamed… he heard furniture crashing to the ground in the next room… suddenly it stopped almost as quickly as it had begun.

'What was it, Peter? What happened?' She was sobbing; he could feel her shaking… shaking with terror.

'An earthquake,' he said. 'I think it was an earthquake… and… and I think I've cum.'

Chapter 4

Peter walked down the main street. The sun was shining brightly, and the Bucharest spring had arrived. A flower seller sat on the pavement with a huge array of brightly coloured flowers, displayed for potential buyers. Behind her, in stark contrast, was a building or rather the shell of a building. Half of the building had collapsed making it look like some sort of grotesque doll's house. Rooms, complete with their tables, chairs and beds, were exposed to the world. The remains of staircases went upwards from floor to floor. At one side was a pile of rubble almost two stories high, two stories that had once been ten stories. The same images were scattered throughout the city. Bucharest had lost fifty tower blocks that night. At least 1500 people had died according to official figures. In the opinion of the diplomatic community the figure was probably twice as much. Now, two weeks later, the city was beginning to move again.

Mavis and Peter had been lucky. Cracks had appeared in the walls of Mavis' flat, but the building had survived the earthquake. They had dressed quickly and left the building. People were already walking around in the streets. All were consumed by a stunned silence. Perhaps this was due to the lack of traffic on the streets, perhaps it was just a shared sense of calamity, but people just walked, and walked in silence. Peter and Mavis made their way to the Embassy that, they reasoned, would be the centre of operations, that would be where they would be told what to do.

On the days following the earthquake Peter had been busy. At first, he had had to help with the immediate tasks, of establishing whether members of staff were safe, answering questions on the whereabouts of British citizens and answering calls from the press. These tasks were not normally his responsibility, but for a few days everyone had to take turns at dealing with the most urgent issues. Now, two weeks later he was beginning to deal with his own area of responsibility. Assessing the damage to business and the Romanian economy, advising British businessmen on whether it was safe to visit and how they should maintain their commercial interests, and preparing lists of goods and services that Romania might need immediately and for reconstruction. It was only now that Peter had time to start thinking about his own situation. Images of the earthquake kept coming back to him, the shaking, the rumbling, the fear, but more and more another memory began to intrude – he had ejaculated. Yes, he was sure, he had ejaculated as the earthquake struck and, when he had done so, he had been inside Mavis.

The more he thought about it the more certain he became. What did it mean? What were the consequences? Could she be pregnant? He wondered where she was in her menstrual cycle. He was no expert in such matters, but he thought he had read somewhere that for at least half of the month pregnancy could not occur. He asked himself if Mavis had dropped any hints. She had not been concerned that he did not have a contraceptive, so that probably meant that she knew she was safe – or did it? What if she did not mind getting pregnant? What if the pink underwear had been a deliberate trap? What if… But it was no use speculating he would just have to wait, wait and hope, hope and pray.

Tom Briggs walked purposefully past the two Romanian policemen at the entrance to the Embassy. He went in the main door and walked up to the desk on the left.

'Morning Phyllis,' he said cheerfully. 'How are you today? Is Peter in?'

'Hello Tom, nice to see you again.' Tom was one of her favourite businessmen. He was always open and friendly and had been visiting the country regularly for his company, which made hydraulic pumps. 'We've had quite a time here since your last visit, what with the earthquake and everything. You were lucky to have missed it.'

'Yes, but I didn't miss it. I was in Constanţa at the time. Never been so frightened in my life.'

'I'm surprised you have come back so soon. Nobody's doing much business at the moment, that is unless they are selling construction equipment or medical goods.'

'Well actually I still haven't been home, I've sort of been on holiday.'

'Holiday? Tom, you never cease to amaze me. What an earth are you doing, taking a holiday in Romania at a time like this?'

'Well I met this girl and… well that's what I want to talk to Peter about.'

'Oh, that explains everything. It's love that has kept you here. Is she pretty?'

'Very, is Peter in?'

'I think he's with the Ambassador, but he shouldn't be long. Stefan is in if you want a word with him whilst you are waiting.'

'Fine, I'll do that. See you later.' Tom walked back towards the front door and turned right into Stefan's office. Stefan was reading at his desk and looked up as he came in.

'Hello Tom. What brings you here? Not much going on, although give it a few more months and I should think they will be buying again.'

'Well, the main reason I am here is that I'm hoping to get married.'

'Married? Romanian girl?' Stefan was looking at him intensely, his expression revealing nothing of his thoughts.

'Yes, Romanian. I need advice, I know it's not always easy to get permission.'

'No, it's not. Some people have waited years. The country has opened up a bit since the earthquake. We need the international aid. It's possible that things might ease for a while, but it won't last.'

'You mean we might stand a chance if we act quickly?'

'Possibly. Who is she?'

'She's an interpreter in Constanţa. She's gorgeous and her name is Suzana, Suzana Cuza.'

'So at least she speaks English?' Stefan's gaze didn't flicker, but his trained mind was moving rapidly analysing the information. Quite a coincidence, young Suzana seems to get around. But why should she choose Tom, and why now? He didn't have to wait long for an answer.'

'Yes, she speaks English perfectly.' Tom looked at him earnestly, trying to come to a decision. 'Look Stefan can I tell you something in strict confidence.'

'Yes, if you want to.'

'Well Suzana… that is… she's pregnant. Do you think that will help with getting permission?'

'It depends,' Stefan gave him a deep searching look which made Tom shiver inside. 'And is the baby yours?'

'No, no, good heavens no. I would never have taken the risk. No, she told me about it before I proposed.'

'Before?'

'Yes before. Look it's not what you think, she's a decent girl. She hasn't explained exactly what happened, but it's quite clear that she was not a willing party to it.'

'You mean she was raped?' Stefan now seemed to be interrogating him and Tom was beginning to resent it.

'No… I don't know… Anyway that's her business and mine. All I want from the Embassy is advice.'

'Sorry Tom, I didn't mean to pry.' Stefan's voice had become soft and silky. 'I had to ask you because those are the questions the authorities will ask, and the answers may well influence their decision.'

'Oh, it's OK Stefan. Sorry if I sounded touchy. It's just that it's all a bit hard to take in.'

'But you are sure that you want to marry her?'

'Absolutely.'

'Hello Tom, Good to see you. Phyllis said that you were in here.' Neither of them had heard Peter enter the room. Tom turned to greet him.

'Peter,' he said holding out his hand.

'And what is all this I hear about romance and marriage. Phyllis is quite overcome. She thought she was in with a chance.'

'Yes, Stefan was just advising me on the local situation, but I wondered if you would fix me up with a meeting with the Consul. Here,' Tom took his wallet out of his pocket. 'I've got a picture of her. Isn't she lovely?'

'Certainly, I'll arrange for you to see Alan… Alan Parsons, the Consul.' Peter held out his hand and took the photograph from Tom. 'Yes, she's cert…' Stefan watched as the colour drained out of Peter's face. 'Yes, she's lovely,' said Peter trying hard to compose himself. He handed the photograph back, but Stefan could see that his hand was shaking.

'And she's going to have a baby,' said Stefan cheerfully. 'But unfortunately, it isn't Tom's.'

'Peter, I need to talk to you.' Mavis walked into Peter's office, her face looked even rosier than usual and there was a look in her eye that made Peter feel uneasy.

'Fine, have a seat.' Peter waved to the chair in front of his desk.

'Not here, I need to talk to you in private. Will you come round after work' It was not a question, but more of a command. Peter had been trying to avoid going to Mavis' flat. At first it had been easy as the earthquake had kept them all incredibly busy, but gradually Peter's excuses became less convincing and he knew it was only a matter of time before they had a showdown. Peter had decided that he had to end the relationship. Perhaps now was the time. Mavis wanted to talk, so talk they would. Peter would tell her how he felt and try to convince her that there was no mileage in continuing.

'OK,' he said. 'I'll be round at seven.'

'Promise,' she said slightly surprised that he had succumbed so easily.

'Yes, I promise.'

'OK,' she said, satisfied by his reply. 'I'll see you later.'

Stefan picked up the telephone on its third ring. It was Giorgiu Babu and once again he marvelled at the Colonel's efficiency. He had posed the question only two days ago and here, it seemed, was the answer. After the usual exchange of greetings Stefan asked if Giorgiu had any news.

'Yes,' came the reply. 'She is certainly pregnant.'

'Are you sure?'

'Certain, and what is more I can tell you pretty much when it happened.'

'Really,' said Stefan. 'I'm impressed. That would certainly be of interest.'

'According to my contact, it would have been the second or third week of January.'

'Now that is interesting. How an earth did you find that out?'

'I thought you would be interested, that would seem to place it at about the time you and your Embassy colleague were in the area. As for how I know, her doctor told me.'

'*Her doctor?* What on earth happened to patient confidentiality?'

'Well you don't worry too much about such matters if you have been messing around with your teenage patients for twenty years and don't want to go to prison.'

'I see,' said Stefan with a laugh. 'I should imagine you can count on his co-operation again then?'

'Certainly, what do you want?'

'Well, it might be worth doing a little paternity test. How about a sample of the baby's blood? Once it's born of course.'

'I'll see what I can do.'

'Thank you Giorgiu, I'm grateful.'

'It's a pleasure Stefan, but I would still like to know exactly what you are up to.'

'All in good time,' he replied with a just audible chuckle.

Peter opened another can of beer. Soon it would be time to go to Mavis' flat. Soon he would have to tackle the issue of their relationship once and for all. He had already drunk three cans of beer, and wondered why it was that he needed Dutch courage before letting Mavis know his true feelings. One part of him did not want to hurt her, in fact there had been times over the past few weeks when he had almost liked her. Fate had not dealt her a fair hand, but to her credit, she was always ready to take the world head-on. Even Jack knew he could only push her so hard, the quality of her work was good but if she felt she was being taken advantage of then woe betides the perpetrator. The Management Officer had already learnt the hard way. He had insisted that her flat could not be redecorated. He had explained that they were in Romania and when in Romania… She had smiled sweetly and returned half an hour later with a copy of the Diplomatic Service Procedure, open at the appropriate page, and a draft letter to the Head of the Foreign Office Estates Department. 'Perhaps you could ask them how you can do your job in such a difficult Post' she had said. He had succumbed, the following week the painters moved in. It had been the same with the new fridge and the worn-out bed, initial resistance had been challenged and overcome. Others had begun to notice and had secretly admired the way she had handled the notoriously intransigent Management Officer.

Still, Peter was quite sure that he did not see his future with Mavis. He had, in fact, recently noticed a rather attractive young officer at the US Embassy. She had long blond hair and had chatted to him freely when they met to discuss earthquake reconstruction aid to Romania. She had even asked him if he was married or had a permanent girlfriend. He had replied that he was still looking. Once he had settled matters with Mavis, he would give her a call.

Finally, at half-past seven he decided that he really must go. He went down to the garage and got into his car. He was feeling a little bit tipsy and wondered whether he ought to walk. He decided that he could not arrive any later, so drove out into the street. As usual the traffic was very light, so he arrived at Mavis' door just over ten minutes later. The door opened almost at the moment he touched the bell.

'You're late,' she said.

'Sorry, I...'

'And you've been drinking.' She looked at him in a slightly disapproving way. 'Never mind, come in, sit down and I'll get you an orange juice.'

Peter entered the lounge just managing to conceal his growing irritation. Orange juice for Christ's sake, who the hell did she think she was? He was not a child. He stayed standing for a few minutes to assert his independence; but took the proffered orange juice and drank it down quickly.

'Peter please, do sit down. We really do need to talk.' Her voice had changed to a softer more conciliatory tone. If he didn't know her better, he would have thought she was pleading with him.

'OK,' he said sitting down. 'What do you want to say? When you have finished, I have something to tell you.'

She came and sat beside him on the settee and turned to face him. She stretched out and took hold of his hands in hers. Peter thought about pulling them away, but decided that there was no need to hurt her unnecessarily. He was going to do that later anyway. He looked at her and rather to his surprise a large tear rolled down her cheek. She opened her mouth to speak, closed it again and leant towards him. At last she spoke, at first almost silently and then in a clearer determined voice.

'Peter, we are going to have a baby.'

'You… you are going to what…' It was not a question it was a shocked reaction as his mind tried to take in the news. Deep down it was the news he had been dreading, something that he knew was a possibility, but which work, and hope had pushed from his mind. He remembered the rumble of the earthquake and the sudden, sticky release. But still faced with her statement he could not accept it as a reality.

'I said that we are going to have a baby.'

'You… you mean you are pregnant?'

'Yes, I mean I am pregnant. That is what having a baby means. I am pregnant and you are the father.'

'Are you sure?'

'Yes, I'm sure. I have been to see the Embassy panel doctor at the clinic.'

'And you are sure it's mine?' he regretted saying it almost before the words came out. He knew it had to be his and he knew when it had been conceived, but even then he clung to a straw.

'Yes,' her voice hardened and raised just a little, her eyes flashed with anger. 'Yes of course I'm sure it's fucking well yours. Who else do you think I've been to bed with?'

'Sorry, it's just it was a bit of a shock. What are you going to do about it?'

'I'm not having an abortion if that's what you mean and it's not what I am going to do about it, it's what *we* have to do.'

'Well… what are we going to do about it then?'

'We are going to get married of course.'

'Christ! Married? But…' Peter was genuinely shocked at the statement of the obvious. Marry Mavis, that was the very last thing he wanted to do. 'But I don't want to get married.'

'You should have thought of that before you made me pregnant,' the softness had now completely gone. Mavis was at her hardest and most uncompromising. 'You could at least be a bit more of a gentleman about it.'

'Sorry… look,' it was Peter's turn to plead. 'Can't we think about this for a while?'

'Yes, you have until tomorrow, and my advice is that you had better propose to me then, that is if you value your precious Foreign Office career.' She stood up. 'Anyway, I think you had better go now. It doesn't look like you will be very good company tonight.'

Peter stood up and left with the very minimum of formalities. He drove home fast swerving to miss the odd car and pedestrian; half hoping he would have an accident to escape from the nightmare that confronted him. He let himself into his flat and went straight to the fridge and took out a can of beer. He knew that drinking was not the answer, more than at any time in his life he needed a clear head. He sank in the armchair and opened the can, then he began to think. First of all, he decided, it was pretty clear that the child was his and that Mavis intended to keep it. He was also certain that she would insist on marriage. Until tonight, Mavis' marriage prospects could not have been good, now she had the opportunity she was not likely to let it go. He asked himself if he could just refuse, after all it was a free country. What would the Office say? They would certainly disapprove, but it could hardly have been the first time it had happened. Perhaps a note would go on his file and his posting would be cut short, but that would not be a major problem it did not have long to run anyway. Would it damage him in the long term? He thought not. He had almost made up his mind to resist her threats, then he thought of Jack. The more he thought the more he realised that Jack would take a hard line. It was Jack, after all, who had asked him to look after the girl. She was Jack's secretary and he was fiercely loyal to his personal staff. Jack's wife, Sheila, was deeply religious and would ensure that Jack did not slip in his resolve. If Peter resisted and refused to marry Mavis, he could be sure that his Confidential appraisal report would damn him for the next ten years. He could, of course, complain officially that the report was prejudiced by outside factors, not based on his work. But he knew it would be no good, the Office disliked people complaining, and the senior officer almost invariably won. Jack was, in any case, a very experienced operator. The report would be written in such a way that every criticism would be supported by the facts, or would be an ambiguous allusion which other professional operators would read with the utmost clarity. Peter knew that the choice was marry Mavis or say goodbye to promotion for several years, by which time he would have missed the boat. To add to his misery was the news that Suzana was pregnant, and he could not dismiss the fact that he might have fathered her child as well. Stefan's attitude was worrying too; his almost unsubtle hints of a deeper knowledge of events were making Peter feel increasingly uncomfortable. He sighed deeply and took another long swig of beer.

'Congratulations, I've just heard the news,' Stefan came beaming into Peter's office.

'Err, thanks,' Peter tried to smile, as he shook hands for the umpteenth time that morning. The news of his engagement to Mavis had gone round the Embassy like a bush fire. Everyone seemed delighted for them, even if one or two were a little puzzled. Eventually, in a few weeks' time, as Mavis's figure would surely thicken out even more and the news of the pregnancy would circulate, they would have their answer as to why a good looking, ambitious officer with a promising future had settled on a dour and unattractive Embassy secretary. For the moment they would respond to the natural pleasure of romance and the consolation that there was more to Mavis than her outward appearance.

'You really are a dark horse Peter. I would never have guessed it,' Stefan's smile remained on his face, but there was still some hint in it that made Peter feel uneasy.

'Oh well, you know, love moves in a mysterious way,' Peter replied, with a lightness he did not feel.

'It certainly does. Anyway, I'm very pleased for both of you.'

'Thank you.'

'You have arranged for the blood test yet?'

'Blood test? What do you mean?' Peter looked at Stefan sharply, but Stefan's expression gave no hint that his question had been the least bit unusual.

'Don't you have to have a blood test in the UK before you get married? We always do in Romania.'

'No... I don't think so, I've never really thought about it.'

'Well it's often a good idea, puts one's mind at rest. I had one before I got married. At least I was able to be sure that I hadn't brought anything unwanted into the marital bed.'

'I hardly think that's likely in my case,' said Peter coldly.

'Oh, I'm sorry old chap, I didn't mean to imply... It's just a routine precaution in my country.'

'Well routine or not, it's not a precaution that is necessary in my case,' but again Peter knew that Stefan had struck a nerve. He had taken no precautions with Suzana and it was just possible that he might have contracted something. The thought horrified him, and he felt a cold numbness in the depths of his stomach.

'I'm sorry I brought it up, I certainly didn't mean to upset you.' Stefan's voice was smooth and conciliatory.

'I am not upset; I have nothing to be upset about. I don't have any problem with you bringing it up. It's just not our custom in the UK.' Peter began to feel that he was protesting too much and it was time to regain the high ground. 'By the way are those reports you promised me ready yet? I know I asked you at short notice, but I do need to get them in tomorrow's bag.'

'Yes, they are right here,' replied Stefan handing him a batch of neatly typed papers. 'That was what I came in to give you.'

'Oh… err… thanks,' Peter took the proffered papers, once again feeling that Stefan had got the better of him.

'When is the *happy* day?' asked Stefan.

'We are thinking of early June,' Peter replied coolly, not liking Stefan's deliberate emphasis on the 'happy'.

'Oh dear, I will probably miss it. I am meant to be accompanying the Romanian trade mission on reconstruction to London during the first two weeks of June.'

'What a pity,' Peter did not feel it was a pity at all. Until relatively recently he had got on very well with Stefan but, since their East coast trip, the man had been getting more and more under his skin.

'Anyway, I shall be thinking of you both,' said Stefan, standing up to leave. 'And, by the way, if you do decide to have a blood test let me know. I can arrange it with total discretion, that is unless you would prefer to use the Diplomatic clinic.

'I hardly think that will be necessary thank you,' replied Peter in his iciest tone, but deep down he knew it might be necessary and he might just take up the offer.

It was a lovely day for a wedding. The sun shone brightly, and the guests mingled on the Ambassador's lawn. The ceremony had gone quite well under the guiding hand of the Embassy Chaplain. Mavis had looked almost pretty in her wedding dress. Her heavy frame still masked the slight swelling of her belly. No one yet seemed to have guessed the reason for their speedy betrothal or, if they had, they had kept their suspicions well away from Peter. Peter's mother, Mavis's parents and her brother had all come out for the wedding. Mavis herself had been sweetness itself since the day he had gone to her and proposed, just as she had suggested he should. She had accepted him with a certain grace and without any obvious show of triumph. Peter had decided that if marriage was inevitable to save his career then he had better make the best of it. He even found himself looking forward to the birth of the baby, he was going to be a father and he rather liked the idea.

The Ambassador made a witty speech praising the qualities of the young couple. He was sure that they would have a fulfilling and exciting life in the Service, and he was proud that in his Embassy the match had been made and another Diplomatic Service husband and wife team created. Everyone then toasted the happy couple and came up as singles or pairs to congratulate them.

'Can I have a word?' The question was asked almost silently as Arthur Deane, the MI6 Head of Station whispered his congratulations.

'Err yes,' Peter was not quite sure whether Arthur meant now or later.

'Meet me on the terrace in, shall we say, half an hour.'

'Fine,' said Peter looking at his watch. 'What…' but before he could ask Arthur had already moved on. Peter continued to shake hands, but with much less interest than previously. What did Deane want? And why all the mystery? It was probably nothing; these people always made things sound more dramatic than they deserved. Still Peter could not keep his mind off the forthcoming meeting. He thought of all the things it could be. Perhaps one of his businessmen had been compromised; maybe he wanted to know about one of his Romanian contacts in the Foreign Trade Enterprises. Then he thought of Suzana. Could it be about her? He shivered and then consoled himself that any personal security breach would be handled by the Head of Chancery and not by Deane. Still he waited anxiously until twenty-five minutes had passed and then whispered to Mavis 'I'll be back in a minute.'

'Sorry to drag you away from the party Peter,' Deane emerged silently from the shadows and stood beside Peter.

Peter jumped slightly and turned to face the newcomer 'That's alright Arthur. What can I do for you?'

'How well do you know Stefan Teduscu?'

'Well,' Peter was taken aback by the question. 'Fairly well I suppose, we work quite closely together.'

'Do you know him socially?'

'Not terribly well. I've met his family once or twice.'

'You went on a trip to the East Coast with him in February, didn't you?'

'Yes,' replied Peter, trying not to sound too concerned by the mention of the fateful trip.

'Did he say anything unusual to you?'

'No,' Peter hesitated. 'No, I don't think so. What sort of thing?'

'Anything, anything at all that sounded odd.'

'No.'

'Did he give any indication about what he thought of the regime?'

'No, I don't think so. Only the usual Romanian jokes about Ceaușescu.'

'Do you think he was a loyal Romanian citizen?'

'I've really no idea. We talked mainly about work.'

'Thank you, Peter. Sorry to interrupt the wedding. I just needed a quick word before you left for your honeymoon. I will want a more detailed chat when you get back.'

'Can I ask what all this is about?'

'Well I expect there is no harm in telling you, you'll find out soon enough anyway. Do you know where he is at present?'

'Yes, he's in London with the Romanian Trade Mission.'

'Yes, he's in London, but not with the Mission. You see he has defected.'

'Christ,' Peter was stunned by the news. 'You mean he's claimed political asylum and left his family here.'

'No, he took his family with him, which rather bears out the claims he has made to our people in London.'

'What claims?' Peter was trying hard to take it all in.

'He claims that he is a Colonel in the Securitate. Please keep that bit of information to yourself. If you think of anything that might be of interest, please let me know.'

BARBADOS

SOME TWENTY YEARS LATER

Chapter 5

Peter looked out of the window of the British Airways jet and watched his future home come into view. This was what he had worked for all his life, his own post. He was British High Commissioner designate to Barbados and the East Caribbean. Very soon he would present his credentials and would be able to drop the 'designate'. In practice, he would be seen as carrying out the full role from the moment he set foot on Barbadian soil. He had spent the last three years in London as the Under Secretary responsible for information and culture; not perhaps the most prolific job in the Office, but certainly one at the centre of activities. Before London he had been Consul General in Geneva, a pleasant, if undemanding, job. Now as High Commissioner, the Commonwealth equivalent of an Ambassador, he had finally made it. Do this job right and perhaps at the end of it he would be Sir Peter. In the old days an automatic knighthood would have come with the job. Now, after successive governments had chipped away at the honours system, it was almost a rarity. He would have to perform and be noticed if the coveted accolade was to be his.

He turned to look at his sleeping spouse beside him. Mavis' eyes were closed. Her mouth was wide open, and she was snoring lightly. He looked at her silently for several minutes, wondering whether to wake her. Nobody could call Mavis a handsome woman, but she had improved with age. Her complexion was now smooth and clear and, although not a slim woman, she no longer seemed to have the heaviness that had been so evident when they had first met over twenty years ago. Marriage suited Mavis. She had gladly given up work when their first child was born and had resigned from her job in the Service. These days a young couple would be expecting Personnel to find them joint postings, but that was not the way of things when they had married. Mavis had enjoyed being a Diplomatic Service spouse. She was still the scourge of Management Officers but, as Peter had risen in the Service, this was not thought to be unusual. Many senior wives suffered, usually deservedly, from reputations of being demanding and fussy dragons. Mavis underscored her dragon-like status with a mischievous sense of humour. She had been known to make a Management Officer wriggle like a worm on a hook and then to throw back her head, roar with laughter and ask him to sit down and share tea and cake with her. Mavis had, after all, once been a member of the junior staff herself and she could empathise with anyone doing a difficult job in trying circumstances.

Peter turned as a hand tapped him on the shoulder.

'Look Dad, you can see the beach. It looks great.'

'Yes Jack, it looks great. I think that is the East Coast that's why the sea is so rough. The breakers come straight off the Atlantic.'

'Hadn't you better wake Mum?' Jack's twin sister Becky asked.

'Maybe,' said Peter turning back towards his wife.

'No need, I'm awake. Come on everyone let's tidy up before we land.'

'No time,' said Jack. 'The seat belt sign has just gone on.'

'Any excuse,' retorted his sister.

'It's not an excuse everyone knows that you shouldn't start messing about with things once the signs on.'

'Oh, be quiet you two. Let us at least start a new country with a bit of peace and quiet.' Mavis' voice was stern, but they knew that she was not really cross. Jack and Becky were ten just under half the age of their elder sister Annabelle, who was studying medicine at University. Their birth had not been planned, Peter and Mavis had just got complacent and, after a boring night out at a cocktail party, had relaxed in front of the television and not bothered to go upstairs to the bedroom. As their protection against such mishaps was kept in the drawer in the bedside table, neither of them had considered the possible consequences of making love on the settee. It had been a bit of a shock when Mavis discovered that she was pregnant again. The shock had been compounded when the first ultrasound revealed that there was not one mistake, but two swimming around in Mavis' womb. Now they had the twins, neither Peter nor Mavis would have given them up for the world.

Andrew looked at his watch. He was a tall fair-haired young man. He looked as if he might be an athlete and had the air of competence and confidence about him. He had been in Barbados for just over a year as the Second Secretary responsible for political matters. He was looking at the sky towards the East.

'There it is,' he said.

His companions turned their heads in the direction of his pointing finger.

'Aye, that's it alright. Let's hope he hasn't missed the bloody plane.' Angus McMullen was the Deputy High Commissioner, one of Her

Majesty's Diplomatic Service's vast contingent of dry Scots.

'I should think London would have let us know by now if he had,' observed the third man, Colonel Simon Perrigrew the Defence Attaché.

'Aye, I suppose you're right. Then again that would depend on whether he let them know and whether the wee lassies in communications could be bothered to send a telegram.'

Andrew smiled quietly to himself. He knew very well that if the High Commissioner had missed the plane then London would have told them. Angus knew it very well too, but he always enjoyed himself by anticipating small disasters. Andrew knew that there was no point in responding to Angus' pretended concerns. He left this to simpler folk like the Colonel.

'They would have telephoned then,' persisted the Colonel.

'Aye maybe, then again maybe not.'

'I really think they would have Angus. I mean if they are not on the plane it would be most embarrassing, most embarrassing. I mean what would we say to him?' Colonel Perrigrew nodded towards the Head of Protocol, who had come to represent the Barbadian Government.

'You would have to tell him, Simon, that the High Commissioner had missed the plane.'

'Me?' protested the Colonel. 'I really think, Angus, that it would be more appropriate coming from you. Protocol and all that you know or, if not you, then Andrew. As Defence Attaché it's not really my job to handle protocol.'

'Don't worry,' said Andrew, feeling that it was time that he put a stop to all the nonsense. 'I'm sure he will be on the plane and if he's not I will speak to the Head of Protocol myself.'

'Oh, thank you Andrew,' responded the Colonel, with genuine relief.

'What about these laddies outside?' asked Angus turning to Andrew. 'Will they cause any problem?'

'I hope not,' Andrew replied. 'They are from the sugar co-operative. They feel Britain has not done enough to discourage European beet sugar producers from getting quotas cut. There's less than a dozen of them, but perhaps I'd better have a quick word with the Head of Protocol. We can't ask them to stop a free demonstration, but it would be worth one or two of the airport police being on hand just in case of trouble.'

'Yes Andrew, I think that would be wise.'

Andrew walked over to the Head of Protocol, who listened carefully and nodded his agreement.

'That's fine Angus,' said Andrew returned to the side of the Deputy High Commissioner. 'He'll sort it out.'

'Good, let's walk down to the tarmac, the plane's about to land.'

Peter stepped out of the aeroplane cabin into the bright sunlight. It took a few moments for his eyes to adjust, and to note with satisfaction the small group of awaiting officials. In the old days the line-up would have been much longer, with every officer holding diplomatic rank expected to attend. Now a count of three, plus one local, was quite good. He walked slowly down the steps and stretched out his hand to the tall, bespectacled, distinguished-looking Barbadian at the bottom.

'Welcome to Barbados, Mr Parker,' intoned the official.

'Thank you, it is a great pleasure to be here,' replied Peter, putting on his best diplomatic smile.

'The Prime Minister asked me to express his warm greetings. He is looking forward to seeing you later in the week.'

'Please express my thanks to the Prime Minister and tell him that I too am looking forward to our meeting,' Peter felt something of a shuffle behind him and rapidly took the hint that Mavis was growing impatient. 'And may I introduce my wife Mavis, and my children, Jack and Becky.'

'A great pleasure to meet you,' said the Head of Protocol, with a little bow.

Peter then ushered the small group forward to meet his staff. Angus he had already met in London during his briefing.

'Hello Angus, good to see you. I don't think you have met Mavis.'

'Glad to see you got here alright Peter. Nice to meet you Mrs Parker.'

'We were worried in case you might have missed the plane,' interjected the Colonel.

Angus gave him a shrivelling look and waved towards him with his hand, 'and this is Simon Perrigrew, the Defence Attaché. They usually send a sailor to Barbados, so Christ knows why they sent a soldier this time. Probably inter-service rivalry, isn't that so Simon?' This was a sore subject and Angus noted with satisfaction that his arrow had struck home. Serve the bugger right for his silly fuss about the High Commissioner missing the plane.

'Oh, err well we do sort of take things in turns. I mean it's up to the Ministry of Defence and...' Simon petered out, as he did not quite know how to justify the system of buggins turn that sometimes seemed to be a feature of his chosen career.

They completed the introductions and walked slowly over to the terminal building, the Head of Protocol collecting their passports, on the way, to facilitate immigration. Becky took an immediate interest in Andrew, who she conceded was probably a little old for her. Nevertheless, she lost no time in telling him about her extremely pretty sister Annabelle, who would be coming out from medical school in ten days' time.

Peter followed Angus through the crowds of people towards the airport exit. Mavis and the twins struggled to keep up whilst Andrew and Simon did their best to ease their way. The High Commission driver, a large cheerful Bajan, had arrived and taken over the baggage trolley. As they emerged once again into the bright sunlight they were met by a photographer, who pointed his camera at Peter and began adjusting the focus. A fat man in a scruffy white suit stepped forward.

'Mr Parker, a few words please. Geoff Forrest, Daily Star.'

'Err, yes,' Peter paused, and gathered his High Commission colleagues about him. He needed to make a good start and that meant co-operating with the press. 'With pleasure, fire away.'

'How do you feel about taking over as High Commissioner?'

'Delighted, I've always wanted to come to Barbados.'

'And what do you hope to achieve whilst you are here?'

'Well, Barbados, and the Caribbean generally, are very important to the United Kingdom. We have strong historical links and many common interests.'

'And what are those interests?'

'We have a strong Caribbean community back home, and I shall be doing my best to develop bilateral trade and contacts in other areas.' Peter was pleased at the benign thrust of the questions which allowed him to say the right thing. One more question and he would be able to excuse himself and get his tired family to the Residence.

'And what about sugar?'

'Oh yes sugar,' Peter cursed under his breath. He tried to remember the phrases of the 'line to take' which had been set out for him by the Department. He suddenly became aware of a group of young men with placards who had begun to move forward. They hoisted their placards which were inscribed with various slogans. Peter became aware that the words 'sugar' and 'quotas' were liberally mixed with phrases such as 'Death to the imperialist pigs' and 'Fair quotas or else.' As Peter fought for words, the small crowd began to chant -

'What about sugar, what about sugar, what about sugar.'

'Well my Government wants to see fair sugar quotas…'

'Rubbish,' yelled one of the youths.

'Yes, rubbish,' yelled another.

'It's really a matter for the European Union…' Peter looked around for assistance from Angus and Andrew. Andrew moved forward to whisper in his ear. Peter listened gratefully as Andrew rapidly gave him the words he had been searching for. Peter turned back towards the reporter and the chanting group. He opened his mouth to speak, but his words were brutally cut off as something soft and mushy landed with a splat on his half-open lips. A second mango hit him on the chest, then a third. He looked down to see the blotches of orange mess on his clean white shirt and a small river of juice running down his tie.

'This way High Commissioner,' it was Andrew pulling his arm, trying to lead him away from the group which were now moving forward, their eyes glinting as they sensed their quarry was about to make a run for it. Peter went to follow, but his path was blocked by a huge worker with a cane-cutting machete. Before Peter had time to react, something flew past his arm and the man let out a blood-curdling scream. Almost in slow motion he saw the man double up, his face twisted in agony, his hands clutching his groin. Mavis was standing next to him; her face set in a look of determined satisfaction. Her British Airways bag had done the trick, one mighty underarm swing and their path was clear. Peter was barely aware of the flashing cameras or of the white helmeted policeman who moved in to break up the group of demonstrators. Within minutes he was in the Jaguar, leaning back exhausted against the soft green leather upholstery. The little line of official cars sped out of the airport gates and headed towards Bridgetown.

'High Commissioner,' said Andrew, walking into Peter's office. 'I think you will wish to see this.'

'I expect so,' replied Peter, taking the proffered newspaper. 'How bad is it.'

'Not so good, but it could have been worse.'

Peter laid the copy of the Daily Star out flat on his desk and glanced down taking in the whole of the front page. His winced as he read the headline:

BRITISH HIGH COMMISSIONER PARKER GETS A STICKY WELCOME

Underneath taking up the full top half of the front page was a picture of himself. His mouth, shirt and tie were covered in mango and mango juice. Just below his picture was another piece of bold type announcing to the world:

BUT HER LADYSHIP SCORES A BULL EYE

And there, clearly for all to see, was a picture of Mavis, her face set in a determined frown. The picture had been taken just after the point of impact. The huge black Bajan was doubled up, his face screwed up in pain, his hands clutching his testicles. Mavis was at full stretch holding tightly onto the British Airways bag, which was starting the return swing from its hapless target.

'Hmm,' said Peter. 'Couldn't be much worse.'

'Well at least it diverted their minds from sugar quotas, there's only a very brief mention of the subject on page 10.'

'I expect that's some consolation,' said Peter thoughtfully. 'But what will London think? Her Majesty's Diplomatic Service Wives are hardly meant to go about castrating the locals.'

'They'd probably say that she landed a well-deserved blow for democracy. Anyway, it's hardly likely that they will see it. The Department doesn't usually bother to read the cuttings we send them, and this is one cutting they are not going to get.'

'But won't one of the UK dailies pick it up from their local correspondents?'

'It's possible of course, but we should be alright. I've spoken to the local stringers and told them we would view it as a personal favour if they would let this one pass.'

'But can you trust them?'

'Some yes, some no, but they all rely heavily on the High Commission for information on what is going on. They know that we might find it difficult to confide in them in the future, if they let us down by passing on a bit of tabloid gossip.'

Peter looked hard at the younger man, trying to detect a sign of smugness, pleasure at his discomfort or even of pride, but there was none. The face only revealed professionalism and openness. The young man was either sincere or a bloody good actor, either way he was clearly an asset. 'Thank you, Andrew, you have done well.'

'What time would you like the office meeting High Commissioner?'

Peter smiled to himself, noting the compliment had not been acknowledged merely accepted as just dessert for good work, and the subject rapidly changed so as not to dwell on it. Yes, indeed an asset. 'Shall we say 10.30?'

'Fine, thank you. I'll tell the others.'

Andrew left the office leaving Peter looking down at the picture of his wife, with a mixture of pride and trepidation.

Peter looked around the assembled faces. This was to be his team, the people on whom he would have to depend during the next couple of years. Andrew, Simon and Angus he had met at the airport. The

Management Officer, Jim Smythe, had also been to see him to discuss his baggage. That left the Commercial Secretary, Fred Forbes, who he had not met and Anthony Tremlett, a rather gaunt man in early middle age, who dealt with a whole range of odd subjects from terrorism to money laundering.

'Thank you all for coming,' Peter began, although he was all too well aware that they were there by Royal Command. 'I would like to begin with some comments on how matters are seen in London. I had extensive talks in the Office before I came out, including with the Secretary of State. We can then go round the table and you can let me know what is happening in each of your patches and, in particular, any events that will involve me in the next month or two.' Peter paused and looked around the table to make sure he had their attention. All looked alert and were listening intently. 'Before I begin, however, I would like to warn you,' Peter noted with satisfaction that his words had slightly raised the tension and expectation around the table. 'Any, and I mean any,' he continued, his face impassive and his voice quiet and controlled, 'Any mention of mangoes or bull's eyes will result in an immediate transfer to Ulan Bator.' He felt the intensity rise briefly, and then be replaced by a relaxation of the tension and general laughter at his joke. 'Right, having got that out of the way, let me tell you about London.'

For the next ten minutes Peter outlined what he had learnt during his briefing. There followed a short exchange of views on various points, before Peter asked them for their individual contributions.

As the senior officer, Angus spoke first. Peter noted that his deputy, despite his dry humour, did not merit the close attention of his colleagues. He outlined the programme, that had been organised for Peter to meet the Prime Minister, the American Ambassador and the Canadian High Commissioner. Peter would then need to tour the other Caribbean islands for which he was responsible. On two or three occasions, Angus turned to Andrew to remind him of this or that point. Andrew chipped in again when Angus forgot to mention that the Princess would be passing through in three weeks' time and would be spending a couple of nights at the Residence. Peter was impressed by the young diplomat's ability to prompt his senior, without appearing to do so.

Simon came next, and told the assembly of the forthcoming visit of a Royal Naval destroyer HMS Hopeful. It was a routine visit, but one which would need his colleagues' full support. First, and most important was the need to find sufficient girls and High Commission ladies to entertain the sailors. When Peter asked why the Diplomatic Service always had to do the pimping for the Royal Navy, Simon went bright red and protested that he had not meant to imply that the ladies concerned should do any more than entertain the sailors in a respectable social manner. Indeed, he insisted, his own wife Felicity would be at the forefront of such activities and would personally ensure that all the High Commission ladies were fully protected. Peter resisted the temptation to ask what Simon had meant by 'fully protected' and noted for future reference that he should not make jokes in front of Simon who took everything literally. Andrew had to remind Simon of his second point, which seemed to have totally slipped from the flustered Colonel's mind. The Navy had challenged the High Commission to a cricket match, and net practice was due to begin at the weekend. It transpired that Andrew was the High Commission Captain and already had the reputation of being a fine batsman. There was some talent in the Development Division downstairs, who dealt with aid matters, and one of the High Commission drivers was a pacey seam bowler. Peter agreed that if they found themselves short of an eleven, he would be happy to help prop up the middle order.

After a brief diversion into the world of local budgets, by Jim the Management Officer, and the promise of a private briefing from Anthony Tremlett on 'various matters of interest' the floor was given to Fred Forbes.

'We have a Trade Mission due in three weeks' time,' Fred began.

'Doesn't that clash with the ship's visit and the visit of the Princess?' Peter asked, turning to Angus.

'And the auditors will also be around that week,' Jim Smythe chipped in, with a glare at Angus which suggested that this was not the first time the subject had cropped up.

Peter glanced at Andrew, but the young man was studying the backs of his hands.

'Well err yes, that is true,' responded Angus.

'Couldn't we have put some of them off?' asked Peter.

'Well I did consider it, but everyone seemed keen on those dates.'

'But do we have the resources to cope with four major events in one week?' persisted Peter.

'Well I hope so,' replied Angus beginning to shuffle on his chair.

'Well I can't say I'm too happy about it,' said Peter stiffly 'But I imagine it is too late now to do anything about it.'

'You should have listened to young Andrew six weeks ago Angus,' Anthony Tremlett's quiet voice passed judgement on the hapless Deputy High Commissioner.

'OK,' said Peter. 'We will just have to make sure our planning is right.' There were clearly differences among the small group of men around the table, and now was not the time to acerbate them. 'So, who are the Trade Mission and how many members?' he asked, turning back to Fred.

'The South Eastern Counties Export Club,' replied Fred. 'There are about ten of them. The leader is in financial services, Stefan... something,' Fred began flicking through his papers looking for the name.

'Stefan?' for some inexplicable reason Peter felt an icy chill down his spine. The name Stefan had struck some chord in his memory. He was not quite sure why since there must be thousands of Stefans, even in England.

'Yes, here it is Stefan Teduscu. Originally a Romanian, I believe.'

'Oh dear me,' said Peter mainly to himself, but just loud enough for one or two of the others to turn and look at him quizzically.

Peter opened the door of the Conference Room and ushered in Mavis and the twins. This was to be her first opportunity to meet the High Commission staff, and their first chance to meet her. Peter had wanted to keep it very informal and had laid on wine and sandwiches. His plan was that everyone would have begun drinking and eating by the time his family arrived. They would have already formed clusters and he could then steer Mavis from group to group for a brief chat. As he opened the door, he was mildly surprised by the silence. The reason soon became clear, all the staff were lined up like troops for inspection. The food and drink lay untouched on the side tables. Angus stepped forward towards her.

'Good morning Mrs Parker. Welcome to Barbados. May I introduce you to our staff.'

Peter cursed under his breath; damn the man he had totally ignored his instructions. The staff were all lined up in order of seniority and there seemed no way that he could now humiliate his deputy by publicly overruling him. But Mavis had other ideas.

'Oh Angus, don't be so stuffy,' she squealed, bouncing forward to the centre of the room. 'Come on everyone grab a drink and some chow, and I'll be with you in a mo for a chat.'

For some four seconds there was a stunned silence, then Anthony Tremlett began to clap. In no time at all Mavis was receiving a standing ovation. This was the second time since her arrival in Barbados that she had scored a bull's eye, and her destruction of the Deputy High Commissioner had been equally as effective as her demolition of the union leader at the airport.

Andrew picked up the telephone on the third ring. 'Andrew Walker.'
'Andrew it's me, Meriko.'
'Meriko, hi, still all right for tonight, I hope.'

'Yes Andrew, I'm OK for tonight. You are going to pick me up at 7.'

'Yes, I'll be there at 7 on the dot.'

'Thank you,' she said, as Andrew waited for her to continue. He knew that this girl would not have rung up just for a chat. She must have something she wanted to tell him. 'Andrew,' she said.

'Yes?'

'I'm going back to Japan.'

Andrew closed his eyes, as if he had been struck in the face. 'But, I thought your contract was for another two years at least. What's happened?'

'Well it is, but the UN have offered to send me on a one-year postgraduate course on international development at Tokyo University. I do hope to come back after that, maybe on promotion.'

'But...' Andrew wanted to scream down the phone 'but what about me' but instead he pulled himself together. 'It sounds wonderful, congratulations... but I will miss you.'

'I'll miss you too, Andrew.'

'We can talk tonight, see you at 7,' Andrew knew that he was cutting off the conversation rather abruptly, but he also knew that he couldn't hold back his disappointment much longer.

'OK, see you tonight Andrew,' she said, putting down the phone.

Andrew put the phone down and leant back in his chair. He closed his eyes and tried to take in the gut-wrenching news. They had been going out together for three months, and it was fair to say that he was besotted. Images of Meriko's long shiny black hair and dark brown eyes flooded into his mind. He saw her golden skin, her small perfectly formed breasts, tipped by firm dark brown nipples. He remembered the patch of black hair between her long slim legs, he thought about their last night together.

'Shit, shit, shit.' He said aloud, then turned back to his computer to continue writing the brief on Grenada for the High Commissioner.

Chapter 6

Annabelle was running late. She looked at her watch and it was nearly half-past nine. The flight was due to leave at ten thirty-five. Her ticket said that she should be at the airport two hours before the flight. She knew that this was more for the airline's convenience than for her own, but still she only had just over an hour and the taxi was making heavy weather of the traffic on the M23. Her head was aching too. She asked herself, for the tenth time, why she had allowed her fellow students to ply her with cheap Spanish wine last night. It had been the last day of term before the Easter holidays and it had been somebody's birthday, but then it always seemed to be somebody's something. She tapped on the glass and the driver slid it back.

'Sorry to bother you, but I'm running a bit late.'

'Don't worry luv, most flights are late at this time of year.'

'Yes, but I really am late. Couldn't you go a bit faster?' she tried to sound calm and friendly. The last thing she wanted to do was annoy him. That might make things worse.

'Well I could, if I could fly, but I can't.' he replied with a chuckle. 'If you know how I can get through all this traffic any quicker luv, perhaps you would tell me.'

'Sorry,' she said knowing it was useless. 'I know you are doing your best.' She leant back against the seat and closed her eyes. Her head seemed to be throbbing even harder, and she was beginning to feel a bit sick.

Ten minutes later the taxi drew up in front of the terminal. Annabelle jumped out and ran to get a trolley. To her irritation, the driver had only just started to unload her baggage from the boot when she returned. He watched her as she loaded all her bags on the trolley and then held out his hand.

'That'll be twenty-three pounds fifty luv.'

Annabelle scrabbled through her purse and counted out the money exactly. 'OK?' she said deliberately emphasising the word to show that she did not think he deserved a tip.

'Well I expect it'll have to be,' he said grumpily. 'Most people have the decency to round it up.'

'Well I'm not most people,' she retorted turning away and pushing her cart towards the automatic doors. She heard him shout something none too complimentary after her; but did her best to ignore it. She pushed the trolley faster and held her chin up high. At the very least he would not have the satisfaction of knowing that he had got to her.

'Careful, watch where you are going,' the pretty dark-haired girl had been halfway through the doors with her trolley when Annabelle's trolley crashed into it.

Annabelle watched as her baggage began to wobble and then topple to the ground.

'Shit,' she said. 'Now look what you've done. Couldn't you see I was halfway through the door?'

'*Excuse me*,' said the dark-haired girl. 'I was halfway through the door, and you were still arguing with the taxi driver.'

The reference to the taxi driver struck a raw nerve somewhere in Annabelle's throbbing head, 'I wasn't arguing with the taxi driver and even if I was it has nothing at all to do with you. Why don't you mind your own business you stupid bitch?'

'Well if there is a stupid bitch around here it is certainly not me.' The girl gave a toss of her dark mane, and walked away pushing her trolley towards the check-in. Annabelle was left trying to reassemble her bags on the trolley. The automatic doors did their best to make the exercise even more difficult by periodically opening and closing. Annabelle was not normally an aggressive or abusive person, but at that moment what she would like to have done to the dark-haired girl did not bear thinking about. Finally, the trolley was re-loaded, and she set off in pursuit of her adversary. The girl seemed to be going to the same checkout, but at the last moment moved to an adjacent one. Annabelle, who had been trying to think of further insults if they ended up at the same place, noted with even greater hatred that they were indeed travelling on the same plane, but the girl was in Club Class and she was in Economy.

Andrew looked across the table at the girl. Once again, he felt a pang of regret at what he was about to lose. She was exquisite. He watched as she expertly located a small shrimp with her chopsticks and gracefully transferred it to her perfectly shaped mouth. Her long shiny black hair fell to her shoulders and gently swayed with the rhythm of her eating. She was wearing a simple white blouse buttoned to the neck, but its discretion did not, in any way, limit her sexuality. Her small well-shaped breasts announced their presence against the clear white fabric. Andrew wondered if he should try and persuade her not to go. He knew her mind was made up, but perhaps if he proposed he might change her mind. He had pondered the question of marriage on several occasions over the past few weeks, and almost continually since her phone call. He knew that it would need very little to get him to ask her, but he was aware deep down that she would gently reject him if he did ask. Her thoughts were on her career, and she was not yet ready for total emotional commitment.

'I will miss you Meriko,' he said conscious that he was repeating their telephone conversation.

'I will miss you too Andrew,' her response was totally natural, and she gave no hint that she was aware that they were re-enacting their earlier words.

'Will you come back?'

'I hope so.'

'So do I,' he touched her fingertips with his and looked straight into her eyes. 'Very, very much.'

She returned his gaze and gently returned the pressure on his fingertips. They remained silent for several moments. At last she spoke, her voice gentle and unwavering. 'I like you very much Andrew and I would like to come back,' Andrew could feel his heart beating hard within his chest. 'At the moment,' she continued. 'I need to sort out my career. Perhaps when I do come back, perhaps then we can get back together.'

'And in the meantime,' he asked.

'In the meantime, we should follow our own paths. If we try to maintain a relationship at a distance it will not work. Either we would not accept the separation and I would have to abandon my plans, or we would disappoint each other. It is better for both of us that we stop now and start afresh in the future if our paths come together again.'

'Will you be seeing someone else?' he had to ask the question. Perhaps there was an old college friend in Tokyo and she already knew that she would be going back to someone else.

'At the moment Andrew there is only you. There is nobody else,' she smiled at him gently. 'For the future I cannot speak and...' she paused as if the words did not come easily. 'And if you find someone else before I return, I will understand.'

'You don't think it would be better for us to keep in touch? We could write, even visit for holidays.'

'No,' she said.

Andrew knew she had made up her mind, the simple finality of her 'no' left no scope for further discussion. 'OK,' he said at last. 'But we are friends.'

'Yes Andrew, we are friends.'

Nicu followed the girl, in the very short skirt, into the large modern office.

'Senor Cuza,' she announced.

'Nicu,' the man stretched out his hand. He was short and heavily built. His face was pocked marked and he was almost bald. The Amani suit and white suede shoes failed to change the impression that he was what he had always been, one of nature's thugs. It was there in the eyes, the cruel glint that showed both a willingness to use violence, if it suited his purpose, and the suggestion that, if he did use violence, he would take pleasure in doing so. To Nicu the man was not a cause for disquiet, rather someone to exercise caution with. Nicu was used to dealing with people who lived on the wrong side of the line, which divided civilised human beings from the rest. In fact, he had no difficulty in using violence himself if it suited his purpose. The difference between them was that the man looked a thug, whilst Nicu did not.

'Antonio, you asked to see me.'

'Yes Nicu, I have a little task for you.'

Nicu waited silently for the Colombian to elaborate. Whether or not he was prepared to accept a task was apparently not in question.'

'There is a man who has been interfering with our banking arrangements. He is, I believe, working for others in our line of business. The difficulty is that he is using our outlets and I would like this difficulty removed.'

'Where do I find this man?'

'His details are in these papers,' replied the Colombian handing Nicu a black folder. You will find him at the Grand Hotel in Barbados in three weeks' time. He will be there as a member of a British trade delegation.'

'How would you like the difficulty dealt with?'

'That my friend is up to you,' the Colombian replied, the corners of his mouth curled into the semblance of a smile. 'His activities must stop, with or without his agreement. You will, of course, receive the usual remuneration.'

'I understand,' said Nicu.

They shook hands and the girl returned to escort him to the lift. Nicu considered whether to find out whether the girl was available. He had nothing planned for the evening and she looked as if she knew how to please a man. With some regret, he decided against. She was probably Antonio's property and he had no desire to end up in the sea off the coast of Venezuela. It was only once that he was in the lift and the doors had closed that he glanced at the file. A picture of the man was on the inside cover. Nicu looked at it and the flicker of recognition in his brain caused him to smile to himself in anticipation. He would enjoy resolving this little difficulty.

'Do you have a girlfriend Andrew?'

Andrew turned and looked at Becky who was standing beside him and looking at him earnestly. 'Maybe, then again maybe not,' he replied with a smile. 'And why young lady, do you want to know?'

'Oh… nothing.'

'Good, then the answer is nothing.'

'Oh Andrew, don't be such a pig. You know very well, why I want to know.'

'Could it be anything to do with your enchanting sister Annabelle, that you have been telling me about?'

'You know very well it's about Annabelle,' she said sniffing hard to show her exasperation.

'And does Annabelle know that you are trying to fix her up with a boyfriend, before she has even got here?'

'Of course, she doesn't… and don't you dare say anything to her… if you do, I'll never speak to you again… she can get really mad, and she'd kill me if you told her.'

'Well maybe I won't tell her as long as you stop your matchmaking.'

'OK, but you'll be sorry. When you see her, you will wish that you had my help.'

'Rebecca, stop pestering Andrew,' Mavis had joined them quietly and had listened in to the end of their conversation. 'And if you don't, I will tell Annabelle myself. Anyway, Andrew is here to meet Daddy's new secretary, not Annabelle.'

'Oh, alright Mummy, but I think you are both *really* mean.'

'It's just touching down we can go through now into the Customs area,' said Jack who had been watching out of the large glass viewing window with Peter. 'Come on let's hurry.'

The small party trooped through the security door into the Customs area flashing their Diplomatic passes at the guard on the door. He nodded politely and waved them through with a small gesture of his hand. Becky and Jack ran forward to get a view of the plane, which was now surrounded by various vehicles. A set of mobile steps was being wheeled up against the door of the aircraft. The door opened and the head of a smartly dressed air stewardess poked out. The local British Airways Manager walked up the steps and spoke to members of the crew. After a few minutes, passengers began to file down the steps and walk across the tarmac to the terminal. A small queue formed behind the immigration desk and Peter and his family began to look out for Annabelle. Andrew watched out for an unattached young woman, who might be Peter's new secretary. She had sent a small passport photograph and Andrew did not expect to have any difficulty in identifying the sophisticated looking dark-haired young women.

'There she is,' cried Becky pointing at Annabelle who was nearing the front of the immigration queue. The sisters exchanged waves as the girl presented her passport to the Immigration Officer and Becky ran forward to meet her sister.

Andrew allowed his eyes to follow Becky's extended finger, temporarily pausing from his duty of looking for the secretary. He readily admitted to himself that Becky had been right in her assessment of her sister. Annabelle was indeed a lovely young woman. She had long blond hair and a tanned clear skin. She was wearing a white trouser suit and, although this was not Andrew's favourite choice of garment for the female sex, there was absolutely no doubt that she looked pretty good in it. The suit did nothing to detract from her long slender frame, which was gently curved in all the right places. Andrew looked at her face. She had green-blue eyes, a pert nose and a well-shaped mouth. It was in the mouth, however, that Andrew noted Annabelle's only obvious blemish. It carried a slight, but distinct, pout which suggested that this was a girl who was both spoilt and used to getting her own way.

'Excuse me, you are not from the High Commission, are you?'

Andrew rapidly turned from his scrutiny of Annabelle to the dark-haired newcomer. 'Yes, I am. You must be Daniella Briggs. Welcome to Barbados,' Andrew held out his hand. 'I'm Andrew Walker, Second Sec. Political.' Andrew had added his rank and title as was customary for Foreign Office officials meeting overseas for the first time. Although a rather formal sounding practice, it avoided any potential embarrassment for the newcomer, who would not know if their greeter was the High Commissioner or the High Commission driver.

'It's lovely to be here and a pleasure to meet you Andrew,' she said taking his proffered hand.

Andrew held on to the cool hand slightly longer than he had intended, as their eyes met. Suddenly aware, he withdrew his hand rather abruptly. The girl's mouth moved to form an amused smile and her eyes continued to hold his gaze. Andrew knew that something was happening, his normally cool demeanour seemed to be deserting him. He felt confused.

'Let me introduce you to the High Commissioner,' he said, finally managing to break the spell.

The girl's eyes followed the direction indicated by his hand and she noticeably stiffened. 'Who's that girl?' she asked.

'That's Becky, the High Commissioner's daughter. That's her twin brother Jack with her.'

'No no, not the young girl, the blond girl talking to the High Commissioner?'

'Oh, that's Annabelle. She's the High Commissioner's elder daughter.'

'Oh shit,' Daniella said quietly.

Andrew looked at her quizzically. 'She was on your flight; didn't you see her?'

'Yes,' she replied, her eyes narrowed as she grinned cheekily. 'We met at Gatwick, and I don't think I am her favourite person.'

The restaurant owner stepped forward to greet him as he entered the small anteroom that led on to the main dining area.

'Mr McMullen, how are you today sir? Your table is ready, but your dining companion has not yet arrived. Would you like to wait for him here or go straight to the table?'

'I'll wait for him here, thank you Pedro.' Angus went and sat down on the couch in front of which was a small coffee table. 'And I'll have the usual please, double scotch, no ice and just a splash of soda.'

'Certainly,' Pedro walked over to the small bar and spoke to the barman.

The whisky arrived, served exactly as he had requested. Angus took a sip and allowed the malt to move around his mouth, before sipping again. Although it was only just after noon this was not Angus' first drink of the day. In fact, it was his fifth or possibly sixth. These days he found that a drink or two before breakfast or instead of breakfast set him up for the day. His memory was not as good as it used to be and he found that his morning drink, perhaps topped up from his hip flask during the morning, helped. Angus thought back to the last few days since the arrival of the new High Commissioner. He had nothing against Peter exactly, although he thought the High Commissioner had been rather short with him at the office meeting. Mavis was another matter altogether; the woman was quite out of control. Her behaviour at the airport had been indescribable. When Angus had joined the service the wives of Ambassadors and High Commissioners had been ladies. They knew that they were representing Britain and their husbands, and nothing would have induced them to make a public display. It was really a matter of breeding; Mavis had after all been a typist, so perhaps it was to be expected. Angus' thoughts then moved to the drinks party to meet the High Commissioner's family. He had had it all arranged, everyone lined up just as it should be done. Then that bitch came in and humiliated him in front of everyone. Angus felt his indignation rising and he took another large swig of the whisky.

'Angus, how are you? Good of you to invite me.' Angus' thoughts were interrupted by the voice of his dining companion. He stood up rather unsteadily and held out his hand.

'Geoff, great to see you. What'll you have?'

'A beer will do very nicely thank you Angus.'

Angus called over the waiter and ordered a beer and another double scotch. They chatted quietly sipping their drinks. Although they could not be described as friends, they knew each other quite well and both realised that their relationship could be mutually beneficial. They exchanged views on the performance of the present Government and the prospects for an early election. Angus then briefed Geoff on the latest international meeting on Caribbean security and on the efforts, they were making with the Americans to combat drugs and money laundering. Finally, Angus drained his drink, stood up and waved towards the dining room.

'Let's eat,' he said.

'How's the new man doing?' Geoff asked as they followed the owner towards their table. The table was a corner one next to the window and overlooking the bay. Angus noted with satisfaction that it was some distance from the nearest diner so they should be able to talk in comfort without risking being overheard. Angus waited for Geoff to sit down and then sat down himself before replying.

'Oh, he's doing fine,' he paused and then added. 'So far.'

'Sounds like you don't think much of him,' observed the reporter.

'I didn't say that.'

'No, you didn't, but your approval sounded pretty qualified.'

'You journalists are always seeing disputes when they don't exist.'

'I said nothing about disputes. I just said that from your tone you didn't seem to like him much.' Angus made no comment, so Geoff continued. 'Frankly I thought his comments on sugar at the airport were pretty feeble.'

'Perhaps, but you have to remember that he has just come out,' said Angus, trying to sound loyal.

'Yes, but he must have been briefed in London?'

'Oh yes, he would certainly have been briefed.' The waiter came and took their order, and it was only when they were halfway through their fish course that Geoff raised the question of the High Commissioner again.

'What about his wife?' he asked.

Angus said nothing for a few moments then looking down at the fish on his plate and carefully removing the central bone replied. 'What about her?'

'Well personally I thought she over-reacted a bit at the airport.'

'Off the record,' said Angus. 'I thought so too.'

'She was lucky to get away with it. Anyone else would have been arrested for assault.'

'Pity she wasn't,' chuckled Angus, taking a long swig of wine. 'They were pretty lucky it didn't get in the English press or the Office would have had a thing or two to say.'

'Well you've got your young chap Walker to thank for that,' said Geoff a trifle bitterly. 'He virtually threatened us all with ex-communication, shaft the High Commissioner and no more co-operation.'

'I think that young man is rather overstepping his authority, and it's not for the first time.'

'You mean that co-operation would not be cut off if the story got back home.'

'Well certainly not by me. As I see it a journalist has to do his job and report news. We, on the other hand, have a duty to keep journalists informed on what is happening on our patch.' Angus leaned forward and dropped his voice almost to a whisper. 'It's my personal view that bad behaviour by diplomats or their families should be brought to the attention of the powers that be. If there is no sanction, standards will fall. We are, after all, representing Britain.'

Geoff looked long and hard at Angus, who now leaned back in his seat, drained his glass and beckoned to the waiter for a refill.

'I understand,' said Geoff.

Chapter 7

Peter had enjoyed Grenada. It was a pretty island, and everyone had been very friendly. The British Representative had set up a series of meetings for him with several leading politicians. All were full of enthusiasm for the future and their part in it. Perhaps it was inevitable that an island that had spawned Sir Edward Gairy's Mongoose gang, a socialist revolution and an American invasion should remain a hotbed of political intrigue. The fascinating political situation had added to Peter's pleasure, and as he boarded the LIAT jet he regretted that the visit had been restricted to two working days. He sat down in an aisle seat, opened his newspaper and waited for take-off.

Peter was halfway through the sports page when it occurred to him that they had been standing outside the terminal building for nearly half an hour, the cabin was becoming insufferably hot and he was beginning to sweat. Suddenly a voice came over the speakers.

'This is your Captain speaking. We apologise for the delay in take-off. This is due to minor technical difficulties. These should be resolved shortly, and we shall then be proceeding to the runway for take-off.'

'Leave Island Any Time' Peter turned to the speaker who was beside him, sitting in the window seat. She was a girl who looked barely into her twenties. It took him only a few seconds to realise that she was stunning, and he wondered how it was possible that he had not noticed her before.

'I thought LIAT stood for 'Luggage In Any Town,' he said.

'That too, probably,' replied the girl.

Peter wondered whether to continue the conversation. He was acutely aware that any efforts to keep her talking might look as if he was trying to chat her up. Even a hint of such a thing would be totally inappropriate for Her Majesty's High Commissioner. Even though he had just arrived in the area his face was becoming known to the public, and it was highly probable that at least one person on the plane knew who he was. Not only that, the girl looked even younger than Annabelle. He was old enough to be her father.

'Are you here on holiday?' the girl had removed the decision from him.

'No,' he replied. 'I work in Barbados.

'What do you do?' she asked.

'Err, I'm a Civil Servant,' he said, not wishing to reveal too much.

'Where from? America? England?'

'Britain.'

'How do you like the Caribbean,' she asked.

'Oh, I think it's wonderful, and I like your weather. Not like England.'

'This is my first big trip from Grenada,' the girl said.

'Really,' Peter wondered whether to find out more, but once again the girl pre-empted him.

'I am Miss Junior Caribbean. They are sending me on a trip to Barbados, St Vincent, St Lucia and Antigua. Then, next year, I get to go to America to enter the Miss Americas competition.'

'It must be very exciting.'

'Oh, it is. What's your name?'

'Peter,' he replied, then thinking that sounded a bit familiar added 'Err Peter Parker.'

'Mine's Trixie,' she said, clearly not too worried about sounding familiar. 'How do you do Peter' she giggled, holding out her hand.

'How do you do Trixie,' he said, taking it.

It seemed like no time at all before they were in the air. Trixie chattered away, telling him about her brothers and sisters, school, hobbies and above all her hopes of winning in America. Peter could not help noticing that whenever she got a little excited, about this or that bit of her life story, she would bring her knees up, between the narrow seats, and hug them. Her full cotton skirt would slide perilously upwards revealing the lower part of a pair of very slender thighs. It was probably the effect of the thighs that encouraged Peter to make his comment.

'I really hope you win in America,' he said. 'You are very pretty.'

'Oh, do you think so?' she purred. 'But don't you think my breasts are a bit small?' Trixie leant forward revealing the upper half of two perfectly formed spheres, the light fabric also fell forward giving Peter just a momentary glimpse of two dark brown, pointed nipples.

'Juice and sandwich. Sorry about the delay,' said the Steward dropping a small tray in Peter's lap. The tray hit something hard and began to topple. With deft professionalism the Steward grabbed it to stop it falling. 'Oops sorry,' he said. 'It's a bit bumpy down there.'

Peter found himself going red, but Trixie elbowed him lightly in the ribs and giggled. 'Don't worry, I think he meant the air turbulence.'

'What are you up to this weekend?' asked Andrew.

'Unpacking,' she smiled ruefully. 'My heavy baggage was delivered this morning.'

'That's not bad, you've only just arrived.'

'True,' said Daniella, 'But I don't have much. It's nice to have moved into the flat though.'

'Do you need a hand? I'm not doing anything tomorrow.'

'That would be nice. Are you sure?'

'Yes. I remember when I arrived. I seemed to be living with cardboard boxes for weeks. If you hit it quickly, right at the beginning, it's a lot easier. What time do you want me?'

'Shall we say ten o'clock?'

'Fine, ten o'clock I'll be there.'

'Thank you,' said the girl, turning to go. She got to his office door and turned back to face him. 'Andrew,' she said.

'Yes?'

'You are very sweet,' and with a friendly smile she turned and left.

Andrew turned picked up his biro, and began to check the draft of the programme for the High Commissioner's visit to St Vincent. The telephone rang and he picked it up. 'Andrew Walker,' he said.

'Oh, Andrew it's Annabelle.'

'Hello Annabelle, how are you settling in?'

'Fine thank you. Listen Mummy wondered if you would like to come to tea on Sunday?'

'That would be nice, but I'm afraid I can't. I'm accompanying the High Commissioner to St Vincent on Sunday. We have to be at the airport at quarter to six.'

'No problem. I've already spoken to Daddy. He says it would be fine for you to go to the airport from here in his car.'

'In that case I'd love to come. What time do you want me?'

'Shall we say three o'clock?'

'I'll be there at three then, complete with suitcase.'

'Suitcase? You're coming to tea not to spend the night,' Annabelle then dropped her voice to a seductive whisper and added. 'Unless you want to that is.'

'My suitcase for St Vincent, I meant.'

'Oh, sorry. Yes of course. I'd forgotten. See you Sunday.' The phone went dead and Peter held it thoughtfully for a few moments before returning it to its cradle. What did she have in mind? Only yesterday he had seen Meriko off at the airport. Now, less than twenty-four hours later, he had arranged to spend Saturday with Daniella and Sunday afternoon with Annabelle. He would have to watch his step.

He heard the clatter of the letterbox and the familiar sound of envelopes dropping on the carpet. Stefan put down his coffee cup on the kitchen table and tightened the cord round the waist of his dressing gown. He had put on weight. He was no longer the fit, Securitate Colonel in his early thirties who had defected from his native Romania for a new life in the West. He had, however, done well in the intervening couple of decades. His house in Esher in Surrey was worth at least half a million, he owned a Jaguar and Rodica had an Audi. Young Stefan junior had had a good education and gained a good degree at Bristol University. His sister Chrissy was now on her way to her degree in English, before doing her Post Graduate teaching degree. The long hours he had spent being interrogated in safe houses in the English countryside and the years looking over his shoulder at shadows had been worth it. He was now a successful British businessman and, since the fall of Ceaușescu in Romania, no longer feared the risk of reprisals from his former masters. Stefan walked into the hall, bent down and picked up the mail. He returned to the kitchen, took another sip of coffee and began to sort it out.

There were the usual batch of bills and junk mail, several letters to Rodica and the children and one or two business letters, that had not been addressed to his office. Finally, he got down to two items, the first a thick brown envelope bearing the familiar 'On Her Majesty Service' motive in blue with a tiny symbol in the corner to indicate re-cycled paper. The second was an airmail envelope liberally covered with stamps from the Turks and Caicos Islands. He opened the official envelope first. It was from the Commercial Officer in Barbados and covered the draft programme for the Trade Mission he was going to lead. He glanced rapidly at the closely typed sheet, neatly laid out in date order. He was about to return it to its envelope for future scrutiny when an item on the first page caught his eye. 'Opening address by the High Commissioner, Mr Peter Parker C.M.G.' Could it be the Peter Parker? The Peter Parker he had known all those years ago. The Peter Parker who had visited the East Coast of Romania with him, jumped into bed with a local girl, and fathered her child. Stefan stood up and went into his study. He took out a copy of the latest Who's Who and went through almost fifty entries under 'Parker'. Although none of them were listed as High Commissioner in Barbados, it was clear that there was only one who fitted the profile of a newly arrived High Commissioner and that was the Peter Parker who had served in Bucharest as a young man.

Stefan went back into the kitchen, sipped his coffee and opened the other envelope. It was a letter from his partner who ran the Caribbean end of his business. Filip Mendez. The letter did not bring good news; instead it carried two dire warnings. American Government investigators had been asking questions about the company. One American, who Filip counted as a friend, having accepted favours from him both in cash and kind, had warned him that a raid was likely of their offices in the next few weeks, to look for evidence of money laundering. Filip had shredded all incriminating documents, but it was only a matter of time before matters got out of control. Secondly, and perhaps of even more concern, the opposition from Venezuela was taking a close interest in their activities. Filip had received a visitor late one night. The visitor had said very little, but just enough to convey that Filip and his partner were unwelcome in the area, unless they abandoned their current business activities. The suggestion was that they should find some other way to make a living and, if they didn't, then they would not be living long enough to enjoy any living they made. The man had left saying that Filip and Stefan had only a few weeks to decide where their future lay. Filip ended up by saying that Stefan should come out to visit, but that he should not do so for a month as he, Filip, was being watched and it would be better not to make others think they were panicking.

Stefan took a long sip of his coffee and sat back in his chair. Clearly it was time to think about retirement. Filip was right, both the authorities and the opposition posed severe problems. It was perhaps fortunate that in less than two weeks he would be leading a Trade Mission to the area. This would give him some cover and possibly some protection. Some of the Mission members would be going to other islands, after Barbados, so he could visit various banks where he and Filip had accounts. If there were any problems, he could call on the assistance of the local British Mission. Peter Parker would be useful; both to give him respectability and to buy time before an official investigation took place. He must check the documents that he had brought with him from Romania. Documents that, at first, he had obtained in case they might be useful for his defection, but which, in the event, he had not used. Then there was Filip. Could he trust him? Filip's reasons for suggesting that he should not come out for a month seemed pretty flimsy. Better not to tell him that he would be there within two weeks, just in case his partner had ideas about clearing some of the company's bank accounts into his own. Stefan selected a date five weeks ahead and prepared a fax to Filip to say that that was the date when he would arrive.

It was true that Daniella did not have many possessions, but there still seemed to be an awful lot of boxes. Daniella had told the packers to put everything together in the second bedroom, so she and Andrew opened each box and carefully unwrapped its contents. Daniella would then decide which room she wanted the items in and together they would transfer them to their new home. Very quickly there was a huge pile of wrapping paper.

'Obviously they charge the Foreign Office by volume,' observed Andrew. 'I've never seen so much wrapping paper.'

'At least nothing is broken,' replied Daniella. 'At least, not yet.'

'True,' said Andrew. Then pointing to a large fairly thin box asked, 'What's in there?'

'Oh, that will be my pictures. Let's open it and you can help me put them up.'

The case was solid and well protected but with the help of the hammer and screwdriver that Andrew had brought with him he managed to get the top off. The box contained six pictures. The first was a beautiful drawing of a donkey.

'Wow, I like this,' said Andrew. 'Who did it?'

'It's by a Romanian artist called Grigorescu. That icon is Romanian too.'

'It's lovely,' Andrew picked up the icon and examined it closely. 'Where did you get it, it must be worth a fortune.'

'They belonged to my Mother. She gave me them as a going-away present. She was originally from Romania.'

'So, you are Romanian? That must be where you get your classic Latin looks from.'

'Don't be silly,' she said giving him a friendly prod in the ribs. 'Anyway, I'm only half Romanian, My Dad is a Geordie and proud of it.'

'Ah, I thought I detected a bit of a Geordie accent. All those short 'A's.'

'*Andrew*,' she squealed, 'you had better watch out. Git yersell on the wrong side of a Geordie man, an yer'll live to regret it.'

'Sorry, sorry. You have the sincere apologies of a Southerner. I shall never again question the language of a Geordie, and most certainly not of a Romanian Geordie.'

The cushion hit him on the head, and he retaliated with a ball of packing paper. Soon they were in full battle until finally they fell together in a heap on the mound of wrapping paper. 'Enough' she commanded, still laughing. 'Back to work, you lazy Southerner.'

Andrew stood up and held out his hand to help her up. She took it and pulled herself to her feet. For a few seconds they were off-balance as they steadied themselves among the pile of wrapping paper. She fell towards him a little and instinctively he caught her in his arms. Their eyes were only a few inches apart and for a frozen moment they locked. Andrew found his lips moving towards her mouth. Her lips were moist and inviting. He felt all the thrills of that first kiss, a kiss that stirred in his memory from adolescence, but this was better, oh so much better. Daniella drew back as Andrew released her.

'Sorry,' he said.

'Don't be,' she said, then with a charming little giggle added. 'But come on, you are here to work.'

Andrew nodded his agreement and went back to the box of pictures to remove the other four. Three were landscapes in watercolour; the fourth was a portrait in oils of a very pretty woman, with dark hair, in young middle age.

'Are these by Grigorescu too?' he asked. 'They are very good.'

'No silly,' she said, a little frown appearing on the corners of her mouth. 'They're mine, I paint a bit in my spare time.'

'They really are very good. You are quite an artist. Who is the lovely lady with the dark hair?'

'Thank you,' she said, 'That's my Mother.'

'You ought to take it up professionally.'

'Don't be daft, lots of people paint. Come on stop wasting time,' her tone was mildly reproachful, but he could see that she was pleased. 'We've got to get this place shipshape, the High Commissioner said he might pop in, when he gets back from St Vincent, to see how I have settled in.

Andrew arrived at the door of the Residence and rang the bell. The door opened almost immediately, but instead of the butler a young girl appeared.

'Hi Andrew, wait until you see Annabelle. She has dressed herself up especially for you.'

'Becky,' Andrew said sternly. 'If you don't behave yourself, I shall turn right around and go home.'

'You can't,' she said gleefully. 'You have to go to the airport with Daddy.'

'Yes, I can. Once I tell your father what you are trying to do, he will agree to meet me at the airport. He will probably send you off to bed as well.'

'Oh alright. Stop making such a fuss. Anyway, Mummy is waiting for you on the veranda. Annabelle is still upstairs - *getting herself ready for you.*'

'*Rebecca.*' Andrew's voice carried all the authority of a professional man in his prime.

Becky sniffed and turned away. 'Follow me please.' She said, with studied coolness.

Andrew smiled to himself and followed her on to the balcony.

'I hope Becky has not been bothering you,' said Mavis, greeting him warmly.

Andrew looked at Becky who glared at him. 'Oh, not at all. *Children* never bother me.' Andrew watched as his barb struck home. Becky sniffed again loudly and sat down in a cane chair, deliberately not looking at him.

'Have some tea,' Mavis hid her smile, reckoning that perhaps Becky had been put in her place sufficiently for the time being. She went over to the trolley and poured him a cup, complying with his request for milk and no sugar. Andrew sat down in the chair next to Becky and waited for the thaw that he knew would come. Suddenly he was on his feet again, his eyes blinking to make sure they were not deceived. She was an apparition. At the airport her hair had been long and blond, but showing the results of a long and exhausting journey. At the High Commission, when she had come with her family to meet the staff, it was tied back, and she looked every bit the young lady doctor that she was soon to be. But now, on the Residence balcony, she was transformed. Her hair fell loosely to her shoulders like golden corn. She was wearing a light white cotton dress with a blue print, the blue seemed to pick out the blue flecks in her blue-green eyes. The light fabric touched gently on the curve of her breasts, clung to her small waist and hinted at the slender line of her legs.

'Annabelle, you look lovely,' Andrew spoke with a quiet sincerity. Annabelle looked pleased, Mavis amused and Becky triumphant. Annabelle had scored and, not for the first time, a young man had been knocked off his feet.

That afternoon a new Annabelle was revealed to Andrew. An Annabelle happy and at ease in the bosom of her family, but more surprisingly an Annabelle who was a fierce idealist. She was a stout defender of the National Health Service, a scourge to the politicians who only saw it in terms of electoral advantage and an advocate for proper care for the elderly. Despite his earlier doubts, Andrew now found that not only did he find Annabelle devastatingly attractive, but he liked her as well.

When Mavis took him to one side, just before he left for the airport, and asked for a small favour, Andrew said that he would be delighted. Peter and Mavis had been invited by the American Ambassador to a dinner to welcome them to Barbados. When the Ambassador heard that they had a grown-up daughter, he invited them to bring her too. He had asked whether she would like to bring a friend or whether he should provide a young American diplomat to make up the numbers. Mavis had immediately thought of Andrew, and promised to let the Ambassador know the next day.

Peter led the way through the swing doors of their St Vincent hotel. Andrew followed, and they made their way across the lobby to the Reception desk.

'Peter,' it was a girl's voice, sweet and clear across the deserted lobby. Both men turned.

'Oh hello,' Peter groaned inwardly as the girl almost skipped towards him, her long dark hair and pink cotton dress swaying as she moved.

'Peter, it's lovely to see you again. I hoped we would meet.' She turned to look at Andrew. 'Well, aren't you going to introduce me to your friend?'

'Err… yes of course,' Peter muttered, a feeling of embarrassment creeping over him. 'This is Andrew Walker. Andrew this is… err… Trixie.' Too late he realised he had no idea of her second name and added 'Err Trixie.'

'Nice to meet you Trixie,' said Andrew, carefully suppressing the smile that was itching to escape.

'I've got to run,' said Trixie. 'They're going to do a photo session in bikinis. See you both later.'

'Fine,' said Peter, but it wasn't.

'I hope so,' said Andrew, not minding at all.

'Let's book in,' said Peter, giving Andrew a firm look, which said 'just one word and you'll regret it.'

Chapter 8

Nicu sat down on the settee and took the small cup of thick sweet coffee from his sister. Although it was over twenty years since Suzana had left Romania, she still liked to serve Romanian style coffee. She rarely got the genuine article; that was a treat that only occurred when she had visitors from her native country. Turkish coffee was, however, readily available in Newcastle and it was close enough to the real thing to be acceptable.

Nicu had stayed in Mangalia for several years after she had left and had gradually progressed in the local party. It was only when Ceaușescu had been deposed by the mob and his beloved Communist party had been threatened by imperialist forces that he moved westward. Unlike his sister, however, his destination had not been England. He had chosen South America. He rapidly discovered that his many Party and Securitate contacts opened many doors. Money and secrecy had always been part of the lives of the Romanian party elite. The money, which was stored in safe havens, ranging from Switzerland to the Caribbean, allowed them to buy their way into many areas of international crime including the drugs trade. The secrecy helped them to disappear without trace. Nicu soon found that he had skills that were in great demand. He specialised in getting rid of embarrassing problems. It would not be fair to call him a paid assassin, as only a relatively small proportion of his problems ended up in that way.

'How is Danny liking Barbados?' 'Danny' was Nicu's pet name for Daniella. Uncle and niece had always got on well, although Suzana had always been wary of her brother's influence on the young girl. To be honest, he had never done anything to cause her concern, but she knew the type of people Nicu hung around with and there would always be a potential for trouble.

'She's only been there a little while, but she did telephone from the hotel and say it all looked very pretty and everyone seemed very nice.'

'Hotel? Don't they give her her own place?'

'Yes, she will have a nice flat. She's probably moved in by now.'

'How many bedrooms?'

Suzana opened her mouth to reply, then closed it again and paused for several moments before speaking. 'Why do you want to know?'

'Oh, nothing,' then seeing the hard glint in his sister's eye added 'I thought I might pay her a visit, after all Barbados is not that far from my office in Caracas.'

'Just as I thought,' Suzana's voice hardened, and she moved closer to Nicu and waved her pointed finger at him. 'Now look here Nicu Cuza, what you get up to is your business and frankly I do not want to know about it, but don't you dare involve Daniella in any way. She is starting a new job, a job that requires total respectability. The last thing she needs is her drug dealer uncle fouling things up.'

'Steady Suzana. Don't jump to conclusions. You know I wouldn't do anything to harm Danny. I just want to pay her a visit. If a man can't visit his own niece, it's a bit much. Anyway, I'm not a drug dealer, I'm a businessman.'

'Businessman!' Suzana snorted. 'That can mean anything. All I know is that three of the people you used to call friends are locked away for dealing. Maybe you're not involved yourself, but I don't like your choice of friends.'

'Trust me,' said Nicu standing up and putting his arms around his sister. 'You have my solemn promise that I will do nothing that could affect Danny in any way.'

'Well you had just better not,' she said taking his arms in her hands and pushing them away. 'If you do anything to harm Daniella, Nicu, you will have me to deal with and don't think I wouldn't have you put away for it, brother or not.'

The sun beat down on the parade ground. It had rained heavily throughout the night, and the sun seemed to have made little impact on the several large puddles that remained. Peter watched, from the VIP stand, as the military band played Colonel Bogie and a series of other popular pieces as it marched. Behind the band was a contingent of policemen, still wearing the white Colonial uniforms that had typified British rule. They were followed by contingents of sailors, sea cadets and girl guides. As each group passed in front of the platform, on which stood the Prime Minister and other dignitaries, they moved their heads smartly to the right and saluted.

The puddles were beginning to cause a problem. The band and the policemen had ignored them, marching on with great discipline. Their marching helped disperse the water a little but, where this had been achieved, the result was mud. Their boots were soon covered in mud and the policemen had large brown streaks across their white uniform trousers. The following groups were more circumspect. The sailors split their column in an orderly fashion joining up again after each obstacle. Once or twice the pairing seemed to go awry and as some of the sailors realised that they had changed partners they made little shuffles to re-align. The following cadets watched and then sought to mimic their seniors. Unfortunately, they were marching three abreast so, as each outer line moved away from the danger, the central line was left with several options. The lead cadet had to make the choice. At first, he veered to the left and then to the right; changed his mind and decided to march on, braving the water like a true warrior. The cadets following him had snaked behind him left and right, before taking individual decisions. Some adhered to the left column and some to the right, some ploughed on through the water, others attempted to jump. The resulting splashes sent the outer columns further out, only to return rapidly to the centre as dry land was reached. The returning cadets tended to be quicker than their wet counterparts, so incoming bodies collided with ones that were still dodging and jumping. The Girl Guides, based on the hypothesis that women are brighter than men and don't self-destruct so easily, stopped short of the danger area and formed a cluster of pointing, giggling girls. The band marched proudly on oblivious of the pandemonium behind them until they too, having completed a full circuit were faced with the problem of what to do with the group of Girl Guides blocking their path. The crowd began to fall into the spirit of the exercise and began to cheer. Finally, a red-faced Colonel in Chief leapt from his place on the platform, next to the Prime Minister, and yelled at the top of his voice.

'Attention!' Everyone froze until the Colonel continued in a succession of barked orders. 'Police Unit; About Turn; Halt; Form up in ranks of three; Stand Easy. Marine Band; Left Face; Four paces forward; Halt. Gradually a pattern began to take shape and the Colonel stood hands on hips looking at his handy work. All contingents were now lined up facing the platform, the Band played the National Anthem and the Prime Minister began to speak.

'Is it usually like this?' whispered Peter to Andrew.

'Well it doesn't usually rain so hard,' came the diplomatic reply.

Soon it was over, and Peter and Andrew thanked the Chief of Protocol who was overseeing the diplomatic guests. They decided to cut across the parade ground as a short cut to reach their parked car. Several thousand other spectators had also converged on the ground, so it became quite a difficult act of navigation to maintain direction and avoid puddles. Suddenly a large ripple arose in the crowd just ahead of them; several people were running towards them. There was a scream and a shout and a young man, with a beard, appeared swinging a machete in front of him. The crowd scattered, some squealing some laughing.

'Let's get out of here,' urged Andrew. 'He's high on something, alcohol or ganja.'

'Wait,' commanded Peter. 'Look.'

Andrew turned back towards the man just in time to see the cause of Peter's concern. The man had lunged into the crowd and grabbed hold of a girl. The girl was Trixie. Andrew was stunned by what happened next. The High Commissioner leapt forward and with every ounce of strength in his body punched the man full in the face. The man fell like a stone pulling Trixie down on top of him. Peter pulled her free, and the sobbing girl fell into his arms.

'Come on Sir, let's get out of here before the press arrive,' quickly and with great presence of mind Andrew ushered the pair rapidly to their waiting car and installed them in the rear seat. He jumped in the front next to the driver and told him to take them straight to the hotel. Peter slumped back on the seat, he found that he was beginning to shake from a mixture of fear and exhaustion. But he also felt exhilarated; deep down some element of the macho male stirred inside him. He had acted with speed and bravery, and he had won. The girl was leaning up against him.

'Thank you,' she said. He turned towards her to reply, but the words froze in his mouth. Something was happening and he could not quite believe it. Her hand had moved down to his lap and was gently squeezing his penis through his trousers. He wondered whether to protest, but instead lay further back in his seat and closed his eyes.

Sir Percival stood up and the assembled group of senior officers took their cue from him and collected their papers and prepared to leave.

'Derek, can you spare me a few moments,' Sir Percival asked, addressing his request to the Chief Clerk, Sir Derek Porter.

'Certainly Percy,' replied Sir Derek sitting down again. The Private Secretary hovered briefly, to find out if he was required, then on receiving the unspoken nod from the Permanent Under Secretary, quietly left the room closing the door behind him.

'I take it you've seen this?' Sir Percival tossed a red-topped tabloid newspaper onto the table between them.

'Yes, not exactly the sort of publicity the Office needs at the moment.'

'How well do you know Parker?'

'Fairly well. We worked quite closely when he was heading Information Division.'

'Yes, I've talked to him a few times of course, but I was still in

Washington during most of his time here.' Sir Percival frowned. 'What do you think we should do about it?'

'Well it's unfortunate, but not really his fault. I know his wife, Mavis, too. Bit of a character so I'm not completely surprised. Does sound as if she may have been provoked into doing what she did. I agree that we cannot just ignore it now it's in the Press. Better ask Peter to send a detailed report. He should have done that before, but clearly hoped we would not hear about it.'

'Yes,' said Sir Percival. 'That was very foolish of him. Another mistake like that and we may have to consider how well equipped he is for the job. This time I'm prepared not to make too much of it; but send him a telegram asking him about the full circumstances. Oh, and Parliamentary Unit tell me that Marcus Smith has put down an Oral PQ to the Secretary of State asking about sugar quotas. You had better let Parker know and tell him to let the Department have some notes for supplementaries.'

'Marcus Smith? Sugar quotas are not his usual subject,' observed Sir Derek. 'It sounds like his supplementary will be about Mavis Parker.'

'Exactly,' said Sir Percival. 'Oh, and you had better send the telegram Personal and De-cypher Yourself.'

'Of course,' replied the Chief Clerk.

Daniella was busy. The High Commissioner had left her with plenty of work to do for his return, and she had to begin the invitations for the Reception he was going to hold for the Trade Mission. She looked up as Angus McMullen came into her office.

'Daniella, I've got some dictation for you. Perhaps you could come to my office in, shall we say, ten minutes.'

Daniella looked at him in amazement. Angus had his own Secretary and there seemed no reason why he should call upon her services. 'But can't Alice do it? I have rather a lot to do for the High Commissioner before he returns.'

'No, Alice can't do it,' he sneered. 'I have given Alice the day off. She was very busy whilst I was Acting High Commissioner. I need some work doing and when Peter is away, I am the High Commissioner, so you will kindly do as you are told.'

'Very well,' replied Daniella, trying hard to suppress the tears of anger that were welling up inside her. It was true that Angus was in charge during Peter absence but, as Peter was still working in the area, he was not Acting High Commissioner. He had no right to take her over, unless he had agreed it with Peter in advance. Had this been the case Peter would have mentioned it. Still she would have to work with the man in the future and it would not be wise to cross him.

Ten minutes later Daniella walked into Angus' office, holding her notebook and pencil. Angus indicated to a chair in front of his desk and she sat down. Angus walked over to his office door, closed it and then returned to sit down behind his desk. She looked up expectantly, her notebook open, her legs neatly crossed. Angus was looking at her. In fact, to be more precise, he was looking directly at her crossed legs. She adjusted her skirt, pulling it firmly down over her knees, she glared at him with just enough hostility to indicate her displeasure at his intrusion into her personal space. Angus cleared his throat and began to dictate.

Daniella found herself becoming more and more irritated as she neatly transcribed his words into shorthand in her notebook. The first letter was to the Foreign Office about the routine repair of a shredder, a job that should have been delegated to Jim Smythe, the Management Officer. The second was a letter to the Canadian Deputy High Commissioner thanking him for a darts evening he had held two weeks ago. The third, which nearly caused her to explode, was a letter to his Golf Club in the UK renewing his membership. Daniella decided that if the next letter was either trivial or personal, she would protest in the strongest possible terms, regardless of the consequences. Angus stood up, however, and walked over standing just behind her chair.

'Perhaps you would read them back to me please,' he said. Daniella flicked back to the first letter, although not happy about his demand she felt that if she complied quickly, she would be able to leave. She began to read. Angus leant over her and she got a strong whiff of stale whisky. She began to read more quickly, even more anxious to escape.

'You know, you may be a bit prickly, but you are a pretty young lassee.' Daniella ignored the remark and read on even faster. Suddenly he was leaning right over her, his mouth pressed up against her ear, his hand moving forward, first squeezing her breast and then trying to slide it down into her top. Daniella squealed and tried to struggle to her feet. She recoiled as a full blast of whisky struck her in the face. She grabbed at his hand, which was trying to get into her bra.

'Let me go you foul bastard,' she hissed. But Angus pressed on, both hands now trying to fondle her breasts.

'Come on. Don't be such a prude. It's not the first time you've led a man on, and it won't be the last.'

Daniella fought hard, wondering whether to scream, when the door opened.

'Oops sorry,' said the voice of Anthony Tremlett, disappearing again and closing the door behind him. Daniella wanted to cry out as her hope of salvation disappeared. Angus was temporarily off balance; he drew away red-faced and breathing heavily. Daniella decided to rush for the door, but before she could do so it opened again.

'Daniella, I have to give you your security briefing. Could you go to my room? I will be with you in a moment.' He opened the door to her and ushered her out. 'Angus a word in your ear please.' And the door closed leaving Daniella outside. She made her way to Anthony's office and waited, still shaking, outside the locked door.

Five minutes later Anthony appeared. He opened the door and invited her in.

'Sorry about the security briefing, I just needed to get you out of there. I will need to have a word later, on security, but that can wait. Now, as for our drunken Deputy High Commissioner, I leave it to you whether you report him to Peter on his return. You could, of course, speak direct to Personnel if you prefer it. For the moment I've dealt with him and he will think twice before he tries anything like that again. However,' Anthony gave her a friendly smile, 'if the filthy sod does anything at all that is out of line you just have to let me know, and I personally will see that he is on the plane faster than you can say Jack Robinson. I'm sorry that you have had to put up with such behaviour on your first posting. Believe me, there are not many like him in the Service and even he was a bit more of a Gentleman before the drink got to him.'

'Thank you, Anthony,' she said, feeling a little bit better. 'I am grateful.'

'You're more than welcome. And don't forget I am here if you need me. If you decide to report him formally you would be quite within your rights.'

Peter turned over towards her; she was facing the other way. He sat up slightly, leaning on his elbow and allowed his eyes to wander slowly from her shiny black hair down the curve of her back, across her small firm buttocks down her slender thighs and slim legs to her coffee coloured feet and then back up again. He stretched out his hand and touched the nape of her neck, then allowed his finger to gently trace the journey previously followed by his eyes. As he reached her buttocks, he opened his hand wide and gently squeezed. Trixie stirred and murmured like a contented cat. He leant forward and kissed her on the back of her neck. He felt his erection growing and pushed it between her buttocks.

'Naughty man,' said Trixie pulling away and turning towards him in one smooth movement. She brought her lips to his, kissed him hard and thrust a searching tongue into his open mouth. Soon he was on top of her again, repeating for the third or fourth time that night the exhilarating journey inside her. Afterwards they lay side by side, allowing their bodies to enjoy the sweet calm that followed the completion of their lovemaking.

'God, look at the time,' Peter suddenly awoke to the reality of the day, his calls on the Prime Minister and Leader of the Opposition were less than an hour away.

'Me too,' she squealed. 'I've got another photo-shoot at half-past nine.' She gave his penis one last squeeze and jumped off the bed, then dropped to the floor and began to search for her pants. Peter looked at the crouching girl and made to leap off the bed towards her. 'No, too late,' she said getting up quickly, pants clutched in left hand, bra in right. She dodged around him nimbly into the bathroom and closed the door.

Soon they were dressed and stood together holding each other.

'Can I see you again?' Peter asked.

'Yes.'

'When?'

'I'll be in Barbados next week, at the Grand Barbados.'

'It was nice,' said Peter.

'Yes, it was nice,' she replied kissing him. 'Ask for me at the hotel.'

'I will,' he replied.

Trixie opened the door and peeped out; the coast was clear. She stepped quickly out into the corridor. At that moment the door of the room opposite opened.

'Good morning,' said the man, turning and walking towards the lift.

'Morning,' Trixie replied, following him towards the lift.

The man held the lift door open and she stepped inside.

'Holiday?' he asked.

'No,' she replied. 'I'm here on a publicity tour as Miss Junior Caribbean.'

'Interesting,' he replied. 'I might be able to help promote your career,' he put his hand in his top pocket, took out a card and handed it to her.

'Thank you,' she said, taking the card and looking at it. 'Thank you, Mr Forrest, or can I call you Geoff?'

The Registry clerk walked into Angus' office. Angus beckoned to him to come forward to the desk, where he was reading the English papers that had just arrived in the bag. One had pleased him greatly. On the front page was a picture of Mavis foot outstretched, the sugar worker was doubled up, intense pain clearly etched on his face. The headline in bold black letters read 'Her Ladyship stands by our man in Barbados'. Inside Angus read with great glee how the badly briefed High Commissioner has fluffed his lines on sugar quotas and how his wife had ridden to his rescue with size ten boots. Having revelled in the incident in the news section of the paper, the editor had then added his views in the leader column. Many readers, he argued, may accept the need for highly paid diplomats swigging their cocktails at public expense. Few, however, would condone our public servants indulging in this sort of embarrassing spectacle. The editor finally concluded that the High Commissioner should be relieved of his duties and replaced by someone who knew how to behave.

'Yes?' asked Angus.

'We have just received an Immediate 'Decypher Yourself' telegram from London, 'Personal' for the High Commissioner. Do you want me to ask Communications to copy it to St Vincent?'

'No, there's no need. Just set it up and I will be up in a minute to decypher it.'

'But, it is marked 'Personal' and it's from the Chief Clerk.

'I said that I would deal with it.'

'OK, but I still think…'

'You are not paid to think, you are paid to do as you are told.'

Angus knew that he was breaking all the rules. If in doubt he should have telephoned London explaining that the High Commissioner was away and asking for instructions. The telegram could be about anything, even about himself, but he was fairly sure it would be about the Mavis incident. Angus went up to the Registry and decyphered, and read, the telegram. It was even better than he had hoped. A Parliamentary Question, that was really the icing on the cake. The reply would take all his drafting skills. He had to sound as if he was supporting Peter; but do everything possible to make the situation worse. He licked his lips in joyous anticipation of the task ahead.

Daniella opened her personal mail that had come in the bag. As she had hoped there was a letter from her mother. There was also a Bank statement and a note from Overseas Allowances Section about her allowances. Finally, there was a letter from Uncle Nicu. She looked first at the Bank statement and worked out how much she could expect with her new allowances. She would have to be careful with her money for a while, but it should be manageable. She then read the letter from her mother who gave her all the latest news of friends and family. She ended up by saying that Uncle Nicu wanted to visit her and, whilst she did not want to tell her what to do, she should only agree to his request if she felt comfortable with it. Daniella smiled to herself, Mum was always watching out for her and she was always worrying. She then opened the letter from Uncle Nicu and began to read.

My dearest Danny,

I was delighted when your Mother told me you had been sent to Barbados. It's a great place, I know you will like it. What was especially good news for me was that you can come and visit me in Caracas. It's almost next door. I hope you can get some leave in the summer and come and stay with me for two or three weeks. I have a nice apartment overlooking the Avila with a private swimming pool down below. We can also go and visit the Angel falls in Canaima, it's wonderful there. One of my friends has a plane we can borrow for the trip.

Anyway, more of that later, what I want to ask you now is a small favour. I have to visit Barbados for a couple of weeks, and it occurred to me that I would be much happier staying with my niece than shut up in some stuffy old hotel. What do you think? It would be lots of fun exploring the island together (when we are not working that is). If it's OK with you, give me a ring on the number above. (Feel free to reverse the charge).

Looking forward to seeing you,
Your affectionate uncle,
Nicu.

Daniella didn't hesitate. She picked up the telephone and within moments was talking to her uncle. She told him that she would love to see him and would be delighted to have him as her honoured guest.

Chapter 9

Peter knocked on the door and waited. He had returned from St Vincent the previous day. Today was Sunday, and he had not yet been to the High Commission. Now was an opportunity to kill two birds with one stone. He had promised to visit Daniella to see how she had settled into her new flat, but he also wanted to know if anything important had happened in his absence. Peter was glad to be back in Barbados, St Vincent seemed like another world, but another world that would not let him go. He kept seeing flashes of her in his mind, her delicate coffee-coloured skin, her pert little breasts, the clutch of black hair between her legs. She had excited him more than he could ever remember having been excited. She had brought back his youth. Just thinking about her made him excited again, and it made him young again. He so much wanted to see her again, and yet there was guilt, he was consumed by guilt. Although his marriage to Mavis had not started as the most romantic of marriages, it had survived. Mavis and he had grown together. She was his soul mate and his affection for her ran very deep. The sexual side of the marriage was good too; they knew how to satisfy each other and had their own secret ways of meeting each other's needs. Peter had remained faithful for over twenty years. But now there was Trixie, what should he do?

His thoughts were interrupted by the door opening. Daniella stood there, smiling and looking lovely. Peter had not yet begun to analyse his feelings towards this girl. If he were to do so, he would have realised that it was not sexual, but that there was a feeling of warmth and knowledge developing between them. The feeling had been there almost from the beginning, something rare, something indefinable.

'High Commissioner, it's really kind of you to come,' she opened the door wider to let him in. 'You must be terribly busy.'

'Not at all, it's my pleasure.'

'Can I offer you a drink, tea or coffee perhaps?'

'A cup of tea would be lovely thank you.'

'Have a seat, I'll be right back.' Daniella disappeared into the kitchen and he heard the kettle begin to boil and the rattle of cups. He began to let his eyes wander around the room. The office provided the basic furniture and Daniella did not have a huge amount of possessions, but it quickly became clear that the girl had taste. His eye caught a landscape in watercolour, and he stood up and went over to it to examine it more closely. It was beautifully done, the artist clearly had talent and a wonderful sense of colour. He moved to a second landscape, which was even better. He could see that the artist's technique was developing and wondered who they were. He stooped and looked at the name neatly painted in the corner. 'D. Briggs' that was Daniella's family name it must be a relation, or even Daniella herself. Intrigued he moved to the next picture; it was a drawing of a donkey. Peter did a double-take in amazement; it was a picture he knew. The donkey looking slightly knock-kneed, with pointed ears and a heavy backpack. It was a Grigorescu print, he would have staked his life on it. How strange to find such a picture among an English girl's belongings. If the Donkey surprised him the next picture almost made his heart stop. The oil painting of a pretty dark-haired woman had all the familiarity of a ghost from the past. The woman was older than the Suzana he remembered, but the likeness was too great for it to be anyone else. If he needed any further evidence that it was his own past that he was seeing, it was there in front of him hung neatly beside the oil painting; there was no mistaking the icon.

'Here we are, tea and biscuits. Do you take sugar?' Daniella's voice behind him brought him crashing into the present.

'Err no sugar thank you,' he took the cup and sat down. His mind was racing, 'Briggs' of course Tom Briggs, he had married Suzana. He looked at the girl, she had her mother's dark hair and fine looks. His look became a stare as out of the middle of her face a new truth dawned. She had Annabelle's nose. His began to feel hot, his head began to swim. He had to get out of here. He staggered to his feet. Daniella was staring at him with a mixture of surprise and concern.

'I'm sorry my dear… I must go… I don't feel well.'

Daniella moved towards him and put a steadying hand on his arm, she saw a tear run down his face, something was terribly wrong.

'High Commissioner, you can't go like this. You're not well; sit down. Drink some tea. I'll ring for help.'

'No, no, no. I'm all right. It just… I'm sorry I can't explain. At least not now. You're right the tea will make me feel better.'

He drank his tea as quickly as he could and, despite her protests, gave his thanks and left. He got into his car and sat in the driving seat as his brain sifted through all the information it had just acquired. Whichever way he looked at it, one fact was clear. Daniella was his daughter.

'Angus, it's Geoff, Geoff Forrest. Sorry to trouble you at home, but something has come up that might be of interest to you.'

'Not at all. Always good to hear from you Geoff,' Angus replied. 'What can I do for you?'

'Well perhaps it's what can we do for each other.'

'I'm listening.'

'What do you know about Miss Junior Caribbean?'

Angus thought for a moment. 'Can't say I've heard of her, doesn't ring any bells.'

'Well she is coming to Barbados tomorrow and she is coming from St Vincent.'

'So?' asked Angus, but he was already sensing that Geoff had something of interest.

'So, she was staying in the same hotel as the High Commissioner and young Walker.'

'That doesn't mean anything. There aren't many really good hotels to stay at.'

'But it might mean something if…' Geoff paused to maximise the effect of his news.

'If what?'

'She was seen leaving the High Commissioner's room.'

'Christ, are you sure?'

'Did I not see her coming out of his room with my own little eyes?' Said Geoff pleased with the reaction so far.

Angus began to weigh up the evidence, and his training as a diplomat took over. 'There could be a simple explanation, she might have been delivering a message, for example.'

'At seven o'clock in the morning?'

'Yes, I agree that is a bit odd, but even so there could be an explanation.'

'Angus my friend,' Geoff dropped his voice to a hoarse whisper. 'I can tell if a girl has been fucked, and believe me this girl had just been fucked.'

'OK, I'll take your word for it,' Angus was not at all sure if Geoff's crude contention was correct. Then another thought occurred to him. 'Err, how old is this Miss Junior Caribbean?'

Geoff laughed. 'Good question.'

'And the answer?'

'Well I can't be really sure,' replied the journalist. 'Let us say that to enter the Miss Junior Caribbean competition contestants must not be more than eighteen. If I had to make a guess this one is probably seventeen. She's quite well developed. Then again you never can tell these days, she could be younger.'

Angus whistled. 'That's serious,' he said.

'Who for?'

'The High Commissioner, of course,' replied Angus.

'I thought you would like to see the man in difficulty.'

'I didn't say that,' said Angus.

'Let us just say that the man has not treated you fairly since he arrived, and you would not lose any sleep if he got what he deserves.'

'Well I can't really argue with that,' Angus replied, with a touch of self-righteousness in his voice. 'What does this girl look like?'

'I can't really fault his taste,' replied the journalist. 'She's a little stunner. Wouldn't mind having a go myself. There is a picture of her in the Sunday Star by the way, Page 7.'

'Are you going to do anything about it?'

'If you mean go for her myself; no. It's too risky. As for putting your man in the spotlight again, the answer is, not yet. Not enough evidence you see, my editor wouldn't risk the litigation. Still I know what the little girl is interested in, fame and fortune. If he doesn't treat her right, I am sure she would love to tell her story.'

'Well, let us hope he treats her right,' said Angus, without sincerity. 'Thank you for the information. I will let you know if anything comes my way.'

They exchanged farewells and rang off. Angus sipped his whisky thoughtfully. This was dynamite, enough to finish the High Commissioner off permanently. He went and got his copy of the Sunday Star and turned to page 7. He looked at the picture of the girl. This could be the answer to a problem he had been pondering. He must get into the office early in the morning.

Peter went into the High Commission half an hour early. Daniella was not in yet, so he went and got his own trays from the Registry, and began to look through the papers that had arrived in his absence. He was not quite sure how to deal with the problem of Daniella. He was nervous about seeing her again. He had had a very restless night. First, he had struggled with the question of whether his conclusion the night before, that Daniella was his daughter, was correct. The circumstantial evidence was pretty strong. He decided that there could not be much doubt that Daniella was Suzana's daughter, the pictures and her surname were proof of that. The gap in the evidence, however, was whether he was her father. There was nothing to say that Suzana had not slept with someone else at about the same time. It was true that Daniella and Annabelle had similar noses, but that could be just coincidence. After all, neither girl's nose resembled his own. He then went on to consider the consequences of Daniella being his daughter. He could hardly go to Mavis and Annabelle and say, 'Oh by the way, my new secretary is also my daughter.' But that would not be necessary, clearly Daniella was unaware of the relationship, and she already had a father. The problem boiled down to whether he could live with the knowledge, and still retain a natural working relationship with the girl. It did occur to him that if he did have to have another daughter, he could do much, much worse than Daniella. In fact, he felt a small thrill of pride that she was his daughter, and the thought of working close to her was really quite satisfying. Above all, he decided, he must not do anything at all that might hurt Daniella in any way, nor must he hurt Mavis or Annabelle. Then he thought of Trixie 'Oh dear me' he muttered quietly to himself, dropping his head into his hands. Quickly his professional mind took over and he straightened himself up and picked up the first paper out of his tray.

The first paper was a note from Angus. Peter began to read becoming more and more angry, first at the note and then at the attachments.

Peter, it said,
I thought I had better deal with this in view of the urgency. They require the information for a PQ. I tried to get hold of you in St Vincent; but was unable to make contact. I have explained in my reply that I was replying on your behalf and would show you the reply, so that you can add any comments if you wish. I hope this is acceptable.
Angus.

It certainly wasn't acceptable. He was almost sure that Angus had not tried to contact him. He turned to the exchange of telegrams. The one from London was pretty bad. The tabloid article was devastating. Angus' reply only made matters worse. Angus had set out the sugar policy in detail, hardly necessary, as all the information was available in the Department in London. He had then added that 'It was hardly surprising that the High Commissioner was wrong-footed by the press on such a difficult subject, before he had had time to find his feet.' It made him sound like an idiot, who had not briefed himself and was not capable of handling the press. On the incident involving Mavis, Angus had commented 'It was perhaps understandable that Mrs Parker, exhausted after the long journey, over-reacted and misconstrued the intentions of a democratic demonstrator. Her actions are certainly to be regretted, but I am sure she meant well.' There was no mention that the demonstrator was a huge individual wielding a machete. To cap it all Angus ended the telegram by saying 'I am sure the High Commissioner would wish me to apologise, on his behalf, for the considerable embarrassment this incident has caused, both locally and in London. Equally we apologise for the failure to report the incident so that action could have been taken to limit the damage.'

'Damn the bloody man,' he cursed throwing the papers in his pending tray. He realised that Angus' reply had put him in an impossible position. It was true that he had fluffed his lines a bit on the sugar question, but he was fully briefed and about to respond when the mangoes had struck. Mavis had dealt efficiently, if controversially, with what might have been a life-threatening situation. He certainly would not have made the grovelling apology that Angus had given on his behalf. The problem now was that if he were to go back and try to restate everything, he would sound defensive. If he tried to withdraw the apology, he would appear defiant. The opportunity to present the facts had been lost. He decided to write a factual report by bag recording the events, without comment. He would send this to the department and copy it to the Chief Clerk.

He resolved to have it out with Angus at the first opportunity, the man was not going to get away with it. He was still the High Commissioner and he could make life difficult for his deputy. The next paper made him think again. It was a press cutting from the Sunday Star. 'Peter' he read 'You may find this of interest. This young lady may well be worth inviting to the cocktail party for the ship's visit. I am sure the sailors would welcome the presence of a local celebrity. Angus.' The headline read 'Miss Junior Caribbean comes to Town' above it was a picture of Trixie in a swimsuit. Peter didn't have to be a detective to realise that somehow Angus had discovered about his relationship with Trixie. He also knew that Angus now considered himself to be untouchable.

Señora Mendez was hysterical on the telephone, and Stefan did his best to calm her down. Perhaps it was an accident, the tides can be quite tricky around the islands. But she had insisted that was not possible. Filip was a strong swimmer; a champion in his youth. He swam every morning and had never had a problem until yesterday, when his body had been washed up on the beach. The police had said it was a normal drowning, perhaps he had got cramp. But she knew better, her Filip had been murdered. He had been acting very strangely lately, destroying documents, looking under his car in the mornings, checking every door and window in the house at night. What was to become of her and the children? He had always been a good provider, but she knew nothing about his business. There was not much money in their bank account, but she knew he had money somewhere. Stefan promised to make sure that she was all right. He would come and see her in less than three weeks' time. He was sure there was money to look after her and the children, he just needed a little time to sort it out. In the meantime, she should take the children and go and stay with her family. Let him know where they were as soon as she was safe, but don't speak to anyone else. She had thanked him, but her sobbing remained in his ears, even after she had put down the phone.

Stefan gave a deep sigh and went to make some coffee. At least one problem was solved, whether he could trust Filip. But the news was not good, this had all the hallmarks of a contract killing. If they had got Filip, he must surely be on their list too. It was also noticeable that they had not waited after giving Filip a warning. He would have to be careful, very careful. Unfortunately, the precise instructions he and Filip had given to the banks, for transferring money, required one of them to attend in person. He had to visit them himself. He went up to his bedroom and stood on a chair to take the package from the top shelf of the wardrobe. He unwrapped it and gently stroked the cold metal. The revolver had been with him since his Securitate days. Since his arrival in England, it had only been out of its package for regular cleaning and oiling. Now he must be ready to use it again. He took out another small package and opened it. He ran his finger along the back of the smooth blade and carefully touched the point, knowing that the stiletto was razor-sharp. He removed the strapping that he had used to fix the knife to his calf and placed it next to the stiletto.

Security on aircraft had been getting tighter and tighter in recent years. He could not risk carrying the items on his person. Even his hold baggage might be examined. He had, therefore, to find a way to get the gun and knife out to the Caribbean. No doubt he could acquire similar instruments of protection when he arrived, but there was something comfortable about having his old friends with him; friends that had served him well in the past. He knew the accuracy of the gun and the balance of the knife, as if they were extensions of his physical self. He picked up his diary and flicked through for a number, then went to the telephone and dialled.

'Department of Trade and Industry,' announced a bored female voice.

'Charles Montague please.'

'Putting you through.'

'Montague,' said a male voice.

'Charles, it's me Stefan Teduscu, South Eastern Counties Export Club.'

'Stefan, how can I be of help?'

'I have a small package to get to Barbados for the Trade Mission, I wondered if you could get it sent out by bag for me.'

There was silence on the line as Charles considered the request. 'That might pose a bit of a problem Stefan,' he said. 'The Foreign Office is a bit tough on the use of the bag, evading Customs, that sort of thing you know. Couldn't you send it by courier? We would be prepared to pay if it is for the Mission.'

'Yes,' said Stefan. 'I thought of that and, if there is no alternative, that is what we will have to do. Thanks anyway.'

'I am sorry not to be of help,' Charles sounded genuinely put out by his inability to help. 'What is in the packet?'

'Oh, nothing much. It's just the presents we want to give to the Barbadian Minister of Trade and the President of the local Chamber. I just felt it was a bit political and could be embarrassing if the Customs opened it up.'

'Ah,' said Charles. 'Look, I'll give it a shot, maybe in the circumstances the Foreign Office will agree. I'll ring you back within half an hour.'

Twenty minutes later Charles was back on the phone sounding very pleased with himself. He had convinced the FCO and they had agreed. Stefan should get the parcel to him by first thing tomorrow and it would go in the next day's bag. Stefan thanked him and rang off. He smiled to himself. You could usually get your way with Civil Servants if you knew how to ask. He went off to prepare his parcel with a spring in his step.

Bramley Smith had been a politician. He had also been a very heavy donor to the presidential campaign. The President had been grateful and now Bramley enjoyed the comfort and prestige of being US Ambassador to Barbados and the East Caribbean. Peter did not approve of the American system where career diplomats are leapfrogged by those providing political favours. The British system, which depended on the years of experience obtained through many years of serving in far-flung places, usually gave better results. There had been cases where American Ambassadors had not even known the basic facts about the country in which they were about to serve. Bramley was not one of those cases. Since his first courtesy call on the Ambassador, shortly after arriving, Peter and Bramley had had several longer discussions. Peter had been impressed by the Ambassador's sharp mind and his deep knowledge of the Caribbean.

The small group was greeted at the door by the butler, who led them into the sitting room where Bramley and his wife and a young Embassy couple were waiting. Peter introduced Mavis and Annabelle. Andrew already knew the Ambassador quite well and had met Mrs Smith at several social occasions. The young couple was introduced as Mark and Samantha Benton, a Political First Secretary and his wife. The Ambassador explained that he had not invited other guests, as he wanted this to be an informal family occasion. This suited everyone, as they had already had their fill of official receptions.

They ate their way through a mini feast of tuna in a mustard sauce, chicken breasts cooked in white wine and a flaming Bomb Alaska for dessert. The conversation was relaxed, and Bramley entertained them with amusing anecdotes of political life and mishaps in America. He and Mavis got on particularly well, sharing the same irreverent approach to life. Bramley congratulated her on her under arm swing and said that he could always arrange for her to join the US Embassy baseball team if she found herself at a loose end. Peter felt somewhat relieved that his American colleague, at least, did not view the airport incident as any more than a humorous distraction to island life. At the other end of the table the four young people also found that they had much in common and Andrew and Annabelle readily agreed to join the two Americans after the dinner at the Harbour Lights, a popular beach bar on the south coast.

After dinner Mrs Smith took Mavis off to show her the tapestry she was making, a hobby she had taken up since arriving in Barbados. The four younger members of the group went out on to the balcony to view the garden and the night sky. Bradley took Peter into his study and poured out a couple of stiff brandies.

'One bit of shop I would like to discuss with you Peter,' the Ambassador said once they were seated.

'What's that?' asked Peter, taking a sip of his brandy.

'I believe you have a Trade Mission due out soon?'

'Yes,' Peter replied. 'It arrives in the middle of next week.'

'Would I be right in saying that the leader is called Stefan Teduscu, a financial services specialist of Romanian extraction,' the Ambassador asked.

Peter looked at him with mild surprise. 'Yes, you would certainly be correct.'

Bradley took a long sip of his drink. 'Can I speak frankly, between friends and colleagues.'

'Certainly,' said Peter, wondering what was coming.

'My people have received some information about Teduscu. I have to say that they have no definite proof of wrongdoing, but there is pretty strong circumstantial evidence that he may be involved in money laundering. Again, I want to stress that there is no proof and I am not suggesting that you should take any action, but I did feel I should let you know of our suspicions. If anything happened whilst he was here it could be an embarrassment for you.'

'Thank you for that,' said Peter. 'I am grateful.'

'My pleasure,' said Bradley, standing up. 'Shall we join the ladies?'

Chapter 10

Annabelle swayed and swung her body to the pulsating rhythm of the brass band. Although not a frequent dancer, Andrew found that his natural athleticism allowed him to keep pace with her. The music dropped in tempo and she fell lightly into his arms, he felt her hair rest against his cheek, and he felt happy. The music stopped and they returned to their seats. The American couple had already used up their energy and had been watching them on the dance floor.

'Well done,' said Samantha.

'You looked really romantic,' said Mark with a grin. Andrew glared at him, with mock outrage, but he saw that Annabelle was smiling.

'Another drink?' asked Andrew.

'No thank you,' replied Samantha. 'We really must go.'

'Annabelle?' Andrew turned to her holding up a glass.

'Yes please,' she said. 'Piña Colada with plenty of ice.'

They bid farewell to Samantha and Mark and sat with their drinks, knees touching, eyes engaged.

'Let's go for a walk on the beach,' she suggested.

'Good idea,' he said. They finished their drinks and stood up. Andrew took her hand and they walked out of the bar into the semi-darkness of the starlit night.

They walked hand in hand along the sandy beach, enjoying the silence broken only by the gentle washing of the sea on the beach. The night was clear, and they began pointing out to each other the constellations in the sky.

'Isn't that Ursa Major,' she asked pointing.

'Where?'

'There, silly,' she said pointing again and bringing his head alongside hers.

'I think so,' he said.

'You don't know? Don't they teach you anything in the Foreign Office?'

'OK, yes, it is.'

'Well you're wrong, it isn't.'

'But you tricked me.' He said, sounding aggrieved.

She didn't answer, but instead swung her face round in front of his and placed her lips firmly against his. As he began to respond she gave him a little push and turned and ran towards the sea. Andrew regained his balance and ran after her.

'Let's go in,' she squealed at him over her shoulder.

'But…' before he could ask the question, she was answering him. Her smart cocktail dress was falling from her body as she ran, and she splashed quickly into the sea wearing only a pair of white pants. Andrew needed no second bidding he scrambled out of his clothes and joined her in his underpants. They played, splashing and giggling in the warm water. The effect of the Piña Coladas rapidly wore off; but was replaced by a deeper more fundamental intoxication. Finally, she ran out of the water, picked up her clothes and lay down on the beach. He followed and lay down beside her. She turned towards him and they were kissing again. This time she did not break away. Nor did she demur when his hands found their way onto her wet, naked breasts.

'Suck them,' she commanded, and he did.

'Let's do it under the stars.'

'I don't have any… err.'

'Here take this,' she said with a sigh.

He took the small plastic packet from her and tore it open. He carefully rolled the thin rubber onto his erection. 'Are you always so well prepared?' he asked.

'Only when I go out with randy diplomats,' she replied.

Peter sat at his desk thinking about the conversation he had had with the American Ambassador. He had to act, and act quickly. The last thing he needed on his patch was a money launderer leading a trade mission. The Department of Trade and Industry were the responsible department, but he was not sure how they would handle it unless he could speak to someone at a senior level. Better to do it through the Foreign Office, they were more sensitive in handling delicate international matters. The problem was that there was no proof. If he put the details in a telegram, he would have to be careful to emphasise that. He decided that he would talk to the Under Secretary in charge of the region, but first he would ask Anthony Tremlett if he had any information. He buzzed for Daniella and she appeared immediately.

'Could you ask Anthony if he is free for a word and then put me through to Philip Cummings in London.'

'Yes, right away,' but she hovered. He looked enquiringly at her. 'Is it all right for me to pop to the airport at lunchtime to meet my uncle? I should be back just after three.'

'Fine,' replied Peter.

'Oh, and a Mr Teduscu… Stefan Teduscu telephoned. He asked to come and see you urgently this afternoon.'

'This afternoon? Are you sure? He is the leader of the Trade Mission, but they aren't due here until next week.'

'I know,' Daniella replied. 'That's what I thought was odd. But it was definitely him and he is staying at the Barbados Hilton.'

'Damn,' said Peter. 'OK, tell him four o'clock. Oh, and don't bother with Anthony or the call to London, at least not until after I have seen him.'

'Fine,' said Daniella, leaving and closing the door behind her.

'Damn, damn, damn,' said Peter aloud. This was all he needed.

Trixie walked up from the beach towards the entrance of the Grand Barbados Hotel. Two Rastafarians whistled as she walked past, staring at her tight shorts and shouting lewd comments in her direction. Trixie gave a toss of her black hair and ignored them. They were just like the types she used to date back home, all mouth and no class. Trixie had moved on; she was now Miss Junior Caribbean a starlet waiting to become a star. She moved in more elegant circles now, only a week ago she had had no less a person than the British High Commissioner at her feet. Trixie frowned to herself, why had Peter not contacted her yet. She realised that he was a busy man, but she also had commitments. She knew that it was only a matter of time until he contacted her, but he would have to hurry up because she would not wait forever. Trixie had another reason for being happy today, it was her nineteenth birthday.

As Trixie entered the hotel, she heard a voice behind her call her name. She turned half expecting it to be Peter, but it was the man in the scruffy white suit who had given her his card in St Vincent.

'Trixie, remember me? Geoff Forrest.'

'Yes,' she replied, without great enthusiasm.

'Fancy a drink?' he asked.

'No thank you, it's so hot out there I need a rest.'

'Oh, come on,' he pleaded. 'A drink will cool you down and I have some ideas for a publicity interview.'

'OK,' she said, his proposition now having rather greater appeal.

They walked along the pier that formed the restaurant area of the hotel and took a seat in the shade. Geoff ordered drinks and took out his notebook.'

'Now I'd like to ask you a few questions about how you became Miss Junior Caribbean and how you are finding it. Let's start at the beginning. Where were you born and how old are you?'

'I was born in Aruba and I am nineteen today.'

'Oh great, happy birthday,' said Geoff, inwardly a little disappointed that her age diminished the size of the High Commissioner's indiscretion.

'And when did you first think of becoming a beauty queen?' This question sent Trixie off on a long monologue about her triumphs, past, present and future. Eventually Geoff decided that it was time to cut in and get the conversation back on track.

'Have you met many interesting people here, Ministers, Diplomats, Ambassadors?' he asked.

'Oh yes,' she said, then seeing the expression of doubt on his face felt the need to offer evidence. 'I do know the British High Commissioner.'

'Of that's interesting,' said Geoff, congratulating himself on his strategy. 'Do you know him well?'

'Trixie's eyes twinkled. 'Let us say that we are just good friends.'

Geoff was delighted with the progress so far; but decided not to push it further for the moment. He did, however, have one ace up his sleeve.

'What a coincidence,' he said. 'A friend of mine has asked me to a Reception at the High Commissioner's Residence next week to meet the Royal Navy, and he particularly asked me to bring you along.'

'I'd be delighted,' Trixie replied, thinking to herself how clever Peter was to find such a discrete way of getting them back together again.

'Percy, I think we had better have another word about Parker in Barbados.' Sir Derek had waited until the other officials had departed from their weekly senior management meeting.

'Yes,' responded Sir Percival. 'I agree, the telegram from his Deputy, McMullen, looked a bit odd. It was almost as if he wanted to put the worst possible spin on the incident.'

'That was how I read it. McMullen was completely out of line, in my view, responding without consulting either Parker or myself.'

'I agree, something seems to be going on out there. Parker is generally a safe pair of hands, but it's not looking that way so far.' Sir Percival stood up and paced across the room two or three times before addressing the Chief Clerk again. 'Is there any way we can get someone out there in a low-key way, routine parish visit, that sort of thing?'

'That's what I was thinking,' rejoined Sir Derek. 'There is an internal audit team leaving on Sunday, the auditors are only at First Secretary level and could not take on the job, but we could attach an Inspector from the

Overseas Inspectorate to the audit. It could be billed as a study to see whether future Inspections and audits could be combined in small posts.'

'Good idea. Please go ahead. If you can get David Bloggs to take it on so much the better. He has a nose for these things and plenty of discretion.'

He was much fatter than Peter remembered him and almost bald. Stefan was shown into his office by Alice, Angus' secretary. Stefan came towards him, hand outstretched and a large smile on his face.

'Peter, how nice to see you again. Bucharest is a long time ago.'

'It is indeed,' said Peter and, with as much grace as he could muster, added. 'And it's good to see you.'

'You look well Peter and you've done well too. I always knew you would.'

'Thank you,' replied Peter. 'I gather that your career has not been without its successes. Have a seat, would you like some coffee.'

'That would be nice.'

Peter went over to the telephone system and pressed a button to summon Daniella. After several attempts he remembered that Daniella had gone to the airport.

'Oh, look I'm sorry, I've just remembered that my secretary has gone to the airport to meet her uncle. I can ask someone else to get coffee if you'll give me a few minutes.'

'No please don't bother,' said Stefan, still smiling. 'I'm perfectly happy without.'

'So, tell me about your business Stefan,' Peter sat down on the chair opposite and looked attentive.

'Well after I emigrated to Britain,' Peter smiled to himself at Stefan's euphemism for his defection. 'I decided to make use of all the knowledge I had on countertrade and compensation trading. Clearly the straight barter arrangements we carried out in Romania were not appropriate in the West, but I did find that countries in Latin America and the Caribbean, with hard currency problems, were happy to pay part of the cost of their imports with their products.'

Peter wanted to ask how he had then gone on to money laundering, but instead said 'Good idea, were you successful?'

'In the beginning, yes. But it soon became clear that there was a demand for other types of financial services in the region, where the profit margin was rather better.'

'Totally legal I hope?' asked Peter, smiling broadly to cover the seriousness of the question.

'Of course, you know me. Never one to sail close to the wind. Not like you, old friend, in your Romanian days, chasing every bit of skirt you could find.'

'What are you suggesting?'

'Nothing more than you were suggesting with your question about legality.'

'I was joking, but it sounds like I might have got closer to the truth than I imagined,' Peter said stiffly.

'Bullshit Peter. You and I both know that there have been false rumours about my activities circulating. Why I bet that in that pile of paper there you have an intelligence report saying that I am laundering drug money. Well I can tell you it is all a load of crap.'

'I think perhaps you had better leave,' Peter's face was flushed, and he was satisfied that the man was indeed a crook. 'And I think you had better resign as leader of the Trade Mission. If you do, I will say nothing further about this conversation.'

'Sorry Peter it just won't wash. For a start I am totally innocent of any wrongdoing.'

There was the sound of a door in the outer office closing and Stefan looked round sharply. Both men listened in silence for a moment, before Peter continued.

'Well I'm sorry Stefan, I am just not prepared to take the risk.'

'Well I'm sorry Peter old chap,' replied Stefan mimicking Peter's tone. 'You will just have to be prepared to take the risk.'

'I have to do nothing of the sort,' said Peter angrily. 'Now please get out of my office.' Peter's hand moved towards the alarm bell under his desk.

'I wouldn't do that old chap,' said Stefan calmly. 'Do you remember a girl called Suzana Cuza, pretty young thing lived in Mangalia?'

'I... I've never heard of her,' but Peter was obviously flustered.

'Well I don't know if you heard from her, but you certainly screwed her and made her pregnant.'

'That's rubbish,' spluttered Peter, but he knew it wasn't.

'No, it's not and what is more you have a daughter and her name is Daniella Briggs, and I have the paternity tests to prove it.'

This time there was no mistaking the slamming of the outer office door. Peter went to the door to the outer office and opened it. The office was empty, but he clearly heard Stefan's voice, through the intercom, asking if anyone was there. Peter returned to his office and sat down.

'Look someone may have overheard us, the intercom was left on when I tried to order coffee. I don't know what they heard or who it was, but I suggest you leave. What is it that you want from me?'

'Let us just say that you don't try and remove me from the leadership of the Mission, that you act completely normally towards me and that you prevent any more false rumours from circulating for at least the next three weeks.'

'I'll see what I can do,' said Peter with an air of total resignation.

Annabelle arrived at the door of his flat looking bright and slightly flushed. She carried a large cool box in one hand and a plastic bag in the other.

'Your cook has arrived Sir,' she announced.

'And a bonny cook she is too,' said Andrew kissing her warmly on the lips.

'Make way,' she said. 'There's work to do.' Annabelle marched into the kitchen and nodded her approval at the spotlessly clean work surfaces. She began to unpack and lay out her food and utensils.

'What's on the menu?' he asked.

'Wait and see,' she said. 'Oh, can you put the Champagne in the fridge please?'

'Wow the best Moet Chandon,' he said looking at the label.

'Yes, stolen especially for this evening from the Residence wine cellar along with this tin of French oyster soup from the pantry. You, Assistant Chef, are free to open the soup can, as I want to spice it up a bit.'

Annabelle then took out four large flying fish and washed them under the tap. She cut off the fins and trimmed the tails with kitchen scissors and then scraped off the scales in the sink. Then with great precision she picked up a sharp knife and cut off the heads. Andrew watched as she slipped the knife into the back and, pressing the knife firmly against the backbone, neatly filleted the fish to produce eight well-formed fillets.

'Gosh,' said Andrew in admiration. 'Where did you learn to do that?'

'Where do you think? Surgery classes of course, although human bones are a bit bigger.'

Annabelle breaded and fried the fish, baked two halves of a large aubergine and fried some sweet potato. She added some fresh prawns to the soup and a sprinkling of pepper and herbs, then gently heated it up before adding fresh cream. Finally, she sliced a black Antiguan pineapple and covered it with thin threads of caramelised sugar. 'If you have any ice cream in the fridge, we can have it with the pineapple,' she said surveying her work with satisfaction.

Andrew ate and drank with gusto. 'That was truly delicious,' he said. 'Would you like some coffee?'

Andrew made some coffee and they sat down together on the sofa. They chatted as if they had known each other all their lives exchanging views on politics, religion and the latest movies. Annabelle leant back against the arm of the settee and lifted up her legs. She smiled as she saw Andrew's eyes follow the movement. It was the signal he needed, and the embrace followed naturally. They did not rush; there was no need. Andrew gently undressed her, and she responded in kind. He took her by the hand and led her into the bedroom. She looked at the bed. The covers were neatly folded back; the sheets were crisp and white.

'Are you always so well prepared?' she asked.

'Only when I go out with High Commissioners' daughters,' he replied.

'Pig,' she said, pushing him back onto the bed and jumping on top of him.

Nicu came into the sitting room. He had gone to have a rest after his journey and was now ready to chat to his niece, who had just returned from work. Daniella was sitting in the armchair, head in hands. She did not look up as he came in.

'Danny, it's your Uncle Nicu here. Why the glum face.'

Daniella looked up and tried to smile, but her effort was to no avail. Nicu walked over to her and put his hand on her shoulder.

'What's the matter Danny? What has happened?'

'Oh, it's nothing,' she replied, without conviction.

'Come on, you can't fool Uncle Nicu. I've known you since you were in nappies and I have never seen you look so glum. I shall go and make you some tea then I am ready to talk if you want to. If you don't want to then I'll understand.'

Nicu went off and returned several minutes later with tea and cake. He handed a cup to Daniella and she sipped it without looking up. Nicu sat down and drank his tea, waiting for her to speak.

'Uncle Nicu,' she said, eyes looking down at her cup.

'Yes, Danny?'

'Can I ask you something?'

'Anything.'

'And you will tell me the truth won't you.'

Nicu hesitated. Had she found out something about his activities? 'Of course,' he replied.

'Is Dad my real dad?'

'Why do you ask?' Nicu was taken aback by the question. He had said that he would tell her the truth, but did she really want to know it. Would not the truth hurt more than a small lie?

Daniella looked at him and spoke slowly and deliberately. 'A man came to see the High Commissioner today. When I got back from the airport they were talking in the High Commissioner's office. The intercom was on and I could hear their voices through it. It happens sometimes, as the High Commissioner still does not know how to use it properly. Of course, I went straight away to switch it off but, as I was about to, I heard Mummy's name. The man called her Suzana Cuza and then he said she came from Mangalia and that the High Commissioner had... had slept with her. But that is not all, he then said that the High Commissioner has a daughter and her name is Daniella Briggs. It just doesn't make sense.'

'Who was this man?' asked Nicu, his voice low and icy.

'I didn't see him, but the High Commissioner had an appointment with the leader of the Trade Commission. His name is Teduscu, Stefan Teduscu.'

Nicu did not show any reaction to the name, but inside his brain it acted like a charge of high voltage electricity. He knew all about this man. As Nicu had progressed in the Party, he had become quite close to Colonel Babu. Babu had once counted Teduscu as one of his closest friends, but that had all changed when Teduscu had defected to the West. Teduscu had betrayed everything, his country, the Party and Babu himself. On one drunken evening, during the second bottle of vodka it had all come out. Babu's early love for Teduscu's wife, Rodica, who had been corrupted and taken to the West. How Teduscu had used Babu to report on Suzana and Nicu. How Teduscu had informed Western agents about him, so that he could never take lucrative jobs overseas under deep cover. Babu's friendship with Teduscu had turned to bitter hatred. Nicu's hatred was just as strong, he could still feel the humiliation of being searched and punched in a dark street; he could still taste the vomit in his mouth.

'Your High Commissioner's name is Peter Parker?'

Daniella looked at her Uncle in surprise, not so much because he knew the High Commissioner's name, but at the way he had responded to her story. It was as if he already knew everything, she had told him and was checking off the details. 'Yes,' she replied, then her voice choking with emotion 'Tell me it's not true.'

Nicu took his niece's hands in his and looked straight into her eyes.

'Danny,' he said at last. 'Your mother was a beautiful young woman, but she was a dreamer. She dreamt that a rich foreigner would come and whisk her away into a new life of romance and excitement in the West.' Nicu paused, choosing his words carefully, he did not want to tell Daniella that her mother had taken Peter Parker into her bed within an hour of meeting him. 'When she met a handsome young English Diplomat, she allowed herself to be seduced by the man and by her dreams. After he returned to the capitol, she discovered she was pregnant. She was too ashamed to tell her lover and resolved to bring the child up herself. But then she met this very fine man Tom Briggs. They fell in love. Tom knew the baby was not his, but he was happy to accept it as his own. They got married and you were born.'

Daniella looked at him, she was not crying but her face was tense. 'Why didn't me mam tell me?' she asked, her distress so great that she reverted to using the Geordie name for her mother, a habit she had grown out of many years before.

'Because she loved you and knew that Tom would be the best father you could possibly have.'

'Yes... but...' Daniella could not continue; it was all too much. Nicu put his arms around her and stroked her hair as she buried her face on his chest and sobbed as if her heart would break. Nicu's thoughts went to Stefan Teduscu, the man who had humiliated him, who had made him grovel in his own vomit. Teduscu. the man the Colombian, Antonio, had sent him to kill. But now Nicu had a much stronger reason for killing Teduscu, the bastard had destroyed the happiness of his precious Danny.

Chapter 11

Andrew knew that he would have to run the gauntlet and there, true to form, she was, inviting him in through the Residence front door. Becky had taken a keen interest in the blossoming romance between Andrew and her sister. She felt a personal responsibility to keep it on track, after all had she not willed it to happen even before Annabelle had arrived in the country. Andrew, for his part, did not really mind, but it had become almost a game to keep Becky at bay. Andrew readily admitted to himself that he and Annabelle were on the way to becoming a couple. He still felt some regular twinges of conscience that he had started seeing Annabelle so soon after Meriko's departure. What was rather more strange, was that he also felt that he was being disloyal to Daniella. After all, he and Daniella had exchanged only one brief kiss since they had met, and that was little more than the outcome of a bit of affectionate horseplay. It was true that they saw a lot of each other at the Office, but that did not mean that he should feel any sense of duty towards her. But he did.

'Hello Andy, come in' Becky smiled benignly as she held open the door.

'Hello Becky,' he replied. 'Oh, and by the way my name is Andrew, not Andy.'

'I prefer Andy, it sounds more sisterly.'

'It may do, but you do not happen to be my sister.'

'Not yet,' she said with a knowing smile. 'Anyway, you will be pleased to know that you and Annabelle have the house to yourselves. You can do *exactly* what you want.'

'Really?'

'Yes really. Daddy is taking me and Mummy to the Crane Beach hotel for the night. Everyone says you get a really good breakfast there and they have a beach.'

'Yes,' said Andrew. The breakfast is really good, but you can't swim there. The sea is too rough.'

'I know,' she said, pulling a face. We are going to collect shells.'

'Becky, it's time you were getting ready. Dad says you have to leave at four, so you have less than half an hour.' Annabelle appeared behind

Becky and ushered the young girl on her way. She leant forward and kissed Andrew on the cheek. 'We can say hello properly later,' she whispered.

Andrew followed Annabelle into the sitting room where her father was sitting reading 'The Times'. 'Hello Andrew,' he said looking up. 'I am taking Becky and the twins to Crane Beach for the night. Give us a breather before everything hits the fan next week.'

'Good morning High Commissioner. Yes, Becky told me she said you and Mrs Parker were going for the breakfast, and she is going to collect shells.'

'Yes, that's about it. I expect I will have to grovel about the beach looking for shells too.'

'I hope you are going to be back for the cricket tomorrow afternoon. We are depending on you,' said Andrew, reverting to his role as High Commission cricket captain. The Royal Navy were now offshore, and their first main event was to be the cricket match.

Peter laughed. 'Yes, of course I'll be back. But don't start placing your hopes on me, it's ages since I played. My off-spin will probably bounce the wrong way.'

'Well that will confuse the Navy's batsmen.'

'What are the rest of our team like?' Peter asked.

'Oscar, the driver is a fine fast bowler, he even had a trial for Barbados a few years back. That should rattle them up a bit. We have Des, the Forestry Adviser from the Development Division, who will open, and a couple of others from down there who are pretty good. Anthony Tremlett bats well and can bowl some good medium pace as well. And one or two of the youngsters from Registry and Visa Section are enthusiastic, but untried.'

'So, given that you're pretty good with the bat yourself, we should be able to give them a run for their money. Who is our wicket keeper?'

Andrew frowned. 'Angus is our regular. On a good day he's pretty good and on a bad day… well let us just say he is not always at his best. He has won the odd match for us by end of innings slogging.'

'Well let's hope tomorrow is one of his good days,' said the High Commissioner, with a deep sigh.

Stefan sat at the bar of the Grand Barbados Hotel. Although he would appear, to any casual observer, to be a normal businessman relaxing and enjoying his evening cocktail, Stefan, as always, was alert to his surroundings. Everyone who entered the bar was briefly scrutinised. This was not because Stefan felt he was in any particular danger at the moment, but rather because of his training and of the many years looking over his shoulder, following his defection. Almost without realising it Stefan began to focus his attention on a figure slumped in one of the chairs in the darkest area of the bar. By moving his head slightly, as he brought his glass to his lips, he was able to see the figure reflected in the mirror behind the bar. What was interesting about the figure, whoever it was, was that it was watching him. Stefan slowly got off his barstool, hitched up his trousers and asked the barman where the bathroom was. Although he knew the answer already, he was pleased to see that the barman waved his hand in a deliberate gesture and pointed to the toilet door. Stefan walked slowly towards the bathroom knowing that the most natural route would bring him much closer to the seated figure. As he passed by the figure showed no interest, although Stefan could feel his eyes fixed firmly on him. Stefan watched the figure with equal apparent lack of interest.

Once in the bathroom he locked the door and sat down on the closed lid of the toilet to assess what he had learnt. So Nicu Cuza was in Barbados and Nicu Cuza was watching him. Although their only personal encounter had been fairly brief and on a dark night long ago, Stefan remembered Nicu well. He had taken a personal interest in the Cuza family before his defection and Colonel Babu had sent him photographs with his reports. Even after his new life in the West, Nicu's activities, with his Colombian masters, had not gone completely unnoticed. Filip Mendez had pointed him out only the previous year, as they shared the sordid pleasures of a Miami nightclub, and said that Nicu was part of the opposition and someone to be watched. If Nicu was taking a close interest in him, Stefan reasoned, then it was not for the good of his health. Stefan got up from the toilet and walked back into the bar.

'Nicu Cuza, isn't it?' Stefan said in Romanian, sitting down next to his compatriot. 'Can I offer you a drink?'

'Thank you, I'll have a scotch,' Nicu replied, as if Stefan's presence was the most natural thing in the world.

Stefan raised a finger and a passing waiter came towards them and took their order.

'So Nicu, what are you doing with yourself these days?' Stefan asked.

'Oh, this and that,' replied Nicu.

'Are you staying here? It's an excellent hotel.'

'No,' replied Nicu.

'Sorry about the last time we met. No hard feelings, I hope?'

'None at all,' replied Nicu, lying with the ease of a professional.

'Well here's to a successful future,' said Stefan, raising his glass.

'And success for you too,' responded Nicu. Nicu downed his drink and stood up. 'A pleasure to meet you again,' he said, neither offering his hand nor a Romanian hug. Stefan remained seated and nodded; he watched Nicu walk out of the bar and remained for several minutes before departing by the same exit.

Matilda, the cook's, lobster salad was delicious, as was the High Commissioner's Frascati wine.

'Tiramisu or cheese and biscuits?' asked Annabelle.

'Cheese and biscuits,' replied Andrew. 'I am playing cricket tomorrow.'

'Spoilsport,' she said. 'I shall have the Tiramisu.'

Annabelle dug into a huge slice of the creamy Italian dessert whilst Andrew put small pieces of Brie onto his Carr's water biscuits. Both washed their choice of dessert down with more Frascati, until Andrew leant back in his chair looking contented.

'That was delicious,' he said.

'Shall we take the next course upstairs?' Annabelle said coyly.

'And what is the next course, coffee?' Andrew asked with a mischievous grin.

'It will be if you're not careful,' she said moving over to him and taking his hand.

'What about the dishes?' he asked.

'We've got maids for things like that.'

'We should at least clear them.'

'*Andrew!* Don't be so bloody infuriating,' and, before he could reply, she broke free and ran towards the door. 'Catch me if you can,' she called over her shoulder, right hand already unzipping the back of her dress.

Andrew's sense of good citizenship deserted him, just for once, and he was on his feet and chasing. She had kicked off her shoes and was already halfway up the large colonial-style staircase by the time he reached the door. Andrew bounded after her, and the Captain of cricket began to gain on her, but she was as nimble as a mountain goat. By the time he reached the pair of silk white panties on the landing she had disappeared.

'Hurry up slow-coach,' the voice came tantalisingly out of the main guest bedroom. Andrew entered the room and she was lying naked on the king-sized bed. 'This is where the Princess will sleep. Let's fuck in the royal bed.'

Andrew stood at the door fully dressed and looked at the inviting image before him. He felt excited by the chase and his manhood was already responding to her nakedness. 'I am not sure that would be entirely appropriate,' he said with an apologetic smile.

'*I am not sure that would be entirely appropriate,*' she mimicked, but there was rising anger in her voice. 'Oh, don't be such a pompous ass and stop playing the little boy diplomat.'

'I think perhaps I had better go,' said Andrew calmly, drawing on every last ounce of self-control and willpower. She glared at him in fury and he met her gaze without flinching.

'Well sod off then,' she said, at last.

Andrew turned slowly and began to retrace his steps. 'Andrew' her voice halted him as he began to descend the staircase. OK, you win. We can go to my room.' Andrew returned to her and followed her along the corridor.

'In here,' her voice now cool. She walked over to the bed and pulled down the covers. 'You'd better get your clothes off.'

'Look, I'm sorry. It just didn't seem right,' Andrew said as he unbuttoned his shirt.

'Don't patronise me,' she snapped. 'Just be thankful I'm prepared to forgive you, this time.'

Andrew did not hesitate, but it was only as he entered her for the second time that Annabelle had returned to being the sweet bubbly girl that he had been beginning to fall in love with.

Stefan bent down and looked at the name, newly printed under the doorbell. He stood up again, well satisfied with his night's work. Following Nicu had not been easy; it had taken every bit of skill he possessed. Nicu had not returned to his base for over three hours and for the first hour, at least, he had been checking to make sure that he was not being followed. Daniella lived in a flat in the small South Coast town of Worthing, the road from the hotel to Worthing was long and, in some areas, exposed. On these occasions, Stefan had to maintain a long distance between them. Several times he thought that he had lost his quarry, only to pick him up again when the geography allowed more cover. His decision, to reveal himself to Nicu, was a risky one. Perhaps if he had not, following him might have been easier. Then again, Nicu would have been waiting, until he left the bar, to follow and perhaps kill *him*. Nicu would now be on his guard, but Stefan could now play a more open game. One thing had troubled him, the possibility that Nicu might have an accomplice. Now that he knew that Nicu was staying with his niece, Daniella Briggs, that seemed unlikely. For the next week, that he was to stay in Barbados, Stefan would have to watch every shadow. The other benefit from the face to face meeting was that he was now absolutely sure that Nicu intended to kill him.

'Ow,' said Andrew, waking up suddenly from a short snooze. 'That hurt.'

'Ready?' asked Annabelle, releasing the clutch of chest hair she had used as an alarm clock.

'I'm not sure if I can?'

'I thought you were an athlete,' she said disdainfully.

'Yes, but there is a limit, even for an athlete.'

'Let me see,' she said sitting up straight, so that the sheet fell away from her body and her breasts were suddenly revealed in the light of the breaking dawn shining through the window. She moved down towards his midriff pulling the sheet right back. Delicately she took hold of his penis by the scruff of its foreskin and held it up like a newly born puppy. 'Mmm, I see what you mean. It might be dead.'

'I hope not,' replied Andrew, with a show of concern.

'Wait,' she commanded, leaping off the bed and disappearing naked into a large built-in wardrobe.

Andrew waited, wondering what this strange girl had in store for him next.

Annabelle reappeared clad in a white doctor's coat; one button fastened in the middle. As she moved, the coat gave alternate views of her creamy pointed breasts and the clutch of fair hair that straddled the top of her long slim legs. Around her neck she had a stethoscope.

Annabelle knelt back on the bed and returned her attention to his withered manhood. She cupped it in her hand and, after deftly plugging the arms of the instrument into her ears, pressed the cold metal of the stethoscope firmly against his penis.

'I think I have a pulse,' she said triumphantly. 'And look it's having convulsions.'

'Oh good,' said Andrew. 'At least it is still alive.'

'I had better give it AR to make sure,' she said.

'What's that,' he asked.

'The kiss of life,' she replied, as she opened her mouth to take him in.

'You are the doctor,' replied Andrew, resting his head back on the pillow, his face showing a look of blissful satisfaction.

David Bloggs placed seven pairs of neatly folded underpants in his suitcase next to seven pairs of identical black socks. He was a neat and methodical man, a bachelor in his early forties. David was not the typical Foreign Service Senior Grade officer, although more and more like him were rising in the ranks. At his Comprehensive school he had excelled academically, being the first in the history of the school not only to sit five

A levels, but to get five A grades in them. He had gone on to Bath University to study mathematics and no one among his peers was surprised when he obtained a First. His tutors were keen that he should remain at the College to follow a career as an academic or, at the very least, do a PhD. But David had other ideas he wanted to travel and to rub shoulders with the wealthy and powerful. The Foreign Office accepted him without much ado and very quickly his Northern accent vanished to be replaced by the indeterminate note of a middle Englander. David's progress had been rapid, his keen intellect and powers of analysis landed him a Private Secretary's job in his mid-twenties. After a spell as First Secretary Economic in Paris he went to Rome as Commercial Counsellor before returning to London as an Inspector. He soon gained a reputation as a smoothy. Whether he was addressing the Ambassador or a clerk in the Registry, his polite but searching questions yielded all the solutions. Although not a mean-minded man he had no difficulty in cutting peoples' jobs, if he felt they were not fully loaded.

David was due to arrive in Barbados the next day with the auditors. He was mildly surprised that his telegram to the High Commissioner had not been answered. Most Heads of Post fell over themselves to pretend to welcome him. Perhaps the absence of a reply was indicative of the way the Post was being run. After all, was not his visit intended to find out what had gone wrong? David continued his packing, whistling the Waltz of the Flowers from Tchaikovsky's Nutcracker without missing a note.

Angus woke up late, his head felt fuzzy and his tongue furry. He looked at his watch it was just after ten-thirty. 'Christ,' he muttered aloud, realising that the cricket match was due to start in less than half an hour. He desperately wanted a drink but knew it would be fatal if he was to keep wicket. Splashing water on his face and squirting deodorant under his armpits and around his groin, he rushed into the bedroom to look for his cricket clothes. 'Fuck,' he squealed, as he was struck by a searing pain around his penis from the alcohol in the deodorant spray. He rushed back into the bathroom and draped himself over the sink to wash it off. Unfortunately, the tap water was untypically hot, and he found the cure to be more painful than the complaint. Finally, he was ready, clad in white shirt and flannels and clutching his cricket bag, with his bat and wicket keeper's pads in. He got to his front door and was about to leave, when he realised that his keys and money were in his office trousers. He ran up the stairs two at a time and began to shake keys, coins and assorted paraphernalia out onto the bed. A crumpled piece of paper fell out of his trousers. He was about to throw it in the bin when the top line caught his eye 'To Immediate Bridgetown'. He opened the paper up. 'Shit, shit, shit, shit,' he shouted as the significance of the telegram dawned on him. It was the telegram announcing that an Inspector would visit with the auditors. They were due to arrive the next day and he had done nothing about it. He remembered the telegram arriving just before the High Commissioner returned from his travels. He had heard of David Bloggs and he had heard of his reputation. His immediate thought was whether his post might be downgraded or cut. It was happening all over the world. He would be sent home and Andrew Walker would cover his job. He had felt so resentful at the prospect that he had felt the need for a drink, so he had stuffed the paper in his pocket and only just discovered it. He hadn't booked a room in the hotel or informed Management to include David Bloggs in the programme, he hadn't acknowledged the telegram or even told the High Commissioner of its existence. Well he would just have to show the bloody man the telegram at the cricket match and if he didn't like it, it was just too bad. He looked at his hands; they were shaking. Just one little sip, he decided, just enough to get the blood moving again. Angus took four large swigs from the bottle of scotch and then filled his hip flask to the top. Screwing on the lid he thrust it into his trouser pocket and rushed out of the door.

Andrew was looking around anxiously at his team and trying to decide which one he could ask to keep wicket.

'Have you done any wicket keeping, High Commissioner?' he asked when Peter came up to him, his face showing an enquiring look at the reason for the delay.

'Me? Good gracious no. Where is McMullen?'

'No sign of him yet... Ah, here he is. Thank goodness.' said Peter, indicating the figure running towards them.

'Sorry,' Angus wheezed. 'Problem with the car.'

Andrew and Peter exchanged glances. Angus looked in a terrible state and they could smell the whisky almost before he reached them. 'No matter,' said Andrew. 'You're here now.'

Peter turned away; trying hard to control himself, but Angus came up behind him and tapped him on the shoulder. 'Err... High Commissioner. You ought perhaps to see this. The buggers in London are sending an inspector over... err... with the auditors.'

'What?' Peter turned sharply and took the proffered document from Angus' hand. He read it quickly and a red flush rose to his cheeks. 'Why haven't I seen this before?'

Angus mumbled something unintelligible.

'Have you replied? Have any arrangements been made?'

'No, sorry but…'

'This is totally unacceptable,' Peter hissed. 'You're a disgrace to the Service.' Peter turned away and walked towards Andrew. 'Andrew, please sort this one out. No action has been taken so far. We can discuss further tomorrow morning.' Andrew and Peter then walked onto the field of play deep in conversation.

Angus looked after them with an expression of blind hatred on his face.

Stefan stood on the boundary watching the British High Commission cricket team take the field followed by the two Royal Navy batsmen. Unusually for a Romanian, cricket had become a passion. Perhaps it was the way that a defection removes a nationality, and raises a feeling for all things connected with the adopted country. Maybe it was the years of walking the corridors of the British Embassy in Bucharest, and hearing the hushed whispers of its diplomats exchanging the latest Test match scores in tones of reverence normally reserved for God or the Queen. It had been a chance remark by the Security Officer at the High Commission, when he had arrived for his meeting with the High Commissioner that had brought him here. 'Would he be attending the match with the Royal Navy?' The Security Officer had asked. This had led to a chat about what needed doing to the England team followed by a firm invitation to 'Come and watch us destroy the Navy.' Stefan had already spotted the pretty dark-haired girl among the spectators; she was accompanied by her Uncle Nicu. He fingered the sealed envelope in his pocket, an envelope he had brought with him in the hope of such an encounter. First, he would enjoy the cricket; later, perhaps, he would go and have a few words with Uncle Nicu.

The Royal Navy were doing well. They had won the toss and chosen to bat. This was not surprising for their star, and Captain, who in his working life was the First Mate, had been a promising batsman and a regular on the Minor Counties circuit. Better to get a significant score posted from the beginning and put the High Commission under a bit of pressure. His plan had borne fruit. Each side was to bat for twenty-five overs. After twenty overs the Navy had reached 120 and still had five overs in hand. Their Captain was still at the wicket and had already scored 78. In five more overs he alone could put the match out of reach.

Andrew threw the ball to Peter. 'OK High Commissioner I need you to break this partnership.'

Peter took a short run and gave the ball plenty of air. It was straight and a little wide of the off stump. The batsman allowed it to brush lightly off his pad towards the wicketkeeper. Angus' job was simply to catch the ball in his gloves, but he had other ideas. Instead he launched one gloved hand at the ball and with a flick of his wrist helped it on its way. The batsman ran an easy three. Peter could not believe his eyes, but shrugged, accepting that even the best made mistakes from time to time and Angus was certainly not the best. His second ball was faster and flatter. The batsman was expecting a repeat of the first ball and went down the pitch to hit it to infinity, but he missed. Angus took the ball cleanly and Peter's arms went up in the air to claim the stumping that was about to happen. But it did not happen, Angus stood there calmly and allowed the batsman to get back into his crease. Peter suddenly saw the truth, his wicketkeeper wanted to be sure that the High Commissioner would not have any success, he would have to succeed despite the wicketkeeper.

Chapter 12

Stefan watched the High Commission players leave the field, ready for a short break before commencing their innings. He kept some distance away from the Pavilion, as he did not particularly want to meet the High Commissioner. He could see Daniella chatting animatedly to one or two of the High Commission team, but her Uncle Nicu seemed to have disappeared. When the Royal Navy side took the field and the two High Commission batsmen followed them out, Stefan moved cautiously towards the pavilion. He could see the High Commissioner sitting on the balcony with other members of the team. Daniella was sitting by herself on the grass. Now seemed to be as good a time as any. He walked over to her and sat down beside her. She looked at him faintly surprised and gave an embarrassed half smile as a courtesy to the bald-headed stranger.

'Daniella isn't it?'

'Yes,' she said, the surprise showing clearly on her face.

'I'm a friend of your Uncle Nicu. I thought I saw him over here talking to you.'

'Yes, he was here but he wasn't feeling too well so he went home.'

'Oh, I hope he is alright.' Said Stefan, showing mock concern.

'Yes, I think so,' she replied. 'He is still tired after his journey and probably caught a little too much sun.'

'Pity I missed him,' said Stefan. 'Perhaps you could be kind enough to give him this envelope.'

'Certainly,' said Daniella. 'Who shall I say gave it to me?'

'No need,' said Stefan, standing up. 'It's all in the envelope.' With a brief wave Stefan turned and walked away along the boundary in the direction from which he had come.

Daniella looked at the envelope and then at the back of the departing figure. Suddenly she remembered where she had heard that voice before; it was the man who she had heard through the intercom talking in the High Commissioner's room. She gave a little shiver, hoping against hope that the envelope was not an evil omen.

With Oscar, the High Commission driver, bowling at one end and

Peter at the other, they had managed to restrict the Navy to a total of 132 for four wickets, a fairly daunting total to be achieved in just twenty-five overs. The High Commission started well with Andrew digging himself in and scoring freely. Gradually he began to lose partners, he had a profitable stand of 50 with Anthony Tremlett, until Anthony was run out going for a quick single. When the eighth wicket fell, Andrew was joined by Angus McMullen and only another 21 runs were needed to win. As he walked out to the wicket Angus was swinging his bat backwards and forwards to a rhythm deep inside his head, he was wearing only one pad the straps of which were dangling at the top. The batsman had crossed so Andrew faced the last two balls of the over. The first one he drove firmly through the covers for four, 17 left to win. The last ball of the over was a fast yorker, which dug deep into the dirt underneath Andrew's bat. Andrew firmly dug it out neatly placing it between two of the Navy's fielders. It was an easy single and Andrew began to run. He was halfway down the pitch when he realised that Angus had not moved. Not only was he stationary, but he was down on one knee fiddling with the strap on his pad. Andrew turned quickly and ran back throwing himself full length into his crease as the ball also flew towards the wicket. All the Navy's arms went up in a gleeful chorus, half a dozen voices shouted 'Howzat'. The umpire raised his finger and Andrew, nearly the saviour of his side, was out.

Peter watched the mini drama from the Pavilion balcony. Whilst Andrew was at the crease the High Commission were well placed to win. Now, all that stood between success and failure was Angus McMullen and himself, as last man in. Peter sighed and set off on his way. Andrew gave him a wry smile as they crossed. Peter once again marvelled at the young man's self-control, if it had happened to him, he would probably have gone over and hit Angus over the head with his bat. No sooner had the thought entered his head than he realised that there was still plenty of time for it to happen to him.

The over having finished, it was now Angus' turn to face. Peter looked at him and was surprised to see that he was taking guard, totally unconcerned. It was as if his ludicrous destruction of his Captain's innings had never even happened. The first ball was slightly wide of the off stump. Angus casually swung his bat at it missing by at least a foot. He resumed his stance and patted the ground with his bat. The bowler came in and bowled. Without moving his feet Angus swivelled through 360 degrees, missed the ball completely and collapsed in a heap in front of his wicket. Peter waited for him to stand up, but Angus stayed down. Peter rushed down the wicket and arrived by Angus' side just as the Scotsman was beginning to stagger to his feet.

'Are you alright?' Peter asked.

'Aye,' came the reply.

Peter's eye caught something in the grass glinting in the sun. He bent down and picked it up. Allowing the open silver hip flask to pass briefly under his nose, Peter passed it to Angus.

'I think this is yours and perhaps it explains your behaviour,' Peter spoke quietly and directly to his Deputy. 'You had better pull yourself together man, and if you don't, I shall have great pleasure in making sure that you are back in London within the week.'

'Very well,' Angus' glazed eyes narrowed, as he turned his back on the High Commissioner and then resumed his batting stance.

From that moment it was plain sailing. Something had entered Angus' head, which even the alcohol couldn't eliminate. He set about the bowling like a man possessed. Whether he was seeing one ball, two balls or three will never be known, probably three. If so, it was the middle one he struck five times to the boundary.

'Well done,' said Peter as they walked back.

Angus did not answer, he just looked at Peter and nodded. The hatred was still plainly etched in his eyes.

Stefan had enjoyed the cricket and as he applauded the players leaving the field an elderly man walked towards him along the boundary rope.

'Good match, wasn't it,' the man said.

Stefan looked at the man. He must have been nearly seventy. From his accent he was obviously an islander, but from the white Barbadian community. His face and bald head were covered in little red blotches, some of which had scaly white skin on them. Stefan recognised the symptoms of the slow skin cancer that developed in many of the white-skinned islanders who had been over-exposed to the sun in their youth. He wondered why the man was not wearing a hat then noticed that he was carrying one. 'Yes, a very good match,' he replied with a friendly smile.

'Used to play myself in the old days. Nearly got picked for the West Indies. Used to be different in those days, nearly all whites in the team.'

'Well you have a pretty good team now. Best fast bowlers in the world.'

'Perhaps,' replied the man. 'But the game has changed. All this bowling flat out, no variety any longer.'

'What did you do before you retired?' Stefan asked.

'I used to be a Magistrate until they didn't want me any longer. Put too many of them away. Some of them are still inside. Had to have treatment on this,' he said pointing to his scalp. 'Should wear a hat but it's a bit windy.' He put the hat on top of his head, but it immediately blew off and dropped at his feet. He trapped the brim under his foot and went to bend down to pick it up.

'I'll do it,' said Stefan stooping quickly. Stefan heard the slight sound and a phut as something struck just above his head. As he moved to straighten up Stefan met the elderly man's body coming down. He grabbed hold of the man to help him up, one hand on the man's waist the other supporting his right shoulder, but he felt like a heavy sack. Stefan felt something sticky on his hand as he gently lowered the old man to the ground. He didn't really need the confirmation, but when he looked at his hand it was covered with blood.

Daniella went up to Andrew who had been waiting to greet the High Commissioner and Angus as they came off the field.

'Andrew, that was terrific,' she said. 'And you were great.'

Andrew turned to her and smiled. 'Team effort,' he said. 'Even Angus rose to the occasion in the end.'

'Just in time, after the way he ran you out. Anyway, don't be so modest we wouldn't have had a chance without your innings.' She put her hand on his arm. 'I for one think you are great.'

'Yes, and I think he is great too, and he's all mine.' Annabelle had joined them without either of them noticing. She linked arms with Andrew and began to lead him away. 'Come on,' she said. 'Mummy wants to congratulate you too.'

Andrew did not move immediately, and Annabelle tugged him impatiently. When he still hesitated, she moved in front of him and raising herself on tiptoes kissed him on the lips. Her hand went inside his shirt and scratched his nipple. Andrew gave Daniella an apologetic smile. 'See you tomorrow, Daniella,' he said, moving off with Annabelle towards her mother.

'See you,' replied Daniella, more amused than put out by Annabelle's behaviour.

But Andrew and Annabelle never reached Mavis. A sudden shouting from the boundary stopped them in their tracks. Andrew looked across to see a man waving and shouting. He was trying to hold something up, something that was trying to fall to the ground, something that was undoubtedly the body of a man.

'You missed a lot of excitement at the cricket ground,' said Daniella, slumping herself down in an armchair opposite her uncle, who was lying on the sofa.

'Excitement? You know what I think about cricket. It's about as exciting as watching a tap drip.'

'No not the cricket silly, this was much more dramatic.'

'Oh,' said Nicu, his voice sounding mildly disinterested. 'Not the cricket? So, tell me what was the great drama?'

'Well,' said Daniella. 'We were all chatting after the match and we heard all this shouting from a man on the boundary. Andrew ran to see what the problem was and came straight back shouting to us to call an ambulance and the Police. A man had been shot.'

'Shot?'

'Yes shot. It was an old man, an old white Bajan.'

'Was he killed?'

'I don't think so. It seems he was shot in the shoulder. They took him off to hospital. He seemed pretty old so he might not get better easily. Anyway, the Police asked everyone lots of questions, but they let us go because none of us had seen anything and, with the High Commissioner there, they didn't want to cause any problems.'

'But didn't you hear a shot?' asked Nicu.

'That's the funny thing, nobody heard one. The policeman said it had either been done with a rifle a long way off or the gun had a silencer on. Oh, and another thing, before he was shot the old man was talking to Mr Teduscu. In fact, it was Mr Teduscu that was holding him up and shouting.'

'Mr Teduscu?'

'Yes, you know. The man who said all those awful things in the High Commissioner's office. The one who is going to lead the Trade Mission.'

'Ah yes, Teduscu. And what happened to him?'

'Well he said he had just met the man and had been chatting to him about the cricket when it all happened. He went off with the police, said he was very happy to co-operate.'

'Hmmm,' said Nicu. 'All very exciting. Well Danny, my girl, what have you got your uncle for supper. I'm starving.'

'You men. You're all the same. Just lie there waiting for the women to come home to cook the food.' She leant over and kissed him on top of his head. 'Well you are in luck, I got up early this morning and made some chicken escalopes and some Cou-cou, and as a very special treat I've got a bottle of Tuiça that I found at Heathrow on my way out.'

'Sounds great, but what in the name of Mary is Cou-cou.'

'Ah, *that* is the big surprise. It's a sort of Bajan mamalinga.'

'Great, that's my girl.'

Daniella went to go into the kitchen and then stopped and turned. 'Oh,

I forgot that strange Mr Teduscu gave me an envelope for you, just after you left.' She went to her handbag, took it out and gave it to him.

Nicu waited until he could hear her busy in the kitchen before opening it. He took the sheet of paper out of the envelope and began to read.

My dear Nicu,
It was good to see you again after all these years. Times change and I hope we can both put the past behind us. Life in the West has been good to both of us and there seems no reason why we should not be friends.

Nicu snorted at the thought and carried on reading.

I do realise that our associates have not always been on the same side and it may be that some of your friends see me as an inconvenience. I have therefore felt it necessary to invest in a little insurance, just in case. Four letters have been deposited in London ready to be posted. If I am not back in London in three weeks' time to collect them, they will be dropped in the post box. Let me tell you a little about these four letters.

The first is to the National Criminal Intelligence Service. It describes in great detail some of your activities. It contains some documentation, which should be enough to encourage the authorities to investigate you for drug dealing, money laundering and murder. Of course, you are right in thinking that all this will be hard to prove. It is also true that you may not feel the need to visit England for a while so you can safely ignore the letter as a mild inconvenience.

The second letter is to the Head of Personnel at the Foreign Office. Fortunately, I know him quite well from my Bucharest Embassy days, so he will believe me when I tell him a member of staff has a drug dealer for an uncle and she had him to stay in her official flat in Barbados. He might also like to know that she is related to her High Commissioner and that he had been a naughty boy and a major security threat in fathering her.

The third and fourth letters go to two of our most imaginative tabloids. They will be interested to know that, not only does the little Foreign Office girl have an uncle who deals in drugs and murder, but her dad is the High Commissioner. Nobody knows of course that the High Commissioner has a love child born to a, how shall I put it? Born to a lady of doubtful reputation and conceived when he was on an official Government visit to Mangalia. Sex, drugs and diplomats how could any newspaper resist it, particularly when it is backed up by documentary proof. And all handed to them by the missing Leader of a British Trade Mission.

And where will this leave your pretty little Daniella? Certainly not working in Barbados, even assuming that the Foreign Office don't chuck her out altogether. A ruined career is so sad for a young girl, and I'm afraid the tabloids are not too kind either. They will certainly want their interviews, coupled with one or two very fetching nude poses. I actually managed to get quite a good shot myself through her bedroom window. I passed it on to the tabloids with my report just in case they were interested, that is of course unless I retrieve the letters personally myself.

Best regards
Stefan.

'Bastard,' said Nicu, out loud.

'What did you say?' Daniella re-entered the room looking pretty and wearing an apron. 'Oh, you're reading the letter, not a problem, I hope.'

'No, Danny my dear. Not a problem. Just some chatter from an old acquaintance.'

'Well dinner will be ready soon. Would you like a beer?'

'Yes, please,' replied Nicu, but his thoughts were elsewhere. Teduscu had won this time, but eventually... and when the time came, Nicu would enjoy killing him even more... even if it took him years to do it. In the meantime, it was probably just as well that the stupid old man had got in the way of his bullet. Teduscu was right, the tabloids would have a feeding frenzy if they received his letters and his Danny would be the unwilling victim.

Stefan lay on the bed in his hotel room looking at the ceiling. It had not been an easy day. True he had enjoyed the cricket, but after that things had not gone according to plan. He was sure that, once Nicu read his letter, he would be safe for the time being, at least from Nicu. What he had not bargained for was Nicu mounting his attack so soon. He had been lucky. A gust of wind that had blown off an old man's hat had been enough to save him from certain injury and probable death. Life hung on such slender slithers of chance, turn this way and you have life, turn the other and there is only oblivion. He must be more careful. Stefan realised that his greatest enemy was his own arrogance, his belief in his ability to manipulate the world.

The Police had been polite. He had had the endorsement of the High Commissioner. They had questioned him for nearly three hours before releasing him. Even then they had asked him very politely if he had any plans to leave the island. They had accepted his claim that he had only just met the old man for the first time, moments before the incident. The fact that he was about to lead a bilateral trade mission led them to believe that he was an important and respectable visitor. It was also fortunate that the old man was well known to the Police by reputation. He had been a tough magistrate and there were a number of petty crooks and one or two major criminals who would not weep at his passing. Despite his apparent exclusion from the police enquiries, Stefan still felt uncomfortable. He preferred to keep a low profile and disliked any interest shown in him by the authorities. Stefan had one other cause for giving thanks, he had not yet collected his parcel from the High Commission. Had he been carrying his knife and revolver, when he was questioned, matters might have taken a very different turn. Stefan's thoughts then went to Peter, would the High Commissioner continue to protect him to protect himself or would he crumble? Did Peter have a conscience that might suddenly rear its ugly head and overcome his instinct for self-preservation? Stefan would have to watch very closely for any signs of crumbling.

Peter walked into the Conference Room and sat down. 'Good Morning,' he said.

'Good Morning,' they echoed, some adding 'Peter' to their greetings, others adding 'High Commissioner' or leaving the courtesy unadorned. His regular Monday morning meeting had been extended to include several other members of staff. This was the week in which it was all about to happen, the whole team would need to be on its toes.

'First of all,' said Peter smiling broadly 'The cricket match. Apart from the regrettable incident at the end, it was a great success. You will be pleased to know that the gentleman, Mr Toby White, is expected to fully recover from his shoulder wound. I spoke to the Chief of Police this morning and he is sure the shooting was nothing to do with us. They believe it was a vengeance attack by someone White had put away when he was a Magistrate. Anyway, congratulations to the Cricket team for thrashing the Navy.'

'It was pretty close actually,' slipped in Colonel Perrigrew, the Defence Attaché, struggling hard to balance his loyalty between his long-term Service colleagues and his erstwhile companions in the High Commission.

'Yes Simon, quite right. But it was still a great victory.'

'Oh, certainly High Commissioner, I won't quarrel with that. A very great victory indeed.'

'I would now like to talk about the week ahead,' said Peter realising that it was time to drop the cricket match before Simon bogged the issue down with greater analysis. 'The auditors arrive this afternoon accompanied by David Bloggs an Inspector.' Peter glared at Angus over his glasses and Angus looked down and shuffled his papers. 'Andrew,' Peter turned towards the young man on his right. 'Any luck with sorting out his visit.'

'Yes,' replied Andrew. 'I spoke to him on the telephone last night. He sounded very relaxed and looking forward to his visit. He did hint that he was slightly surprised that he had not heard earlier, but I thought it better not to react. Excuses always sound worse than leaving a doubt in his mind about which end screwed it up.'

'Quite right,' said Peter.

'The hotel, transport and office arrangements are all set up.'

'Good. Well done Andrew. At least one of us is on the ball.' Angus received another withering look and Anthony Tremlett coughed or it may have been a guffaw, whatever it was, it was just loud enough to let everyone know that he had done it deliberately.

'Tonight,' continued the High Commissioner we have the cocktail party for the Navy. Simon, I hope you have all the arrangements in hand?' The Colonel nodded vigorously and opened his mouth to speak, but Peter continued talking so he closed it again. 'Andrew, I would like you at the front door. We are expecting the Minister of Defence and the Chief of Staff. There may be one or two other Ministers, one can never be sure. Simon will need to be with me in the receiving line so it would be helpful if you could greet them and bring them over.'

'Fine,' said Andrew.

'Angus, I suggest you stay in the garden and look after the band.'

'But…' Angus spluttered in fury at the intended insult. The band hardly needed looking after and even if they did it should not be by the second most senior officer in the Mission. 'But I do have my own contacts, you know.'

'Well perhaps you could look after the band as well,' said Peter smoothly, ignoring another eruption of suppressed mirth from Anthony.

Angus glared at Anthony, who looked away. He remained silent, brooding on his revenge and, of one thing he was certain, his revenge would come.

Peter then turned to Fred Forbes, the Commercial Secretary. 'Fred, how are we doing on the Trade Mission?'

'The programme is all arranged High Commissioner. As you know the Leader, Stefan Teduscu is already in town. He is coming in to see me this afternoon, mainly to pick up a parcel that came to him through the bag, but we will also go over the arrangements. The rest of the Mission arrive on Wednesday. We will give them a briefing after lunch, and you are entertaining them at the Residence for the evening Reception. It would be helpful if you and Andrew could come to the briefing.'

'Fine,' said Peter, then looking at his Deputy added. 'You had better come to the briefing too Angus.'

'Are the band playing for the Trade Mission too?' asked Anthony innocently.

Everyone laughed and Angus reddened. 'No,' replied Peter. 'They are not. Perhaps Anthony, we could have a word later about the Mission.'

'Certainly, High Commissioner. I did, in fact, want to talk to you about it.'

'Oh, by the way,' Peter turned back to Fred Forbes. 'What was that you mentioned about a parcel for Teduscu?'

'The Department of Trade and Industry have sent him some gifts for the hosts through the bag. He rang up to say that he would like to collect them. I told him that would be fine.'

'Odd,' mused Peter. 'Leaders don't usually send such things through the bag and Teduscu himself knows how tight the rules are. Have you opened it?'

'No, I hardly think I can open parcels addressed personally to the Mission members. They may contain confidential Commercial information.'

'But Teduscu said it contained gifts. I should know about anything being handed over officially. Better bring the parcel to me. I will give it to Teduscu after you have finished your meeting with him.'

'OK,' said Fred, and Anthony nodded approvingly.

'That leaves the Princess. She arrives on Wednesday too. Is everything in order Andrew?'

'Yes, no problems, except...' Andrew had a momentary vision of Annabelle lying naked on the Princess' bed. 'Except what we do with her whilst the Trade Mission Reception is going on.'

'Good point. I'll have a word with her. If she is willing to make a short appearance it would please the Mission members and, if you Andrew can pass the information informally to the Barbadians, it would probably bring a few more Ministers out of their hutches.'

Chapter 13

'Daniella,' said the Security Officer entering her office. 'Any idea what I should do with this?'

'What is it Terry?'

'It's a letter to a solicitor in Greys Inn Road. The Postman brought it in, said that they couldn't deliver it without the full address. They forgot to put London or England on it you see. I said, no problem, I would write London on it for him. But he said that would not do, because it was a recorded delivery and they would have to receive it again properly from the person who had the receipt. I said that seemed a bit daft to me because everyone knows Greys Inn Road is in London, but he said be that as it may, regulations were regulations and you can't have any old person writing bits of address on registered mail. So, I told him I was not any old person, I was an official at the British High Commission. Well he said he was not disputing that, but did I have the original receipt. So, I told him, no, but I would sign for it and make sure it got to Mr Teduscu whose name is on the back, care of the British High Commission. He said that he wasn't sure if he could give it to me to pass on, as I didn't have the receipt. Well I got a bit annoyed and told him that if he didn't hand it over, he wouldn't get his usual bottle of whisky when Christmas comes around again. So, he said I could have it if I signed, which I did, and here it is.'

'OK leave it with me,' said Daniella deciding that was the least complicated course of action with Terry.

'Sure?'

'Yes, sure.'

'Thanks,' said Terry, handing over the package. 'They get really bureaucratic when it suits them. You wouldn't believe the bother I had importing my car. I don't know if I told you but…'

'Yes, I remember,' cut in Daniella having already heard the story three times before. She gave him a big smile and stood up. 'Look Terry, you'll have to excuse me, but I have to get the papers ready for the High Commissioner.'

'Next time then eh. I could do with a chat. It gets pretty boring down there.'

'Yes, next time.'

No sooner had Terry left than Anthony walked in. He looked at the expression on her face and asked. 'Are you all right? You look like you've got the whole world on your shoulders.'

'Yes, I'm fine. I've just had a dose of the Terry's.'

Anthony laughed. 'Oh, I see. He's a nice chap, but he is inclined to go on a bit.'

'Yes, just a bit. Oh, it's not really him it's just that so much is happening at the moment.'

'Office or personal?'

'Both.'

'Ah, well in a way that's why I'm here. I wondered if you would have dinner with me tomorrow night, at the Treasure Beach… or somewhere else if you would prefer.'

Daniella looked at him. He suddenly looked younger, more boyish, not quite the cynical and confident middle-aged man she thought she knew. 'Office or personal?' she asked.

'Well I hoped it would be personal.'

Daniella hesitated. Did she want to go out on a date with Anthony? What about Andrew? She had rather hoped… but then he seemed to have got entangled with her half-sister… her half-sister, what was she thinking about? Did she really believe that Annabelle was her half-sister? She looked at Anthony; he was standing there patiently waiting for an answer. 'Can I let you know tomorrow morning?'

'Yes of course. Tomorrow is better than a rejection.'

'It's not a rejection. It's just I'm a bit confused at present.'

'Andrew?'

Daniella looked at him in surprise. He obviously didn't miss much. 'That's part of it,' she said defensively.

'I can wait,' said Anthony. 'Until tomorrow.'

'Until tomorrow.'

'Do you have a minute, High Commissioner?'

'Yes, Anthony, do come in.'

Anthony Tremlett came in and sat down on one of the two armchairs indicated by the High Commissioner. Peter sat down in the other.

'I thought we had better have a word,' Peter began. 'I would appreciate it if you didn't openly make fun of Angus. I know he asks for it, but he is after all Deputy High Commissioner and you can't expect younger officers to respect him if senior officers are openly contemptuous.'

'Yes, Peter, you are quite right. I'm sorry. I will try and resist in future for the good of the Mission.'

'Fine,' Peter replied. 'That was really all I wanted to say. You said you wanted to speak to me about something?'

'Yes, about Stefan Teduscu.'

'Teduscu, what about him?'

'Well I've had a report from London, which does not show him up in a very good light. And… well… my American colleagues have even greater doubts.'

'What is the problem with him?'

'Probably money laundering, possibly hooked up with traffickers.'

'Cocaine?'

'Yes, that's what the Yanks think.'

'Any proof?' asked Peter.

Anthony paused and looked thoughtful. 'No, nothing concrete, but plenty of circumstantial evidence. His partner Filip Mendez was recently dragged out of the bay on Grand Turk, in the Turks and Caicos Islands, looked like a professional hit.'

'That doesn't mean Teduscu was involved.'

'No, but it does mean he is a risk. Do we really want someone leading a Trade Mission who might embarrass HMG by being exposed as a crook or who might be targeted by drugs barons? We should tell him we would prefer that he drops out of the Mission.'

'That's for me to decide,' said Peter, rather more sharply than he had intended.

Anthony looked at him in surprise. 'Yes, of course, High Commissioner, but I should have thought it was very much in your interest to avoid any embarrassment.'

'Yes, of course it is,' said Peter quietly. 'However, in my judgement the chances aren't very great of anything happening this week. It would be very difficult getting rid of him at this stage both with the rest of the Mission and with the Barbadian Government. What's more he might not agree to go quietly. Frankly I prefer to take the risk.'

Anthony looked at him thoughtfully. 'You served with him I believe in Bucharest?'

'Yes, I did, but that is not why I think we should leave matters as they are for the time being.'

'Very well High Commissioner,' Anthony said stiffly. 'As you say it's your decision.'

'Yes, it is. Thank you, Anthony, I now have things to do.'

Anthony took the hint, stood up and left the room without any further comment.

Daniella went towards the Commercial Section to drop off the envelope to Fred Forbes. As she passed the Reception she was arrested by a familiar voice.

'Danny.'

'Uncle Nicu, what brings you here?'

'I thought I might come and take my favourite niece out to lunch.'

'You only have one niece.'

'Yes, but if I had a hundred nieces you would still be my favourite.'

'Flatterer. Where are you taking me?'

'Pizza?'

'OK, but that means you expect me to drive.'

'Yes,' said Nicu. 'There is no such thing as a free lunch.'

Daniella drove her car along the beach road towards St Lawrence Gap where her favourite pizza restaurant was situated. She had left her large handbag open at Nicu's feet. Nicu had been eyeing a large brown envelope poking out of her bag.

'What is this?' he asked pulling the envelope out of her bag and looking at it, back and front.

'Do you mind. That is official mail. Please put it back.'

But Nicu did not put it back, instead he ripped it open and looked inside.

'*Uncle*,' she shouted. 'What are you doing. I could lose my job.'

But Nicu didn't take any notice; instead he examined all the contents and said very quietly, his voice managing to communicate to her that this was no idle prank, but something much more serious. 'Where did you get this?'

'I was taking it to the Commercial Section to be given back to Stefan Teduscu. Apparently, the Post Office returned it because the address was incomplete.' She sounded puzzled and a little angry, but still responded to her Uncle's urgent tone.

'Listen Danny. You will have to trust me. This envelope contains papers that concern us, and you will have to believe me when I tell you that Teduscu is out to do us great harm.'

Daniella was silent for some time. 'OK,' she said at last. 'But don't think I am happy about it.'

Fred Forbes showed Stefan into the High Commissioner's office.

'You said you would like a word with Mr Teduscu, High Commissioner.'

'Yes Fred, thank you,' said Peter, holding his hand out to Stefan. 'Good to see you again Stefan.'

'Would you like me to stay,' asked Fred.

'No, thank you Fred. I'm sure you have enough to do at the moment. Go and have a bite of lunch.' Thus, the Commercial Secretary was despatched in traditional Foreign Office fashion not with the message that he was not wanted, but that his time was too valuable to waste. In fact, Peter did not want any witnesses to the conversation he was about to have with Stefan Teduscu, and there can be little doubt that Stefan shared his sentiments exactly.

'Have a seat Teduscu,' said Peter, waiving at the chair in front of his desk.

'I see that we are no longer on first name terms,' Stefan's mouth twitched into a lopsided smile revealing several yellowing teeth.

'As far as I am concerned your assumption is perfectly correct. You lost all right to be treated with courtesy when you came into my office last week and attempted to blackmail me,' said Peter icily.

Stefan's smile widened. '*Attempted*, actually I thought I had succeeded.'

'I shall ignore that remark,' said Peter with as much dignity as he could muster, well aware that Stefan's remark was close to the truth.

'Well, to what do I owe the pleasure of this summons? Are you about to tell me to go to hell and damn the consequences? Have you bought your retirement house yet by the way?'

'I asked to see you because of this,' Peter produced a parcel from his desk drawer and put it on the desk. The parcel had been opened and the contents removed.

Stefan's smug smile dropped for a moment, and he spoke with a touch of genuine anger. 'That parcel was addressed to me personally. You had absolutely no right to open it. However, if you hand over the items that were in it, I shall not pursue the matter further.'

It was Peter's turn to sound angry. 'How *dare* you? I have every right to open a parcel sent to my High Commission by Diplomat bag. You have the audacity to try and smuggle arms through official channels, and then to question my authority when you are caught red-handed.'

'Well, what do you propose to do about it?' Stefan spoke calmly, having regained his composure.

'What you have done is a criminal offence, I shall have to consider carefully what action to take.'

'Consider away, but just remember that you have as much to lose as I have.'

'I may well decide that my integrity is worth more than avoiding a little unpleasantness. I have nothing more to say for the moment. Let me show you out.'

'Could I first have my belongings please.' Peter did not answer, and the two men stared at each other with mutual loathing. Finally, Stefan shrugged. 'OK, you win, for the moment.' He turned and went towards the door.

As he was leaving the building Terry the Security Officer called after him. 'Oh Mr Teduscu, did you get your package alright?' At first Stefan thought he was referring to the parcel that had come in the bag, but then Terry gave him chapter and verse about the returned package from the Post Office.

'Miss Briggs took it to give back to you,' Terry explained at the end of his monologue.

'Where is she? I'll go and get it from her.'

'Oh, she went out to lunch with her Uncle Nicu. I think she still had it with her because I did not see her go to the Commercial Section. Shall I ask her to contact you when she comes back?'

'No, don't bother,' said Stefan. 'I'll get in touch with her myself.' But he knew that it was unlikely that he would see the package again, and that in all probability Nicu would now feel free to resume his attack. He would have to act fast, very fast.

Peter stood up as David Bloggs entered his office. 'Good flight?' he asked holding out his right hand.

'Yes, thank you Peter. I hope you don't mind me calling you Peter. We have met but, if I remember correctly, only on a course in 86,' replied the Inspector, shaking the proffered hand warmly.

'Yes of course David. I must say your memory is pretty good, I knew that we had met but couldn't remember the year or occasion.'

'Well it does get difficult in our life, always on the move and dozens of new faces.'

'Yes indeed. Have a seat. It's good to see you and welcome to my patch.'

'I expect you are wondering what I am doing on your patch?' said David.

'No, not really. I thought it was something to do with a pilot scheme, co-ordinating the activities between Inspectors and auditors.'

David laughed. 'Now we both know that you have been around long enough not to buy that one.'

'Well, OK. Why are you here?'

'Can't you guess?' David asked, looking directly at the High

Commissioner.

'Sugar, tabloids and my wife?' asked Peter pressing his lips tightly together as if to prevent any further revelations.

'Yes, that is certainly part of it Peter,' the Inspector continued to maintain direct eye contact. 'That in itself would have been noted, but it needed something more to prompt this visit. If you add to the airport business a rather odd telegram from a Deputy obviously out to shaft his boss then, seen from a distance you understand, there might appear to be a certain loss of control.'

'Yes, I can understand that David.' Peter replied, feeling that the Inspector's frankness was leaving him totally exposed.

'So, I hope you won't mind my moving about a bit, chatting informally to staff. That sort of thing. Please understand that I am here to help, not to criticise or make waves. Sometimes in life, even in the Foreign Office, circumstances make it desirable that those working in the field can have the benefit of advice from the Centre. This may or may not be one of those occasions. I hope you will ask your staff to be as open and co-operative as possible. We can continue to link my visit to the audit as far as everyone else is concerned. For my part I will try to keep you fully informed as my discussions progress. I very much hope that, when I leave Barbados at the end of the week, we can both look back at this as a storm in a teacup, and that I can report to London that there is nothing more to be said.' The Inspector delivered his little speech in a tone of deep sincerity and reassurance. In fact, Peter felt more alarmed than reassured. London must be pretty concerned to send a messenger with such a blunt message. However, he was also aware that he had to maintain the fiction and phrased his response accordingly.

'Thank you, David, I am most grateful for your frankness and I can assure you that you have my full co-operation and that of my staff.'

'I expected nothing else from you Peter. Now where does this Deputy of yours hang out?'

Angus had not had a drink all day, and to make sure that yesterday's whisky had truly gone he had brushed his teeth five times and gargled with mouthwash four times before he even reached lunchtime. The next week of his life was going to be difficult. If Bloggs got the slightest hint that he could not stay off the bottle he was doomed. He knew that the likes of Tremlett would delight in trying to blacken his name with the Inspector, so he had to remain sober, serious and cool. He desperately wanted a drink and constantly had to put his hands in his pocket so that no one would notice the occasional bouts of shaking. He did have one bad moment when he was talking to the rather delicious press assistant in her office. He had felt his hands begin to shake and had put them in his pockets. Unfortunately, the shaking did not stop, but intensified. The girl had looked at the shaking and moving in the front of his trousers and had come to totally the wrong conclusion. '*Mr McMullen*,' she exclaimed. 'Just what *exactly* are you doing? Please do not come into my office and start behaving like some bad Bajan boy. I really thought you wus a Gentleman.' Angus had blushed deeply, and his already red nose had gone even redder. If he apologised, she would believe she had been right in what she thought she had seen. If he did not, she might think him rude and become antagonistic. In the end he mumbled something unintelligible and beat a hasty retreat.

Angus returned to his office to find David Bloggs waiting for him at the door.

'Ah Angus,' said the Inspector. 'Free for a brief chat?'

'Of course, you must be David Bloggs.'

'Sorry, I should have introduced myself. Well now,' he said sitting down in the comfortable chair and facing Angus across the desk. 'How is Barbados treating you?'

'Fine, thank you. What can I do for you?' asked Angus. 'Can't say I understand the idea of joining up the Inspectorate with internal audit, seems to me that they have totally different functions. Cost-cutting exercise, I suppose?'

'Ah yes, I quite agree. Actually, Angus, that's not really why I'm here.'

'Oh really?' said Angus, feigning surprise. 'That's what London told us.'

'Quite right, quite right… but they could hardly have said that they were sending someone to find out why the Deputy High Commissioner had sent a telegram which virtually said the High Commissioner was an idiot who should not be doing the job, could they?'

Angus flushed, 'I certainly didn't say that,' he protested.

'Didn't you?'

'No, I did not, I said…'

'You said that he had arrived unbriefed, made a total cock-up in dealing with the press at the airport and that his wife had behaved atrociously. To cap it all he had deliberately suppressed the information and thus prevented London from carrying out an exercise in damage limitation.'

'Put the way you put it, perhaps it doesn't sound too good,' said Angus, feeling inwardly delighted that his message had been correctly read in London.

'That's how *you* put it.'

'Well it wasn't how I meant it to sound. I was just telling the truth.'

'Really?'

Angus flushed again. 'Yes, really. Are you calling me a liar?'

'No, of course not,' said the Inspector calmly. 'Let's consider the situation in a different way. Do you like the High Commissioner?'

'I neither like nor dislike him, he has only just arrived.'

'Changes are always difficult,' said the Inspector sounding sympathetic. 'I know myself, one Head of Post leaves who you get on with well and another arrives with new ideas. Can be quite irritating, shaking everything up and making changes.'

'It's not like that at all,' said Angus, feeling tension rising in his own voice.

'What is it like?'

Angus paused and tried to slow his racing pulse. 'Look,' he said at last. 'I admit I don't particularly like the man, his style, his attitude. There's no crime in that. He does think he knows everything, even though others have been in the country for much longer.'

'Well, I'm afraid that's life. He is after all the High Commissioner.'

'Well I don't see the point of your bloody well coming out here. You've obviously made your mind up already to take his side. It's bloody typical of the Office,' Angus said bitterly. 'They always support the Mafia at the top.'

'I am not taking anyone's side; I am just here to establish the facts. I should have thought that as someone already doing a senior job that you would have wanted to be part of that Mafia, as you call it, yourself.'

'Fat fucking chance of that.' Angus said, realising that every remark he made was digging him into a deeper hole.

'I think perhaps Angus that we should talk again later when you are feeling calmer.'

'I am *bloody* calm,' Angus hissed.

'I think not,' said the Inspector standing up. As he went to go out of the door he turned and made a final comment. 'Oh, one other thing Angus. You had better drop in and see the Doctor. You look like you have a fever coming on the way your hands have been shaking.'

Angus shut and locked the door after David Bloggs had departed. He sat down at his desk, head in hands. Finally, he sat up and opened the bottom drawer of his desk. The hot feeling of the whisky going down his throat made him feel better, much better.

Stefan walked out of the courier company office. They had guaranteed that his packet would be in London by lunchtime tomorrow, Tuesday. He would be able to telephone his Bank and confirm that it had arrived and that they understood his instructions. He had waited to see if Daniella would contact him, but she had not. The little bitch was as bad as her uncle. It had been tiresome having to make up the package again. Fortunately, he had copies of everything, so nothing was lost. He had decided to deposit the packet with his Bank this time instead of his solicitor, just in case, as Nicu now knew the Greys Inn Road address. He now had to make sure that Nicu did not find him, before he could confirm that his threat to expose Daniella was in place again. He had taken the precaution of changing his hotel and had decided not to attend the cocktail party for the Navy taking place that evening. Tomorrow, he would hire a mini-moke and explore the North of the Island. The following day, Wednesday, was the first official day of the Trade Mission and, after that, he would no longer be able to keep a low profile. The Wednesday evening reception for the Mission at the High Commissioner's Residence would be the ideal place to meet Nicu again and to let him know that he had better give up any further thoughts of trying to kill him. The Residence reception was ideal, Nicu would hardly be so stupid to do anything there with the whole world looking on.

Nicu had had some difficulty getting Daniella to agree not to do anything further about the packet. Finally, he convinced her by showing her some of the contents. She would not have agreed just to protect herself; to not hand over a packet belonging to someone else went against all her principles. But she did not want her father dragged through the tabloids, even though Peter had so far not acknowledged her existence. She had thought long and hard about the problem of her relationship with Peter and was close to making a decision.

Nicu opened the small plastic bottle and looked at the three white pills it contained. The man in Caracas had told him that one pill would kill a fully grown man, and kill him quickly. The beauty of the pills was that the death would look like a heart attack, unless a very sophisticated post-mortem was carried out. Nicu decided he would take the pills with him to the Navy Reception at the Residence. If Teduscu was there, then he would somehow put one in his drink. When the bald-headed, overweight Stefan collapsed, everyone would automatically think it was a heart attack. For the death to take place at the Residence was a masterstroke. Nobody would suspect anything and, in all probability, the local authorities would not wish to inconvenience the High Commissioner by insisting on a post-mortem. If Stefan was not there, then he would just wait until the Trade Mission Reception on Wednesday and do it then.

Chapter 14

The High Commissioner's Residence looked splendid. The Navy had arrived in force at six-thirty, ready for the seven o'clock start. All were dressed in their tropical whites; many bedecked with medals from the Falklands and the other campaigns, HMS Hopeful had participated in. By five to seven the receiving line was in place. Peter and Mavis stood flanked by Simon and Felicity Perrigrew on their left, strategically placed to greet the guests first and pass them along the line, and the Captain and First Officer on their right. The band had assembled in the pagoda in the garden and had already begun playing their repertoire of popular tunes.

High Commission staff had been instructed to arrive ten minutes early to act as co-hosts. All had complied except for Angus and Anthony, who had still not arrived as the sitting room clock struck seven. Andrew was in place in the entrance hall tasked with the responsibility of greeting Ministers and other VIPs. At five past seven Angus came in puffing heavily. He nodded briefly to Andrew and went straight to the toilet off the hall. He re-appeared looking slightly less ruffled a few minutes later and began to hover just inside the main entrance. At quarter past seven Anthony strolled in looking very relaxed and debonair. His eyes very quickly lit on Angus and greeted him in a hale and hearty voice.

'Evening Angus,' he announced. 'Thought you were the boy in charge of the band tonight?'

Angus gave him a dark look and didn't reply.

'Something seems to have upset the old boy,' said Anthony, addressing the remark to Andrew, but loud enough for anyone in the entrance hall to hear. Angus reddened but still refrained from commenting.

Andrew smiled and Anthony moved on towards the receiving line. At seven-thirty Andrew saw Angus stir and move forward. Moments later the objects of the Deputy High Commissioner's attention came into view. Geoff Forrest entered, on his arm was Trixie. Miss Junior Caribbean was looking her best. Perhaps not ideally dressed for a formal reception, but there was no doubt that the freshness of youth and her fine looks allowed her to carry it off. She was wearing a white blouse loosely buttoned so that it fell open at the neck, showing off the curve of her breasts to the best effect. The bleached whiteness of the blouse contrasted with a vivid turquoise skirt, cut well above the knee so that her slender legs were free to be admired. Her black hair had been braided and beaded, probably by one of the contingent of elderly ladies who practised their craft on the Barbados beaches, so that it fell to her shoulders in separate lines of bright colour.

Andrew was surprised to see her there. He was sure that she would be a great attraction to the Navy, and perhaps that was the explanation of her presence. But who had invited her? As far as he knew only the High Commissioner and himself had met her. The very thought that Peter had asked her was absurd. Andrew had watched the situation in St Vincent develop with a mixture of fascination and horror. His room in the hotel had been adjacent to the High Commissioner's and there was no mistaking the squeals and squeaks that had filtered through the adjoining wall, for the better part of their final night on the island. Andrew felt that the High Commissioner's behaviour had been stupid in the extreme but, though he was a courageous young man, he had not felt able to risk the High Commissioner's wrath by raising it. He had comforted himself in the knowledge that Peter was a grown man and must have known the risk he was taking. Looking at her tonight, Andrew felt that he could understand how a man, struggling with the threat of advancing middle age, might be prepared to expose himself to such a risk. None of this, however, resolved the question of why she was here, unless Peter had suddenly gone barking mad.

Trixie gave Andrew a huge smile of recognition, and a little wave, before setting off to the ladies' room. Angus was now whispering, in a tight huddle, to Geoff Forrest. As Andrew watched the pair of them, it all suddenly became crystal clear. Angus and Geoff were plotting, and Andrew had little doubt about the object of their machinations. Trixie reappeared and Geoff detached himself from Angus and took her arm. It was now peak arrival time and a small queue had formed leading up to the Receiving line. Geoff and Trixie joined the end the queue. Angus faded into the background, but not before Andrew discerned a smirk of satisfaction on his ruddy red face.

Stefan parked the mini-moke in the High Commission car park. The sun had already set, and he glanced at his watch. It was just after seven-thirty, the reception at the Residence would already have begun, so that there was little chance of his bumping into the High Commissioner or Daniella. He went to the front door and rang the bell. After several minutes Stefan saw a little flash of light in the peephole, in the centre of the door, and the door opened.

'Ah Mr Teduscu, sorry to keep you waiting. I am supervising the cleaners and had to move them out of the classified area before opening the door. To what do I owe the pleasure of your company at this late hour? I would have thought you would be at the Residence with the Navy.'

'Peter did invite me, but I thought I would give it a miss and get an early night,' Stefan replied to the Security Officer. 'Sorry to bother you Terry, but I just wondered if you could let Mr Forbes know that I am doing a bit of tourism tomorrow and will not be able to be contacted.'

'No trouble at all Mr Teduscu. Are you going to go anywhere nice?'

'Well I hadn't actually decided yet. I just thought it would be a good idea to drive around the island a bit.'

'My recommendation would be the East Coast, it's very scenic and you can get a cheap lunch over there,' said Terry, looking thoughtful. Suddenly his face lit up. 'No, I've got a better idea, why don't you take a trip on the Jolly Roger. It's a pirate ship, lots of fun and lots of rum and plenty of lovely ladies to talk to. I'm not sure how easy it is to book, but if you go to the tourist office in town, they will give you all the gen.'

'Thanks, Terry. I might just do that. If anyone asks tell them I have gone for a trip on the Jolly Roger.'

'Glad to be of assistance,' the Security Officer said, genuinely pleased that his recommendation had been accepted. 'Is there anything else I can do for you?'

'Would it be possible to check if there is any mail for me.'

'Sure,' Terry replied. 'Step inside and I'll go and have a look.'

Stefan waited until the Security Officer returned, looking very pleased with himself. 'There was nothing for you in the dip,' he said. 'But then I remembered seeing a parcel, addressed to you, in the High Commissioner's office. It looks like it's been opened and then sealed up again. Problem is I'm not quite sure if I should pass it on without the High Commissioner's say so.'

'Ah, yes,' said Stefan, trying not to show the delight he felt. 'Peter did mention to me on the telephone that something had arrived and promised to have it dropped round to my hotel. I thought it might be some stuff for the Trade Mission, so I asked him to open it. He did while I was holding on the phone and it was Mission stuff, just as I thought. I would be happy to take it with me now if you like. That would at least save your driver a trip.'

'I'll go and get it,' said Terry, reassured that Stefan knew all about it and impressed by his free use of the High Commissioner's first name. 'Our drivers are certainly a bit pushed at the moment. Never known a week like this one.'

Ten minutes later Stefan was heading back to his hotel. He laughed out loud as he glanced at the parcel lying on the seat beside him. Now he had his revolver and knife he felt so much better.

Peter watched, horrified, as the couple moved slowly towards him. He continued to greet his guests, shaking hands and making appropriate comments. As he passed on each guest to the Captain, Trixie and the journalist got closer. What the hell was she doing here? He had felt a bit guilty about not having contacted her. Part of him had wanted to seek her out, visit her in her hotel; part of him wanted to touch her firm, smooth body again. But he had known it would be madness, and he had resisted. Now she was here. Here, in his house, a few yards from his wife and daughter. Here, he was about to meet her again. Not this time as a secret lover, but as the British High Commissioner in front of more than a hundred guests.

'Good evening High Commissioner, I think you have already met Trixie, Miss Junior Caribbean.' Geoff Forrest's voice boomed across the short distance between them. To Peter, it sounded loud enough for everyone in the room to hear.

'Peter, how lovely to see you again.' Trixie stepped forward, hand partly stretched towards him.

'Err... yes. Good evening. It was kind of you to come. I'm sure our visitors from the Royal Navy will be delighted to meet you,' Peter moved his hand forward to meet hers, to complete what he intended to be a formal handshake. But that was not what Trixie had in mind. Instead she placed her hand delicately on his arm and leant forward to kiss his cheek. Now there is nothing improper about the social kiss. The Europeans do it all the time. Depending on the country, the kiss can take various forms, a light mutual brushing of the left cheek, a kiss on each cheek, or, if you are Swiss, a kiss on the left followed by one on the right and then completed by a third kiss on the left. The English, it has to be said, are less keen on the social kiss, although its popularity is growing as more and more cross the English Channel to spend their business and leisure time with their less stuffy continental neighbours.

Trixie, however, had her own version. Her kiss was aimed high on his cheek, so high in fact that her moist parted lips pressed themselves firmly against the lower half of his ear. The kiss was not as brief as the usual social kiss. Peter tried to move back, but the lips seemed to follow. He felt her teeth close and gently nibble the lobe of his ear. He felt a sudden wetness as the tip of her tongue touched his skin slightly higher up. Peter's heart began to beat faster as panic rose within his chest. This was no social kiss; it was an unashamed sexual advance. She was challenging him, with all the craft and scorn of a jilted lover. If she did not withdraw soon, others would become aware of the nature of her challenge. He would be undone, his credibility as Her Majesty's representative shot through. He would be the subject of censure by some, of ridicule by others.

'High Commissioner,' Andrew's voice was loud and clear. 'May I introduce Dr Frederick Rafael, the Minister of Defence.'

To Peter's relief Trixie withdrew, clearly unable to continue her treachery when faced with the presence of a real live Minister of the Crown. Peter knew that he was not out of the wood yet, Trixie had clearly signalled her intentions. She wanted capitulation or revenge and the Minister was unlikely to provide more than a temporary respite. Peter held out his hand and shook that proffered by the Minister. Perhaps he could keep the Minister talking, but for how long?

'Trixie, Andrew's voice sounded genuinely pleased and surprised. 'I missed you when you came in; I was so hoping you could accept my invitation. You already know the High Commissioner; I think I introduced you when we were in St Vincent.' To Peter's amazement Andrew then put his arms around the girl and kissed her firmly on the lips. 'Come let me get you a drink.'

For a moment Trixie stood, frozen to the spot. Then with a wide grin she took Andrew's arm and allowed herself to be led away.

The Minister looked on benignly. 'Ah, what we would give to be young again High Commissioner.'

'Yes, indeed,' Peter replied, hoping that the droplets of sweat, running down his brow, were not too evident.

Terry took a beer off the tray and walked over to join Daniella, her uncle and two young sailors. He had just finished his shift and managed to get to the Residence in time to enjoy the last half of the party.

'Hello Terry,' said Daniella. 'Meet Alan and Ted. They were just asking us how they should spend their day off tomorrow. You have been here longer than us. What would you recommend?'

'Funny you should ask,' said Terry. 'I ought to get a job in the Barbados Tourist Board. Why only an hour ago Mr Teduscu asked me the very same question.'

'And what did you recommend?' asked Nicu.

'I suggested he went for a trip on the Jolly Roger. And what's more, that is exactly what he intends to do; tomorrow.'

Trixie had been even more amenable that Andrew had hoped. She had been under no illusions about what Andrew had done to save the High Commissioner, and he had earned her admiration and respect for his actions. It was true that Trixie had been a little put out by Peter's neglect of her, but she also understood the pressures on middle-aged men who stray. Her little fling with Peter had been fun, and she had been flattered by the attentions from someone of such a high status. But Trixie was not short of suitors, and she doubted if she would have wanted to continue the liaison for long in any event. She also knew that she had been set up by Geoff Forrest and lost no time in relating to Andrew how she had received the invitation. For his part Andrew was in no doubt that the real culprit was Angus.

'Thank you for being so understanding,' said Andrew as the two completed their tête-à-tête on the balcony.

'You're welcome,' she said. 'By the way, you kiss very well.'

'Thank you,' he said. 'I only wish it had been delivered in rather different circumstances.'

'You still could,' she said.

'I would like to, but I'm afraid I am already committed.'

'Pity,' said Trixie. 'I think it's time for me to go.'

'*Andrew!* What the fuck do you think you are doing.' Annabelle's face was flushed and furious, as she stormed towards them. 'I've been looking all over for you since your disgusting exhibition in front of my parents.'

'Annabelle, I'm sorry, I can explain… but…' Andrew was not sure how he could explain, he could hardly tell Annabelle that he had done it to cover up her father's adultery.

Trixie turned suddenly and kissed Andrew full on the mouth. 'See you later darling,' she said.

'Don't bother to try to explain you bastard,' said Annabelle, turning on her heel and storming off.

'Touché,' said Trixie, with a wide grin and a wave.

'Touché,' responded Andrew, managing a smile as the slender Miss Junior Caribbean trotted off.

'Anthony,' called Daniella, as she saw him chatting to a naval officer.

Anthony said something to the officer and came over to her.

'Yes, Daniella?'

'I would like to accept your invitation to dinner tomorrow night. The Treasure Beach would be lovely.'

'Are you sure?'

'Yes, I'm sure… that is if you still want me to.'

Yes,' he said. 'I want you to very much. It's just that I think there was more to the Andrew business than met the eye.'

'It has nothing to do with Andrew,' she lied.

'Well I certainly am not going to argue. Shall I pick you up at seven?'

'At seven would be fine,' she said.

It had been a hard day and Peter was glad to be going to bed. The last guest finally left at half-past ten rather the worse for drink. As is customary, the High Commission staff had to stay to the end and try not to show that their feet were aching, and they were desperate to leave. Mavis had disappeared at ten o'clock and Peter had assumed that she had gone to bed. The bedroom door was closed and when Peter opened it, he saw that the lights were off. Mavis must already be in bed. He moved into the room silently using his kinaesthetic sense to navigate himself into the en-suite bathroom. Peter stripped off his clothes, relieved himself in the toilet, washed his hands and splashed water onto his face. The next problem was to find his pyjamas in the bedroom chest without waking Mavis. He successfully reached the chest and opened the drawer.

Suddenly there was a flash of light and the whole room was lit up. Mavis was standing at the door, her hand on the light switch. She was wearing a white coat, open down the front. Under the coat Peter could see that she was wearing black stockings and a black suspender belt and nothing else. Her large white breasts pushed against the coat revealing, in its midst, a sizeable cleavage, her pubic hair, black and tinged with grey hairs, glistened in the bright light of the bedroom. In her hand she carried a long wooden cane.

The scenario was not new to Peter. It had all started some five years after they had married. During their lovemaking she had playfully slapped him on the buttocks. His response had been as sudden as it had been surprising. When he entered her there had been a new passion and a new urgency; somehow, she had released a powerful urge deep down within him. Afterwards they had lain together on the bed feeling relaxed and intimate. Intimate confessions had followed. It all began, Peter told her, when he was nine or ten years old. His father had been sent abroad for a short posting and he had spent the summer at his boarding school. During that summer he had begun to discover new sensations, feelings which had only been hinted at before. One night he had been lying alone on top of his bed. It was dark and he had allowed his hand to move inside his pyjamas. Suddenly he was bathed in light, Matron was standing there in front of him arms crossed, her face stern. 'Parker,' she had said. 'What an earth do you think you are doing? Go to my room at once.' Peter ashamed and shivering had done as he had been told. Matron had bent him over, telling him he must never again indulge in such filthy habits. She had hit him hard, ten times with a gym slipper, Peter had squealed in pain. Afterwards she had clutched him to her, and he had sobbed into the fullness of her bosom. Matron had forgiven him, but he went back to bed a changed person. It was not the last time he had explored himself, but when he did the image of Matron was usually etched on his brain.

The week after his confession Mavis had coyly produced a cane during their lovemaking. Mavis herself had found their sessions satisfying, not only because it stimulated Peter's performance, but also because it fulfilled a need in her. Until her marriage to Peter, Mavis had hated men. The men, she had desired, had almost never responded to her hints, some had even been cruel making unkind comments about her weight and appearance. Caning Peter allowed her to take her revenge on the whole male species.

'Come here you bastard,' Mavis commanded.

Peter did as he was told, and lay passive and naked on the bed. She beat him as she had never beaten him before. When she had finished, she cradled him in her arms and Peter sobbed real tears.

'You meant to hurt me, didn't you?' said Peter as they lay side by side afterwards on the bed.

'Yes,' she said, simply.

'Why?'

'Do you need to ask?'

'Miss Junior Caribbean?'

'Did you have to fuck her? She's younger than Annabelle.'

'What makes you think I did?'

'Peter,' she sat up suddenly angry. 'It was obvious, she virtually stuck her tongue in your ear. If Andrew Walker had not rescued you, the whole town would have been talking about it by now.'

'Sorry,' he said. 'I really am.'

'You'd better be,' she replied.

They lay quietly together, each deep in their own thoughts. 'Mavis,' said Peter, interrupting the silence.

'Yes?'

'There's something else I ought to tell you.'

'I'm listening.'

'I have a daughter.'

'*What!* You mean you've made the girl pregnant.'

'No, no, a grown-up daughter, from before we met. And now I'm being blackmailed.'

'*Since before we met!* Why the hell didn't you tell me before?'

'Well, I didn't really know actually.'

'*You didn't know!* Peter, I've put up with a lot, but I can't stand lies, for God's sake just tell me the truth.'

Peter told her the whole story, how he'd met Suzana, Stefan's hints in Romania and the final proof Stefan had produced. She looked at him trying to take in the incredible story. Peter watched her face change from scepticism to belief. 'Where is she now?' she asked finally.

'That is the most amazing thing of all. She's here. It's Daniella. I swear to God Mavis, I've only just discovered the truth myself, and I'm sure that she does not know either.'

'I believe you,' she said. 'Now we have to find a way of dealing with Teduscu.'

Mavis looked over at Peter; he was fast asleep curled up on the bed. She gave an affectionate sigh and picked up her pen. Mavis had kept a personal diary since she was a little girl and methodically entered into it all her most private thoughts and experiences. It now ran into many volumes, most of which were stored safely in their house in England. The current diary was almost new; she had begun it on the day they arrived in Barbados. Mavis began to write in her neat girlish handwriting. She wrote about Peter's confessions, first that he had had a brief affair with Miss Junior Caribbean and then about the shocking revelations that he had a daughter and that that daughter was Daniella Briggs. She wrote too about their sexual exploits, of how many times she had struck him with the cane, and how much he had sobbed afterwards and whether she had had an orgasm or not. These bits she always wrote in her own secret code and it is doubtful whether even the mathematicians who had solved the enigma code would have unravelled it. Tonight, she almost forgot, such was her need to confide to her diary the emotional revelations of the evening. She wrote rapidly about how she had confronted Peter, how she had felt the need to hurt him. It was only when she began to record the precise details of their encounter that she realised that she was not using her code. Tonight, they had had sex, she had had two orgasms and he had had one, she had struck him seventeen times and he had sobbed into her bosom for over ten minutes. Overall it received a very good rating. Mavis finished writing and put down the pen; she felt very tired. It had been a tiring day and an emotionally draining night. She slid the diary in the desk drawer; tomorrow she would lock it in her private safe. She picked up her cane, stockings and suspender belt off the floor and popped them into the wardrobe. Tomorrow she would stow them away safely in their special hiding place. She walked over to the bed, lay down beside Peter after kissing him briefly on the cheek, turned over and went to sleep.

Chapter 15

Andrew arrived in the office early, he needed to make sure all the arrangements were in hand for the arrival of the Princess the next day, and the High Commissioner had asked him to keep an eye on the Inspector's programme. He had arranged for David Bloggs to meet the wives at a coffee morning at ten o'clock to answer their questions on the Foreign Office's families' policy. Andrew had agreed to go along too, together with Jim Smythe, the Management Officer. Andrew felt mildly despondent at his breakup with Annabelle; even Daniella had seemed more distant than usual. He did not regret his action the previous night; he liked the High Commissioner and had been pleased to have saved him from what might have been serious embarrassment.

'Good morning Andrew, can I have a word.'

'Of course,' replied Andrew, cursing silently to himself. Why did Inspectors always turn up so early? He would be hard pushed to get everything done in time.

'I won't keep you long, I know you are very busy.'

'Thank you, I'm grateful. I am a little pushed,' said Andrew, genuinely grateful that the Inspector understood his problem.

'You are coming with me to meet the wives, I believe?'

'Yes, certainly.'

'Am I in for a hard time?' asked David.

'I doubt it. This is a pretty happy Post, but you never know. Women can sometimes get worked up about the price of vegetables and the lack of nursery education.'

'Well I'll do my best to reassure them,' laughed David.

'Good luck. I shall try and back you up if the heat gets too great.'

'Thanks. Now I just wanted a chat about things generally. How do you find it here? Any major problems? How do you find Peter Parker and Angus McMullen? Anything, in particular you think I should be aware of?' the questions came out in rapid succession leaving Andrew to reply to them all at once.

Andrew looked thoughtful for a moment. 'That's quite a handful of questions, but I'll do my best to answer them. First of all, Barbados is a great place and I'm enjoying it. I have no major problems. I like Peter Parker, in fact I think he will be a fine High Commissioner, not that there was anything wrong with his predecessor. Angus can be a bit tetchy, but he's fine when you get to know him. And finally, I don't think there is anything I should tell you, in particular.'

David smiled. 'Thinking there is anything you should tell me is not quite the same as whether there is anything, I should be aware of.'

Andrew did not reply, but returned the smile.

'That was quite a performance you put up last night,' David said, rapidly changing tack.

'Performance?'

'Yes, performance. I have been watching you carefully since I arrived. You are an excellent young Diplomatic Service Officer and should go far, that is providing that you do not let your better nature sink you. You are not the sort of officer who dumps a Government Minister, even if the girl is very pretty. And you certainly would not kiss a girl on the lips, at the Residence, right in front of the High Commissioner unless you had a very good reason for doing so.'

'I'm not sure I understand what you mean,' said Andrew.

'Oh yes you are, you know precisely what I mean. I admire what you did. Loyalty is a fine virtue, but don't overdo it. See you at quarter to ten,' and with that David Bloggs left the room.

Stefan put his foot down on the accelerator of the Mini-Moke. On either side of the road, the tall sugar cane formed an impenetrable barrier so that the vehicle appeared to be going much faster than it was. Above him was clear blue sky, and Stefan had a comfortable feeling of leaving all his cares behind. He was no longer young and, although he still enjoyed a challenge, the effort involved in staying alive and well was becoming greater. At first, he had enjoyed the duel with Nicu, it was like a chess game, each having to guess their opponent's next move. He realised, however, that he had got very close to becoming unstuck; an old man's hat, blown off in the wind, had almost certainly saved him from a bullet in the heart. An opening appeared on his left and he swung the steering wheel, turning the car North. As he drove, he continued to consider his options. If he left the island, before the end of the Trade Mission's official programme, there was a strong chance that Peter Parker would pass information about him to the British or American authorities. The fact that he would have suddenly abandoned the Mission and his position as leader would make it look as if he had something to hide. Once he left Barbados, and especially if he was on the run, any accusations he made against Peter would have little credibility. Of course, the High Commissioner could take action against him immediately the Mission left Barbados, but provided he stayed with some of the other Mission members, on their visits to other islands, this was unlikely. Apart from the risk to Peter himself of Stefan making accusations against him, the suggestion that the Mission leader was a crook would be embarrassing for the British Government while the Mission was still formally in the Caribbean. He only needed a few more days in the area to arrange to close accounts and transfer out the proceeds. He must, therefore, cling on to the role of Mission Leader for as long as possible.

Then there was Nicu; the man seemed intent on killing him. He had managed to keep him at bay with threats to expose Daniella, but Nicu was a ruthless man and could not be relied upon to behave rationally forever. Stefan fingered the gun strapped under his armpit. Perhaps the best solution would be to strike first.

Anthony Tremlett was next on David Bloggs' list. He caught up with him in the corridor and, true to form, Anthony suggested that they had their talk over a coffee.

'I expect you have heard why I'm here?' began the Inspector.

'If I hadn't, I would have guessed.'

'Things are that bad, are they?'

'No, not really,' replied Anthony. 'But it is obvious there are problems.'

'Such as?'

'Well for a start the High Commissioner and his Deputy can't abide each other.'

'And whose fault is that?'

'Mainly Angus. He's been going downhill for some time.'

'In what way?'

'Whisky mainly, combined with bitterness and paranoia.'

'You don't mince words,' said the Inspector.

'I don't need to,' retorted Anthony.

'If, as you suggest, the Deputy High Commissioner is, or is becoming, an alcoholic, why hasn't anyone done anything about it?' asked David.

'Good question,' replied Anthony. 'I expect, to be fair the High Commissioner has only just arrived. He probably feels it is a bit early to destroy a man's career.'

'There's no reason why it should destroy his career. I like to think we are more sensitive these days. We would arrange appropriate treatment and when his problem has been resolved he could resume work normally.'

Anthony laughed. 'Great in theory. The man must be nearly 55. Are you telling me that you would send him out to his own Post after a year in London drying out?'

'It wouldn't have to be his own Post. There are plenty of other good jobs around.'

'And which Head of Mission would want a reformed drunk as a senior member of his staff?'

'You are very cynical, Anthony.'

'I'm not cynical,' replied Anthony. 'Just a realist.'

'Well you may be right, but that doesn't excuse leaving a man in his situation in a responsible job. It puts everything at risk, and it doesn't do him any favours either.'

'Couldn't agree more,' said Anthony.

David paused and touched his chin with open fingers. 'Just one more question.'

'Shoot,'

'What was all the business at the Residence about?'

'What business?'

'The pretty young coloured girl who seemed a bit familiar with our High Commissioner, that is until young Walker butted in and spirited her away.'

'Your guess is as good as mine,' said Anthony flatly.

'And what is your guess?'

'Haven't really thought about it,' Anthony replied.

'I'm surprised,' said David pleasantly. 'I had gained the impression that you had views on most things. It appears that you don't mind commenting on the Deputy High Commissioner's weaknesses, but you are more circumspect when it comes to his boss.'

'I am not really aware of any weaknesses as you call them.'

'Perhaps,' replied David, standing up. 'Thanks for the coffee anyway.'

'My pleasure,' said Anthony, confirming the Inspector's view that Tremlett always liked the last word.

The sound of tin cans and kettledrums drowned out the gentle washing of the waves against the side of the ship. A conga had started up, and scantily dressed girls alternated with sweaty young men, as they bounced up and down to the rhythm, forming a never-ending snake of bodies. Several times the line passed close to him and once a little blond in a bikini top and hot pants tried to pull him into the fray. The rum had flowed freely, and almost everyone had supped without inhibition. Nicu, however, was an exception. He was stone-cold sober and more than a little irritated. Terry's assertion that Stefan would be taking a trip on the

Jolly Roger had proved to be totally false. Nicu had not only wasted a day, but he was feeling slightly queasy at the rocking of the ship and the constant noise and music was making his head throb. There was nothing he could do but wait until the ship docked and he could escape to dry land. He looked at his watch and frowned. It looked as if he had another two hours to go. The line was coming round again and Nicu could see that the blond had her sights on him again. He moved quickly away and went to the front of the ship and sat down. At least it was a bit quieter and he could think. It was a pity that he had not been able to deal with Stefan on the Jolly Roger; the sea had no equals in disposing of inconvenient bodies. Now he would have to revert to his earlier plan and settle the matter at the Trade Mission cocktail party.

Angus could hardly believe the audacity of it. That little shit Andrew Walker had calmly come and asked him if he would accompany the Auditors to the Residence where they had to check the silver. Angus had told him in no uncertain terms what he could do with the Residence silver. It was not the job of the Deputy High Commissioner to play nanny to a couple of London auditors. But Andrew had persisted. He pointed out that he, the Management Officer and Mavis Parker had to attend the wives' meeting with the Inspector. He had, he added, cleared his approach to Angus with the High Commissioner and it was the High Commissioner's wish that Angus should take on this small task. Angus responded with a string of expletives, but eventually decided that he had little option but to comply.

Now as he stood in the High Commissioner's bedroom, having handed the Auditors over to the maid and the silver cupboard, Angus wondered whether he might have been hasty in objecting to doing the chore. It was not often that he had unfettered access to Residence Master bedroom, and it was just possible that a quick look round might yield evidence of the High Commissioner's fling with Trixie. He quietly began to open cupboards and drawers. It was when he opened the wardrobe that he first struck gold. Just inside on the floor was a cane, on top of which were a black suspender belt, some net stockings and a white coat. Although not concrete proof, the items did provide some circumstantial evidence of some pretty kinky goings-on. Angus picked up the suspender belt, sniffed it and held it out at arm's length to gauge its size. Disappointed he decided that it would go round Trixie three or four times, it must belong to Mavis. The filthy cow was obviously a sadist; well he for one would enjoy exposing her nasty habits.

Spurred on by his find, he searched more thoroughly, and it was in the desk drawer that he discovered the real treasure, a black leather-bound diary full of neat, feminine script. It didn't take him long to confirm his suspicions about the purpose of the cane, stockings and suspender belt; pity it turned into gobbledegook just as it began to give some details. But there was much better to come. The revelations about Peter and his newly discovered daughter, Daniella, nearly took his breath away. There was enough here, with Geoff Forrest's help, to sink the High Commissioner and his precious wife for good. What made it even more delicious was that it would also allow him to pay back that stuck up little bitch, Daniella. She had falsely accused him of sexual harassment to the obnoxious Tremlett. He would enjoy seeing her squirm when the full details of her lineage were plastered all over the Sunday papers. Angus wondered if he dare take the diary, but it would surely be missed and might alert his potential victims to their fate. Then he remembered the photocopier in the office downstairs, and almost cackled aloud with delight as he slipped out of the bedroom and down the stairs, clutching his precious find to his chest.

Peter had regular lunches with the American and Canadian Heads of Mission, and they took it in turns to host the lunch, either at home or at a restaurant. Today was the turn of the Canadian High Commissioner, Pierre Fournoux, a French Canadian, and he had chosen a local restaurant. Peter marvelled that the Canadians still sent French Canadians to English speaking countries, but he imagined that it was a question of political balance. In practice, it did not make any difference as Pierre came from Montreal and his English was as fluent as his French. They talked through all the usual problems and Peter defended the British policy of supporting the Windward Island banana industry against the large American firms in Central America. They also discussed their combined efforts to combat drugs and to bolster regional security. Bramley Smith briefed them on the latest American moves to provide economic support to the region through the Caribbean Basin Initiative. They then moved on to more parochial matters.

'I see you have a trade mission in town,' said Pierre.

'Yes,' replied Peter. 'They arrive tomorrow.'

'Well if we can do anything for them let me know,' said the Canadian. 'If you'll excuse me a moment I'll just go and settle this.' He picked up the bill, got up and went over to the bar.

'Talking about your trade mission,' said Bramley. 'I see that Teduscu is still leading it.'

Peter felt annoyed that the American had raised the matter again. He felt there was an implied criticism in the remark and, after all, Bramley himself had said that there was no concrete proof of wrongdoing. He tried not to show his annoyance and took a sip of his drink before answering.

'Yes, I was grateful for your information on that. I did consult London, but they felt to ask him to step down might be more difficult than leaving him alone. Typical London attitude. They don't like having to do the dirty work themselves,' Peter said with mock bitterness.

'You asked London? Well I must say their attitude does surprise me a bit. The information we have on Teduscu has hardened up quite a lot since we last spoke, and there now seems very little doubt that he is up to no good. I'm surprised your people haven't had that from ours.'

'Well things can sometimes take a while to move between Whitehall departments. I expect they'll send me a telegram tomorrow. Anyway, it's too late to do anything now.'

'I must say I have to admire you Brits,' said Bramley. 'You really do take things in your stride. If it was me having a trade mission arriving tomorrow led by a money launderer, I'd be shitting myself.'

'An *alleged* money launderer,' said Peter, suppressing an urgent need to go to the bathroom.

'Sorry an *alleged* money launderer.'

Peter sighed to himself. He really must find some way of dealing with the Teduscu problem before the whole lot collapsed on top of him.

Peter returned to his office to find David Bloggs waiting for him.

'High Commissioner,' the Inspector began. 'I promised to let you know how my investigations were progressing.'

'Thank you, I'd be most interested to hear,' Peter was indeed interested and already feeling a bit concerned. He noted that David Bloggs had referred to him as High Commissioner, not Peter. A small thing in itself, but an indication of formality. The use of the word 'investigation' also had a sense of foreboding about it.

'May I begin, by saying that you seem to have a very happy Mission here, and that your staff appear to have a strong sense of loyalty to you personally.'

'Thank you,' replied Peter, feeling even more concerned by the complimentary introduction, which could only mean bad things were to follow.

'I must admit, however, to having some concerns.'

'And they are?' asked Peter, feeling no satisfaction that his instincts had proved to be correct.

'First and foremost, there is the question of your deputy, Angus McMullen.'

'Ah yes, Angus,' Peter was not at all surprised that Angus was at the top of the Inspector's list of concerns.

'The man clearly has a serious drink problem. It seems to me that it is only a matter of time before something goes seriously wrong, either in relation to his official duties or to his health. Frankly, I am surprised that you have not thought fit to do something about it yourself.'

'I confess the problem has been very much on my mind. I hope you will recognise, however, that the situation has deteriorated significantly in the past few days. It would not surprise me if London's decision to send an investigator had not tipped him over the top.' Even while he was speaking Peter was asking himself why he had not taken action earlier. He remembered Angus' veiled hints about Trixie the previous week. That had certainly caused him to treat his deputy carefully. Then there were the many other problems Peter had on his mind, Stefan Teduscu and his newly discovered daughter. It was easy for Bloggs to say he should have taken action, but he was not the one trying to keep all the balls in the air so soon after arriving in Post.

'Be that as it may,' said David, amused by Peter's feeble attempt to pass the blame on to London and, by implication, onto himself. 'But action must be taken now and quickly. I suggest you contact London and ask for him to be withdrawn as soon as a replacement can be found or, if possible, sooner. I, myself, will be making a recommendation to that effect. I suggest you also talk to McMullen, telling him what is happening and reassuring him that the Office will do everything they can to help him through his problems. If you would prefer it, I will speak to him, but I think it would be more appropriate coming from you.'

'No, I will speak to him. I accept your comments and your recommendations.'

'Good,' said the Inspector, remaining seated.

'Anything else?' asked Peter, sensing that David Bloggs had not quite finished.

'I am not quite sure how to put this...'

Peter said nothing, but remained stationary, looking directly at the Inspector. He had seen enough of the man to know that he was rarely uncertain about how to put things.

'I must confess to some concern that McMullen may not be the only problem we have to contend with.'

'Really?' said Peter, disinclined to help David Bloggs with his fishing trip.

'There was that odd incident with Miss err Miss...'

'Miss Junior Caribbean,' said Peter, instantly cursing himself for so stupidly falling into the trap.

'Exactly,' David paused. 'Look we are both grown up. I won't insult you by playing games. I do not believe I was the only person who noticed the girl's odd behaviour when she greeted you at the Residence party. Your staff's loyal attempts to cover up the incident and then to clam up tight when I mentioned it only serve to confirm that my initial reaction, that there was something going on beneath the surface, was not wide of the mark.'

'I'm not sure what you are suggesting,' said Peter defensively.

'Let us say that I am not *suggesting* anything, but I do feel it incumbent on me to remind you that the High Commissioner's job is an exposed one. If you give people, the slightest opportunity to make trouble there is a fair chance that that is what you will get. If it's any comfort I will not formally record this in my report, you should, however, be aware that I will mention it informally and you can expect London to be watching closely if there are any further incidents emanating from this Post.'

'Thank you,' was all Peter could say, but he was not quite sure what he had to thank the Inspector for.

'Well, I must let you get on, Peter,' said David Bloggs with a little nod.

Peter noted, with little satisfaction, that David had now returned to first name terms, having delivered his message. He watched as the Inspector left and closed the door behind him. Peter let his head fall into his hands. 'Oh dear me,' he muttered half aloud, 'Oh dear me.'

Anthony arrived at Daniella's door exactly on the dot. She opened the door and he was pleased to see that she was ready. In fact, she had been ready and waiting for nearly fifteen minutes. She had taken particular care in preparing herself for the evening, her hair was black and shiny, and she had used just a hint of makeup to highlight her eyes, whilst leaving her skin looking fresh and natural. She had taken particular care in choosing her clothes. She had thought hard about what might appeal to her undeniably older escort. Eventually she settled for freshness and discretion. A light white cotton dress, relatively highly cut at the bust and falling gracefully to just above the knees, seemed to fit the bill. To make it look a little more formal, she had added the only valuable piece of jewellery she possessed, an emerald broach, set in silver, with small diamonds surrounding the bright green stone. It had belonged to her grandmother, Annie Briggs, and her father had told her that it was antique and that the stones were particularly fine.

'You look lovely, Daniella' Anthony looked at her approvingly.

'You look rather fine yourself,' she said, noting Anthony's very expensive casual clothes. Seeing him standing there a youthful forty-year-old, looking smart and full of vitality, she realised how glad she was that she had accepted his invitation.

They drove North along the West Coast in silence, but it was a comfortable silence; already they seemed to be at ease with each other's company. Daniella found herself thinking about her escort. In the office he was sharp and cynical always making apt comments at the right moment. She realised how little she knew about him personally. He was clearly unmarried; but did that mean he had not been married or might there even be a wife hidden away somewhere in England. He was also an athlete, although this was usually concealed behind his smart office suits. His job certainly contributed to the air of mystery about him; but there was more to it than the job. There was a sense of mystery and intrigue about the man himself.

'Look,' he said, pointing a finger towards the sea. She looked; the sun was large and beginning to disappear into the horizon. The sky was a blaze of reds and oranges, fighting against the bright blue it had maintained throughout the day. The smooth turquoise water was picking up the colours, changing their hues and textures and reflecting them to form a total picture of natural beauty. There are few things more romantic than a Caribbean sunset, and it was at that moment that Daniella realised that she found Anthony deeply attractive.

'Lovely,' she said.

'Yes, very lovely,' and there was something about his tone that made her think that he was not only referring to the sunset.

Chapter 16

She chose pieces of grilled aubergine covered with cheese and breadcrumbs and lightly toasted, followed by the fresh lobster salad with pieces of tropical fruit. Anthony ordered a bottle of the restaurant's best champagne and they chatted. Anthony had views on everything and a deep font of knowledge to back it up. She had never been out with anyone who seemed so at ease with so many subjects. He was a keen sportsman, having played both cricket and rugby in his youth, but he also liked tennis, skiing, diving and even had a pilot's licence. His passion was wildlife and conservation and in Daniella he found a ready ally. He clearly liked politics, but Daniella was still unsure which party would have his vote as he skilfully dissected the Tories policies on monetarism and on the Health Service, but did not spare the Labour party on education or trade unionism. She wondered if he might be a Social Democrat or a Liberal, but their policies too did not escape his scathing wit and astute analysis. She thought she might easily better him on art, but it was a draw when he demonstrated a detailed knowledge of Russian classical painting. Music too was a shared passion and they had both read many of the same books. But what impressed her most of all was his ability to dispense his knowledge in a way which never for a moment made her feel less than his equal. His self-deprecating humour, tinged with an occasional excursion into the realms of outrageous opinion, made the conversation as relaxed and enjoyable as the food. He clearly had a respect for everyone and everything, but he also despised pomp and refused to accept the right of anyone to have total authority over him or anyone else.

They only discovered one area of potential conflict. Daniella had been brought up a Catholic and, although she no longer practised, still held the basic tenets of the faith. Anthony was an unashamed Agnostic; the authority of a God was as unacceptable to him as the authority of one man over another. If nature is a spectrum, he argued, where man is a more developed form and animals, birds, insects, reptiles and even plants are no different in essence, how can man have a soul and a life after death? Is heaven full of the souls of ants? Daniella did not know, only that it all boiled down to faith and a belief that the wonders of the Universe could not exist by chance. Such was their enjoyment of each other, however, that the difference only brought them closer together by allowing them to maintain their own fierce individuality.

Anthony had impeccable manners and she found that doors being opened for her, and the chair being discretely pulled back to allow her to sit gracefully down at the table, added to her enjoyment of the evening. There was no hint of crude sexual innuendoes or approaches. She remembered being put off by one suitor who had indelicately squeezed her buttock before their date was half an hour old. The sexual approach did come, however, as she leant back after devouring a delicious dessert of cream, ice cream and meringue, he gently placed his hand on hers, looked her in the eye and said how much he had enjoyed the evening. She felt a perceptible tremble deep inside her and she told him that she could not remember an evening in her life that she had enjoyed more.

On their way home, Daniella made a decision. 'Anthony,' she said. 'I badly need some advice. I need to confide in someone I can trust.'

Anthony did not answer immediately, and Daniella waited in silence for his response as he steered the large car smoothly around the bends of the coast road. 'If I can be any help at all I am completely at your disposal.'

'Can we talk over a coffee when we get back?' she asked.

'Of course,' he probed no further, knowing that it was something of great importance to her that had to be delivered in her own time.

'I would prefer to talk at your place,' she said. 'My uncle is staying with me.'

'Fine, as long as you don't mind my awful coffee.'

He parked the car in the garage, and they went up to his flat. The flat was bright and cheerful and immaculately tidy. Daniella looked around and noted with approval his good taste in furnishings, the bookcase full of books and the pictures on the wall. Anthony went over to the CD player and put on a Mozart Concerto, loud enough to hear, but quiet enough not to intrude in their conversation. He disappeared into the kitchen and reappeared with two mugs of coffee.

'Not too bad,' she said, taking a sip.

'I hope not,' he said. 'It's meant to be Jamaican Blue Mountain, but I'm not sure if I trust the label. It tastes a bit bitter.'

'Where did you get it?'

'From a friend in the Jamaican High Commission.'

'Well it must be the genuine article then.'

'Yes, it's probably just the way I cook it.'

'Can we talk now?' she asked.

'Yes, let's go and sit down on the settee.'

They sat down at either end of the settee facing each other, he with his legs firmly planted on the ground, she with hers tucked up on the settee beneath her.

'I'm not sure where to begin,' she said.

'How about at the beginning,' his remark did not sound trite or facetious, but the serious comment of a man who was prepared to sit and listen to the whole story.

'OK,' she took a deep breath. 'My mother was Romanian, and I was born there. About the time of my birth my mother married an Englishman and we moved to England. I always thought of him as my dad, but I have since found out that he is not. My mother was already pregnant when they married; and he accepted me as his child.'

She paused to see his reaction, but all she could divine was that he was listening intently. He acknowledged her pause with the slightest nod of encouragement to continue.

'It was a terrible shock; I love my father very much and to find out that he was not my real father was almost too much to bear.'

'I can imagine,' Anthony said quietly. 'It would have shaken anybody.'

'I found out by accident. The High Commissioner was talking in his office with Mr Teduscu. I had been out, and they had somehow left the intercom on. I went to switch it off and heard my mother's name. Mr Teduscu was threatening the High Commissioner, saying I was his daughter and he would expose him if he did not do as he said. Oh, how much I hate that man Teduscu.'

Anthony put his hand on her arm as she choked back a tear. 'Can it possibly be true?' he asked.

'Yes, it's true,' she said bitterly. 'He was serving in Romania at the time I was born and, what is more, my Uncle Nicu confirmed that he was my father. I have even seen papers that Teduscu was sending to London proving that Peter Parker is my father.'

'Have you spoken to the High Commissioner about it?'

'No,' she said. 'How could I?'

'It might be a good idea. He knows you are his daughter and he probably doesn't know that you know. He is a decent man I think you both might feel better if you talked it over.'

'Do you really think so?'

'Yes. I do.'

'But… but I don't think I could. It might be awful. He might reject me. He has his own family the last thing he wants is another daughter turning up.'

'That might be true, but you are not asking him to take you in as his daughter, are you? You already have a family, and, in a way, you've already turned up. Look,' he said taking her hands in his. 'You can't live a normal life, with both of you holding this big secret between you. You really need to talk it through. If it would help, I would talk to him with you… or speak to him first if you wish. Anything you think might help. But you might find it better to speak to him yourself and I would be there for you afterwards.'

'Would you?'

'Yes,' he said simply.

She thought for a moment. 'I think perhaps you are right. I will talk to him. What about Teduscu?'

'Yes, that is a problem. I shall have to give some thought to what we do with Mr Teduscu.'

'Thank you for being so understanding,' she said, leaning over and kissing him on the lips.

It was a signal to him that she was there for the taking, but he knew she was vulnerable and allowed the kiss to finish naturally. He then moved back and said, 'more coffee?'

'Yes, please,' she said, appreciating his consideration.

They drank their coffee in silence, both deep in their own thoughts, conscious of but comfortable in each other's presence. It was Daniella who broke the spell.

'Can I stay with you tonight?' she asked.

'Of course, the bed in the spare room is made up.'

'No, I mean really stay with you.'

He looked at her for a moment and she wondered what she would do if he turned her down. 'There is nothing I would like better Daniella. But only if you are absolutely sure that is what you want.'

'I am absolutely sure she said,' and this time he did not hold back when they kissed.

Peter woke up early and reviewed the day ahead. The Princess was due to arrive at eleven o'clock, and he would have to be at the airport to meet her. The rest of the Trade Mission members would be on the same flight. Fred Forbes would have to field them. He would be seeing them at three to join in their briefing session. In the evening there would be the reception for the Mission at the Residence. He had to remember to speak to the Princess about that. There was something else he had to do, something he was not looking forward to, he had to talk to Angus McMullen. He wondered if he could leave it for a day or two, but he knew it would be better to deal with the matter quickly. That would also help him get back on-side with David Bloggs. Then there was Stefan Teduscu, should he act or wait? Now that Mavis knew about Daniella, the threat of exposure was a little less potent. But there was still Annabelle and Daniella herself, he would have to tell them before they found out in some other way. He tried to think about Daniella. She was his daughter, but how did he feel about her? He had seen her for the first time only a few weeks ago; did he really want another daughter? How would the Office view a past indiscretion? Perhaps they would be lenient, but David Bloggs had made it clear that he was still under a bit of a cloud and on probation. Better to leave Teduscu until the Mission had left Barbados and David Bloggs had returned to London. Next week, when things would be easier, he could talk to Annabelle and then break the news to Daniella. Satisfied that he had made his decisions for the day, as far as they were within his control, he went into the bathroom, had a shower, shaved, brushed his teeth, got dressed and went down to breakfast.

Just over two miles away Daniella opened her eyes, she blinked, taking in the unfamiliar surroundings seen for the first time in daylight. She was wearing Anthony's pyjama top. She smiled as she remembered how he had insisted that she put it on after they had made love for the third time. He did not want her to catch cold he had said. She sat up, stretched like a contented cat and looked down at her partner. He was wearing the pyjama bottoms. She looked at his naked chest remembering again how strong he was. After they had kissed on the settee, he had picked her up like a feather and carried her into the bedroom. He had laid her gently on the bed and undressed her slowly. She had discovered for the first time the true meaning of foreplay. Daniella had not had many lovers, perhaps seven in total. But the techniques of those she had had, had varied considerably. One or two had fussed and fumbled, others had played macho throwing her down and trying to enter her when she was still dry. One had been kinky, and another had squeezed her breasts and buttocks as if they were bags of putty. Anthony had been different, oh so different. He had stroked her gently, gradually raising in her a feeling of warmth and wellbeing, he had then touched her until she was ready and then, at precisely the right moment, he had entered her. The first orgasm had been intense; the later ones had ebbed and flowed like the summer tide. She knew that she had discovered a skilled and complete lover.

Anthony opened his eyes and looked at her. 'What are you smiling at?' he asked.

'That would be telling,' she said placing a finger on his lips.

'Come on,' he said taking hold of her and tickling her lightly. 'It's time for breakfast.'

'Just one more time,' she said giggling.

'OK, but you're spoiling me,' and he pushed her gently back down on the bed.

They feasted on a breakfast of tropical fruits, followed by imported English sausages and Danish bacon. She teased him about his sources of supply, saying that it was the first time she had met a smuggler. He responded by pouring her another cup of Jamaican coffee.

The shock came as they sat sipping coffee and crunching hot fresh toast, liberally laced with New Zealand butter and French strawberry jam. 'Will you marry me?' asked Anthony.

'What did you say?' the hand, holding the toast, froze just before it reached her lips.

'I said, will you marry me?'

'But… but,' she was so shocked by the question, that her mind would not respond – but they hardly knew each other… but it was their first date… but what would everyone say… but…

'You don't have to give me an answer straight away,' he said.

'But I want to… yes… yes, I will marry you,' she heard herself say, almost as surprised by her answer as by his question.

Angus woke up late, his head was throbbing, and he could not quite remember what had happened the night before. He had not intended to drink, but somehow one small one had led to another. He had eventually staggered into the bedroom and fallen onto the bed going into a stupefied sleep, fully dressed. Now it was morning and he somehow had to get up and go to work. He staggered into the bathroom, his mouth tasted foul and he swilled it out with mouthwash. The mouthwash tasted even worse and he quickly spat it out into the basin. He dressed quickly and went into the kitchen and put on the kettle. He lit a cigarette; it was a habit he had been trying to give up, but somehow his need increased just as his need for whisky. The cigarette seemed to taste of mouthwash, and he began to cough. The coughing would not stop, and he felt a sharp pain in his chest. He staggered over to the cupboard and took out a bottle of whisky, he opened it and took a long gulp. After a second gulp he began to feel better, the pain in his chest had almost gone and the coughing stopped. He made himself some coffee and drank it black. Gradually his spirits rose, was not today the day he would have his revenge? He went and got the copies he had taken from Mavis' diary, put them in an official brown envelope and wrote Geoff Forrest's name on the outside. He would see Forrest at the Reception and give him the envelope. Perhaps he had better telephone him to make sure he would be there. He went to the phone and rang Geoff Forrest's number. He cursed as he got the answering machine and left a message saying that he had some information that would be dynamite and to make sure that he attended the Trade Mission Reception. He looked at his watch it was already nine o'clock, he was late.

'Where the hell is the bloody man?' Peter muttered. He wanted to speak to Angus McMullen before he had to leave for the airport to meet the Princess. It was twenty to ten and he would have to leave in three-quarters of an hour. He knew that what he had to say should not be rushed, it should be a calm measured discussion. Equally, he was determined to deal with the matter quickly. He knew that anger and frustration were beginning to rise inside him. He went to Angus' office for the fourth time, but the door was still locked. He was about to go back to his office, when Angus appeared. The man looked a sight, there were shadows under his eyes and his face was drawn. His suit was dishevelled and his shoes unpolished. Anyone seeing him in his present state would be hard pushed to believe that he was a senior diplomat. Peter took a deep breath, what had to be done had to be done.

'Ah Angus,' he said, trying to sound calm and friendly. 'Could we have a word please before I leave for the airport.'

It was not a question but a command, but Angus seemed to think otherwise. 'I'm a bit busy at the moment,' he replied.

Peter was flabbergasted; the man's audacity was breathtaking. He wanted to snap back hard, but he retained his self-control. Speaking very quietly and slowly he said 'Look Angus, we need to talk. This is not something that can wait, and it is important. I have to leave for the airport soon and I would very much appreciate it if we can talk now.'

'Your room or mine?' the insolence in his voice was deliberate.

'*Mine*,' Peter spat the word out, his patience finally succumbing to his pent-up anger. The two men stared at each other for several seconds before Peter turned and walked back to his room. Angus followed five minutes later, leaving just enough time to ensure that Peter's fury remained stoked up.

'Well,' said Angus, sitting down.

Peter had rehearsed what he was going to say in his head several times; but faced with Angus he abandoned his script. 'I am recommending to London that you be replaced immediately,' the statement was blunt and direct, no preparation, no softening.

'May I ask why?'

'Yes, you may. Put simply you are an alcoholic and you are a danger both to this Post and to yourself.'

Angus bit his lip. 'I would have thought your own behaviour is hardly a credit to the Diplomatic Service.'

'How *dare* you,' Peter hissed. 'If you think trading insults will help you, you can think again.'

'I don't need to think again. Do what the fuck you like. You can read about why *you* are a disgrace to the Service in the English Sunday papers.' Having delivered his own bombshell Angus stood up and walked out of the room. He went back to his own office and sat down again. He felt that tightness in his chest again, opened his desk drawer and took out a bottle. He took a long swig and immediately felt a bit better. At least he had given that bastard Parker a thing or two to think about.

In that he was quite correct, Peter did not know whether his deputy's remarks had been just an idle threat, or whether Angus had some hard evidence. What was certain was that there were things that, if they became public, could seriously damage Peter's career. He set off for the airport in a far from happy mood.

The plane landed and Peter went out to the aircraft steps, accompanied by Andrew. The plane door opened, and the British Airways Manager went quickly up the steps and into the aircraft. A few minutes later there was a bustle of activity at the top of the steps and the Princess appeared accompanied by her son and a lady in waiting. She came slowly down the steps towards Peter.

'Welcome to Barbados Ma'am,' Peter said, stepping forward.

'Thank you,' said the Princess. 'You must be Peter Parker, the new High Commissioner. I don't believe we have met.'

'No Ma'am, I arrived last month.'

'Ah Andrew, take my coat please. You can give it back to me when I come back next month.'

'Yes, of course,' said Andrew stepping forward and taking the proffered coat. He had met her several times before, and the Princess had already singled him out as a useful and reliable official.

The group went to the VIP lounge where the Head of Protocol took the passports from the Princess and the small group accompanying her. He returned shortly afterwards having passed them through Passport Control. Within ten minutes they were in the High Commissioner's Jaguar speeding towards the Residence. Peter took the opportunity of explaining to the Princess about the Reception and expressing the hope that it would not inconvenience her. She reassured him and said that, although she was indeed tired after her journey, she would endeavour to make a short appearance, if it would help British trade.

'I am delighted to welcome you to Barbados,' Peter began, looking around at the small group of nine businessmen who made up the South Eastern Counties Export Club Trade Mission. 'I would like to say a few words about the political background to the country and the state of our bilateral relations, which I am happy to say are very good indeed.' Peter spoke for ten minutes before turning to Fred Forbes. 'I would now like to hand over to Fred Forbes, our Commercial Secretary, who will tell you about the local market.'

Fred gave a brief tour of all the main issues affecting the market and ended up by stressing the need for the visitors to seek local partners. Peter then took over again.

'Now Gentlemen,' he said. 'If you have any questions, we will do our best to answer them.'

'High Commissioner, I have a question.'

Peter looked at the speaker; he was an insurance salesman called Tom Foley. He was the Deputy Leader of the Mission. 'Yes? Please go ahead.'

'I understand that no arrangements have been made for us to call on the Prime Minister or even the Minister of Trade. Why is that?'

This was a question Peter had been dreading. He had decided that on no account would he take Stefan Teduscu to meet Ministers. If Stefan's activities became known, which in time they would, he did not want to have been responsible for having opened Ministerial doors to him. He had thought hard about what to say if the question were raised.

'A good point,' Peter replied. 'Normally we would hope to take the Mission Leader and his deputy on a ministerial call. Unfortunately, it was not possible on this occasion as they did not have time available in their diaries.'

'Bullshit,' said Angus McMullen loudly, Peter glared at him remembering how he had asked Angus to attend the briefing shortly after he had arrived.

'However, you will be pleased to know that we have invited three Ministers to the Reception tonight so, if their programmes allow it, you should meet them then.'

'They won't come,' said Angus.

Peter was furious and avoided looking at Angus, in case it made him lose his self- control. Above all he had to maintain his dignity. Instead he looked in the other direction, only to catch the eye of a smirking Stefan Teduscu, who was clearly enjoying Peter's discomfort.

'Well Gentlemen, if you will excuse me, I will now hand over to Fred to answer any more of your questions. I have to get back to the Residence to prepare for tonight.' Escape seemed to Peter as the only way out of a deteriorating situation.

'But you haven't given them a chance to ask *you* any questions,' said Angus.

By this time the visitors were beginning to get the message about the relationship between the High Commissioner and his deputy. Several were looking embarrassed, and one or two looked angry.

'I look forward to seeing you all tonight,' said Peter, getting up and leaving the room.

As he closed the door behind him, he heard Angus say, 'I bet he's looking forward to seeing you tonight,' followed by a round of nervous laughter from the assembled company.

Chapter 17

Peter went back to his office and sat down in one of the easy chairs. McMullen was being intolerable and there was absolutely nothing he could do about it. Once that he had told his deputy that he was having him sent home, there was no greater sanction left to use. Well, the consolation was that he would be rid of the man within a week or at most two. Then an awful thought struck him, what if London refused to recall McMullen? What if they preferred his deputy's version of events to his own? Then he remembered David Bloggs, he was going to recommend that McMullen should be sent home. At least they would be sure to listen to the Inspector. For the first time he felt grateful for David Blogg's presence in Barbados. There was a slight tap on the door. Peter wondered if it was Angus coming to apologise. Well if it was, he could think again, nothing would induce him to give the man an inch.

'Come in,' Peter called.

He was surprised to see Daniella and Anthony enter the room. What surprised him even more was that they were holding hands.

'Peter,' Anthony began. 'I hope you don't mind us butting in, but we have some news we would like to tell you.'

'Yes?'

'Daniella and I are going to be married.'

Peter was dumbstruck, as a thousand thoughts rushed around his head. Married? He did not even know that they had been out together. How did he feel about it? What could he say? She was his daughter, but then Suzana and Tom Briggs were her parents too. Where would they marry? He should offer the Residence for the Wedding Reception, but what about Mavis and, more to the point, Annabelle? When should he break the news to Daniella that he was her father?

'Aren't you going to congratulate us?' asked Anthony.

'Err, yes of course. Congratulations,' he managed to say, but he still felt lost for words. Finally, he pulled himself together. 'It's just that it's a bit of a surprise.'

'It's a surprise to us too,' chipped in Daniella.

'Really Anthony, you people never cease to amaze me,' Peter was now fully back to his diplomatic self. 'I get a new secretary and you steal her from me before she has been here five minutes.'

'Well you only have yourself to blame Peter,' responded Anthony, joining in with the High Commissioner's jocularity. 'You shouldn't have let London send you such a desirable secretary.'

'True, now if I was twenty years younger,' he suddenly realised the implications of what he had said. 'I mean… I…'

'I know exactly what you mean. Thank you, she is a fine catch for any man,' said Anthony, who fully recognised the reason for the High Commissioner's confusion and did his best to rescue him.

'I'm not sure if I like being referred to as a catch. It makes me sound like some sort of fish.'

The ice now broken, they all laughed.

'Where will you get married?' Peter asked.

'We had rather hoped to get married here in Barbados,' said Anthony.

'I spoke to my parents this morning and they are happy to come out,' added Daniella.

'You must use the Residence for the Reception, of course,' Peter at last decided to bite the bullet.

'That's very kind of you,' Daniella was genuinely delighted.

'Yes Peter, thank you very much,' added Anthony.

'Well that's settled then,' Peter found himself feeling rather pleased, he was going to host the wedding reception of his second daughter. If only they knew.

'There is something else we would like to talk to you about,' Daniella suddenly sounded serious.

'Go ahead.'

'If I might also explain,' Anthony said. 'That this is not something that concerns me directly. It is about you and Daniella, but as we are about to be married Daniella was very keen that I should be present. I hope you have no objection.'

Peter's heart missed a beat. 'I'm listening.'

'I'm not sure I know where to begin…' said Daniella.

'Daniella has discovered that you are her real father. She also knows that you are aware of it, but possibly only recently from Teduscu.' Anthony delivered his message with the precision of a surgeon telling his patient he only had a few weeks to live. Peter was stunned at hearing the truth spelt out so simply.

'Yes, it's true,' he said at last. He looked at Daniella. 'I'm truly sorry that you should have found out in this way. I hope you will come to forgive me. Although I did suspect that I had had a child with your mother, I did not know for certain until very recently. To find that you were my daughter was an even bigger shock.'

'Do you mind having another daughter,' asked Daniella.

Peter looked at her for a moment and she felt herself shiver deep down inside as he began to speak.

'I confess it was a very big shock to me, and I have thought hard about how it would affect Mavis and Annabelle. Mavis knows already, but I still have to break the news to Annabelle that she has a sister, and of course to the twins. All I can say, with total sincerity, is that I am happy to have discovered another daughter and I could not wish for a better one than you.'

Daniella and Peter looked directly at each other; a tear began to roll down her cheek. He held open his arms and she moved forward into them. They held each other only briefly before parting. It was not the fully-fledged hug of father and daughter, but it was a beginning. Peter felt his eyes watering too and brushed away a tear with the back of his hand.

'Well done, both of you,' said Anthony, deliberately breaking the spell to allow them both to regain their composure.

'I hope you will give your blessing to your daughter's marriage, Daddy dear,' Daniella asked, lightly.

'Yes indeed,' Peter replied, smiling broadly.

Nicu was prepared. Tonight, was the night. He had it all planned, provided Stefan Teduscu turned up at the Residence, as he most certainly would, Nicu would make sure he left horizontally. If things went well, Teduscu's death would look like a heart attack and Nicu would be able to stay with his niece for a little while longer. If things did not go well, he needed to be able to get off the island quickly. Nicu had made contingency plans. He booked a flight out at 9 o'clock and left his baggage at the airport. He had hired a car, paid up in advance, and agreed that it would be collected by the hire company, from the airport, the next day. The Reception started at seven, provided he left the Residence by eight he could still catch the flight out, if needs be. This meant he must implement his plan by half-past seven, at the latest, so he could see if it had been effective or was likely to raise suspicions. He experimented with some of the tablets to make sure they dissolved in whisky. He calculated the dose carefully, to achieve the optimum level of solubility without leaving an obvious residue. Stefan would probably need to drink at least half a glassful to be sure of it killing him. Nicu felt quite excited at the prospect of his evening's work, his only regret was that he may have to leave Daniella without saying goodbye.

Stefan was also preparing for the evening. He would need to speak to Nicu at the Reception and convince him that he had put in place another set of documents. If Nicu tried anything, he should know that his niece would be the one to suffer. One thing did continue to worry Stefan, however, could he trust Nicu to act rationally? What if Nicu's desire to dispose of him was greater than his wish to protect his niece? Nicu was ruthless and reckless, it was also possible that Nicu himself might be in danger if he did not carry out the instructions of his masters. Might it not be better to dispose of Nicu and eliminate the risk altogether? Killing Nicu would, of course, pose its own dangers so he preferred his first idea of protecting himself through the threat to Daniella. Nevertheless, he decided, it was now time to carry his gun and knife with him wherever he went.

Angus was lying on his bed; he really did not feel like going to the Reception. He had told Geoff Forrest that he would be there, and he knew that Geoff was his best chance of revenge. If Parker was going to have him sent home, then he would make sure that the High Commissioner followed not long afterwards. The pain in his chest had not gone away; at times it felt much worse, a sort of crushing tightness. Angus picked up the bottle of whisky off the side table and took a mouthful; it tasted metallic and he coughed. He took out his handkerchief and mopped his brow, which felt clammy and sticky. Maybe he was beginning to get flu or perhaps some local tropical illness. Tomorrow, he vowed, he would go and see the doctor, but tonight he had things to do. He got unsteadily off the bed, took another mouthful of whisky and went into the bathroom. He looked at himself in the mirror, his complexion looked grey and patchy. He suddenly felt sick and went over to the toilet and lifted the lid. He belched loudly and spat into the toilet. He felt the taste of whisky and stale tobacco in his mouth and spat again. He must try and pull himself together. Drawing on all his resources he washed his face and brushed his teeth. He dressed quickly, picked up the brown envelope, checked its contents and went out of the door. As the cool evening air hit him, he felt slightly better, but there was still the uncomfortable feeling of tightness in his chest. He got into his car, switched on the engine and set off towards the Residence.

Peter was back in the receiving line. It was only two days since he had hosted the reception for the Navy, but so much had happened since Monday that it seemed like weeks ago. He was pleased that he and Daniella had finally spoken. Since he had discovered the truth, he had found it difficult working with her, knowing that he was her father and he was living a lie. She also seemed to have been affected as she had become more formal and more distant. Once or twice he had caught her looking at him in a strange way. He had thought that it was his imagination, brought about by his feelings of guilt. Now it was all clear, Daniella had known the secret too and had known it ever since Stefan had first threatened him in the office.

Peter still had the problem of telling Annabelle. He had intended to do it before the reception, but Annabelle had stayed sulking in her room until the first guests had begun to arrive. She had been in a foul mood ever since Monday when she had fallen out with Andrew. Peter wanted to tell her that Andrew had been protecting him, but he did not want to admit to his daughter that he had been having an affair with a girl three or four years her junior. He knew he had to find a way to re-establish Andrew in her good books, but it would just have to wait until after the reception. There was also the problem of Stefan Teduscu, soon he would be rid of him, but he would need to decide whether to set the authorities on him once he had left Barbados.

Andrew appeared at his elbow, interrupting his thoughts.

'High Commissioner, may I introduce His Excellency Dr Rodney King the Minister of Foreign Trade.'

'Dr King, welcome,' Peter held out his hand, at least on this occasion he could greet a Minister without having Trixie draped about his neck.

'Good Evening High Commissioner, a nice place you have here. This is the first time I have had occasion to visit your splendid house. Your predecessor did invite me once or twice, but I was travelling and could not come.'

'Well I am delighted that you were able to make it this time and I very much hope that it will be the first of many occasions.'

There was a sudden bustling in the hall and Andrew leant forward and whispered in his ear, 'The Princess.'

'Ah yes,' Peter turned back to the Minister. 'Dr King, if you would excuse me for a moment, I think the Princess has arrived. If you would like to wait here with Mr Walker, I will go and escort her in and introduce you.'

'Delighted, 'said the Minister, puffing out his chest.

Peter went and greeted the Princess and escorted her into the reception room. He introduced her to Dr King and was gratified that she took the trouble to exchange a few words with him on how much she liked Barbados. This would be credit in the bank for Peter and he knew that he would be able to easily obtain the ear of the Minister for the next few months. Andrew was then delegated to take the Minister off to meet members of the Mission. Peter took the Princess over to David Bloggs in the hope that she might make one or two favourable remarks to him; anything that countered the Inspector's views about him, and his High Commission would be welcome. He had a momentary panic when he realised that David was talking to Angus, Angus was an unguided missile, and anything could happen with him around. He had already committed himself to the introduction and short of suddenly wheeling her away there was not much he could do.

Peter presented David Bloggs and the Princess then turned to Angus. 'Mr McMullen, I hope you are well.'

'Yes, thank you Ma'am,' Angus replied, sounding a little more in control than Peter had seen him in recent days.

'Perhaps you would get me a little glass of my usual.'

'Certainly Ma'am, I have instructed the butler to have it ready,' Angus bowed slightly and went off to get her drink.

'Mr McMullen and I are both connoisseurs of fine Scotch whisky,' said the Princess with unintentional irony.

Peter nodded and smiled weakly. Inside he was fuming. He was not surprised that the Princess knew Angus, she had transited Barbados on several occasions. What had annoyed him was the audacity of Angus in giving instructions to his staff and not alerting him to the fact that the Princess had a favourite drink. Such information could be vital in running a successful Mission.

Angus returned with the Princess' drink feeling very pleased with himself. He knew that Peter would be furious and that heightened his pleasure. The evening was going well, all he had to do now was find Geoff Forrest and hand him the copies of Mavis' diary. His revenge would then be complete. He grimaced as he handed the Princess her drink, perhaps it was the act of bending forward but the tightness in his chest returned suddenly. Tomorrow he would definitely go and see his doctor.

Nicu, with Daniella at his side, joined Stefan Teduscu who was talking to an official from the Barbados Central Bank.

'Stefan, congratulations on your trade mission, it seems to be a great success.'

'Thank you Nicu, it certainly seems to be going well so far.'

Both men knew that their words were only preliminary sparring, before each revealed their true agenda. The man from the Central Bank, sensing that this was something more than a meeting of two acquaintances at a cocktail party, excused himself to go and talk to the American

Ambassador. The two men stood next to each other like two wary cats, each ready to respond to the move of the other.

'I have something to say,' said Daniella breaking the silence. 'Why are you doing this to me and my family?'

'I have no intention of doing anything to you or your family.'

'Well, for a start you are blackmailing my father, the High Commissioner.'

'Blackmail? That is not a very nice word.'

Before Daniella could reply, Nicu stepped forward and took Stefan's glass. 'Your glass is empty, let me get you a drink while you and Daniella talk. What is it Whisky?'

'Whisky soda, no ice, please.'

'Daniella?'

'White wine please.'

Nicu went off towards the bar holding Stefan's empty glass. Although Stefan had allowed Nicu to take his glass, he already found the episode strange. There were plenty of waiters circulating with drinks and Nicu could easily have beckoned one over. Perhaps he wanted to leave Daniella alone with him to discuss her father, but that seemed odd. Nicu would have been more likely to be the protective uncle and stay with his niece. That is... unless...

'I am sorry if I have caused you a problem, Miss Briggs, said Stefan courteously. 'That was certainly not my intention.'

'What was your intention?'

'Shall we just say that in this hard world one has to protect oneself. There are people who want to damage my reputation by telling lies about my business activities. I needed your father's help to prove them wrong.'

'Who should want to do that?'

'Oh, many people. Competitors who are jealous of my success. Even those from the old Romania who cannot forgive me for making a new life in the West.'

'That is no excuse for hurting other people. My father never did anything to hurt you why should you want to hurt him.'

'I don't want to hurt him, young lady. I just needed his help.'

'If he believed that you were acting honestly then I'm sure he would have given that help willingly. You would not have needed to blackmail him.'

Nicu went to the bar and asked for a whisky soda, a glass of white wine and a beer. The waiter poured out the drinks, and handed them to him on a tray. On the left of the bar was a large tropical fern. Nicu glanced over to where Stefan and Daniella were standing. They were deep in conversation and Stefan had his back to him. Nicu moved swiftly behind the fern, took a small bottle out of his pocket, opened it and dropped a white tablet into the whisky soda. He waited until it dissolved, gently shaking and rotating the glass until no residue was visible. Satisfied he emerged from behind the fern and headed back towards Stefan and Daniella.

'White wine,' said Nicu handing Daniella the wine glass.

'Thank you.'

'And whisky soda for you Stefan, no ice.'

'Thanks,' Stefan took the glass and looked at it thoughtfully.

'Well, have you two resolved your differences?' asked Nicu, sounding uncharacteristically jovial. 'In my opinion there comes a time when compatriots abroad have to stick together. Stefan and I have had disagreements in the past, but I think it is time for us to put them behind us.'

'I quite agree,' said Stefan.

'I can't believe what I'm hearing. You men are all the same, one minute you want to kill each other and the next you are drinking buddies. Well I for one do not want to be part of your mutual admiration society.' Daniella turned sharply on her heel and walked off. It was time to find Anthony at least she could rely on him not to betray her.

'Women,' said Nicu turning to watch the figure of his departing niece.

Stefan acted quickly, whilst Nicu's attention was distracted, he collared a passing waiter and put the whisky on his tray.

'I've changed my mind. This is a whisky soda; I think I'll have a beer.' Stefan picked up the beer, and added, 'I haven't touched it.'

Nicu turned back just in time to see Stefan with the glass of beer and the waiter moving off with the whisky soda on his tray. He watched, horrified, as the waiter moved over to a small group of people clustered around the Princess. He recognised three of them, the High Commissioner, his deputy and the visiting Inspector.

Matilda was a large woman, both in stature and in heart. She had been the High Commission cook for thirteen years, and had served as a scullery maid for several years before that. The story goes that she was taken on by the first High Commissioner, when Barbados achieved independence. Matilda would never confirm or deny the story, suffice to say that she knew everything there was to know about the Residence and its past High Commissioners. Matilda had her own way of doing things, and had resisted the efforts of several ladies of the house to change her habits or her menus. Mavis had decided early on in their relationship to do what most of her predecessors had done, namely 'leave it to Matilda'. Matilda had not been well pleased when she was told that there were to be two major receptions within three days. This in addition to the visit of the Princess who normally required Matilda's unfettered attention. She complained loudly to the butler that this would not have happened under some of her previous High Commissioners. They would have made absolutely sure that such important events were properly planned. Her main problem was staff, one or two of her usual waitresses were unable to do both functions, so with reluctance she had to engage two extra young girls who were untried and untested. The girls, Virginia and Prudence turned up on time and were smartly turned out in little black dresses and white aprons. Matilda could only hope that they were up to the job.

So far, the evening was going well. Both the new girls seemed to be performing well, and with only minor prompting went to and from the kitchen bearing large trays, filled with food. Virginia appeared in the kitchen with an empty tray and Matilda set about filling it. In the centre she put a large bowl of her special spicy tomato sauce and surrounded it liberally with small English cocktail sausages. These were a favourite with the expatriate community, who always missed their sausage and bacon when they travelled abroad. Cheese was another scarcity on the island, so one section of the tray was reserved for little sticks, bearing cubes of cheddar cheese and pineapple. The rest of the tray was filled with spicy prawns and devilled chicken pieces, prepared to Matilda's own secret recipe. When the tray was full Matilda gently pushed Virginia through the door.

'Make sure you go first to the Princess,' she commanded. 'And make sure she has some of my devilled chicken pieces.'

Chapter 18

Nicu knew he had to do something. If Stefan were to drop dead of a heart attack nobody would make too great an effort to find out precisely what had happened. If the Princess, or even the High Commissioner, were to drop dead, it would be a different matter altogether. Nicu's chances of escaping would be very small indeed, and no jury would have any sympathy if he were to be charged with murder. His best chance was to reach the waiter before he reached the group round the Princess. If possible, he could retrieve the poisoned glass or, at the very least, relieve the waiter of the whole tray. Nicu launched himself after the waiter with every bit of energy he possessed.

Virginia was pleased with the way the evening had gone so far. This was her very first experience of a major diplomatic reception. She had helped out at some less elevated parties where the drink had flowed, and the customers' hands had strayed onto any pair of passing female buttocks that took their fancy. Virginia's shapely rump had been a frequent target but now, if tonight was a success, she could move up in the world. Matilda had even hinted that there may be a maid's job going at the High Commission in the next month or two, as one of the present maids had managed to get herself pregnant. If Virginia landed such a job, she would never make such a silly mistake, *she* would be much more careful. She had listened carefully to Matilda's instructions, and was now dedicated to the task of finding the Princess as quickly as possible and getting her to eat some of Matilda's devilled chicken pieces. If she was lucky the Princess would make a favourable comment and she would be able to report back to Matilda that the chicken had gone down a treat.

Perhaps if Virginia had not been so single-minded, and dedicated to her task, she would have seen Nicu, as he went to throw himself after the waiter. If Nicu had been in less of a panic, he might have been able to swerve in front or behind the girl. But the girl did not see Nicu, and Nicu did not swerve. Nicu collided with Virginia with considerable force. At almost the same moment Virginia saw, out of the corner of her eye, a large shape coming towards her. Virginia reacted immediately by lifting the tray higher, on her left hand, in just the way she had seen the drinks waiters do, when they move smoothly through a crowded room. This was not a good idea, as Nicu's body striking hers caused her arm to perform a graceful arc, projecting the tray like an old-fashioned catapult in a medieval movie.

The waiter had already arrived at the Princess' group, and four hands stretched out and changed their empty glasses for full ones. When faced with a new drink it is human nature to take a quick sip. This gives the drinker the assurance that their selection is correct, and there is also the extra enjoyment of the coolness and freshness of the new acquisition. It was at about the same moment that the new drinks reached four pairs of welcoming lips, that Virginia's tray and its contents arrived with the group. Tomato sauce, especially when it has been made to Matilda's special recipe, can be very tasty. When sprayed from a great height, however, it is rather less desirable. The bowl landed with a splat on the elegant bust of the Princess; the contents rained down in liberal proportions on her drinking companions. Sausages, shrimps and pieces of Matilda's devilled chicken, together with little pieces of cheese and pineapple on sticks, having initially achieved greater height than the sauce bowl, followed the red rain down.

Nicu still had some momentum left, but he achieved greater acceleration from the right-handed slap delivered to him by Virginia. The poor girl seeing her future destroyed in one cascade of canapés paid back the perpetrator of her misfortune in the only way she knew. Nicu did not really feel the blow, he was too busy trying to regain his balance before he landed firmly on the back of the drink's waiter, who was himself fully preoccupied with the task of trying to keep his tray free from the falling sausages and tomato sauce. The combined force of the drink's tray, the waiter and Nicu knocked down Peter, Angus and the Princess in one blow. All three made forlorn attempts to regain their balance, but by now the floor was so slippery with Matilda's tomato sauce that their efforts were to no avail. David Bloggs, initially the sole upright survivor of the group, took one more sip of his drink and slumped to the floor to join the others.

Nicu was the first to recover. This was partly because he had been on top of the pile and had escaped most of the blizzard of tomato sauce, sausages, prawn, devilled chicken pieces, cheese and pineapple on sticks, plus the broken glass contributed by the drink's waiter's tray of beverages. But, more to the point, it was Nicu who knew more about the genesis of the event and about his own personal part in it than anybody else. Nicu felt the need to make himself scarce. He stood up quickly and announced to the growing crowd that he was going to the bathroom to clean himself up. This did not seem a particularly strange proposal, as even he looked rather the worse for wear. Nicu quickly headed into the hallway and instead of going to the bathroom went straight out of the front door. Daniella, spotting her disappearing uncle, followed him and caught up with him just as he was entering his hire car.

'Uncle,' she cried. 'What is happening? Where are you going?'

'Danny, I have to go. You know nothing, understand. It is better that you know nothing,' and within seconds he was in the car, switching on the ignition and revving the engine.

'But...' Daniella tried to speak over the engaging engine.

'You know nothing Daniella, I'll be in touch,' and with those departing words the car shot off and disappeared through the Residence gates.

Daniella was unsure about what she knew nothing about, but she did know that her Mother's concerns about Uncle Nicu were beginning to look well-founded. She turned and went desolately back into the reception.

Not a lot had changed since she had left to follow her uncle. The number of onlookers had increased, intrigued by the carnage on view. The spectacle was made even more exciting since it included no lesser personages than the Princess and the High Commissioner himself. Some of the fallen had tried to get up, but immediately encountered difficulty with the slippery tomato sauce and the broken glass. Cuts appeared on hands and knees, and it was becoming difficult to distinguish between the original tomato sauce and the new little pools of blood.

Cool heads were beginning to take over; Annabelle, Mavis, Anthony and Andrew, well trained in handling the unexpected, all converged on the scene. Mavis issued brisk instructions to the wailing Virginia and to several waiters who had given up their duties to watch the entertainment. Andrew headed for the Princess and helped her to her feet, with great dignity she made her way up to her room, accompanied by one of the High Commission wives to begin the task of removing prawns and devilled chicken from her coiffure. The waiter managed to extract himself and went to the kitchen to clean himself up. Anthony helped Peter, who looked grim-faced but unhurt, to his feet. Annabelle was left to deal with the two prone bodies who had not yet risen on their own. She first went to David Bloggs and began to examine him.

'Get my medical bag, quickly. It's in the cupboard in my bedroom,' she ordered, seeing her sister Becky in the watching crowd. Becky did as she was bid running up the stairs two at a time.

'Oh my God,' Colonel Simon Perrigrew surveyed the scene for the first time. He had arrived late at the Reception. It had all been Felicity's fault, she had taken far too long to get ready and then had allowed their pet retriever puppy, Pixie, to get out just as they were about to leave the house. It had taken fifteen minutes to retrieve the dog, by which time Simon was swearing loudly and making remarks about why the bloody animal should be called a retriever, when the only retrieving it did was being retrieved itself. Felicity wasn't amused and told him that if he wanted to use military language, he could use it somewhere else. They had driven in silence to the Residence, with Simon showing his fury by excessive use of the accelerator and brakes. As they reached the Residence a car came hurtling out of the gates in the middle of the road. Simon swung hard on the steering wheel and simultaneously applied the brakes. His car swerved and skidded, scratching its side against the bushes and landing up parked inches away from the Residence gatepost.

'Be careful,' said Felicity. 'You could have killed us.'

'I... I... could have killed us.'

'You really must try and control your temper tantrums,' persisted his wife, little realising that she was in danger of pushing her husband to new depths.

'But that *fucking* idiot was in the middle of the road driving like a madman.'

'Don't swear, you know you were going too fast just because poor little Pixie got out. I shouldn't be surprised if he doesn't want to speak to you any more.'

'Nothing would give me greater pleasure than to never speak to your stupid dog again.' Simon had by now parked the car and had arrived on the sacred territory of the High Commission. He bit his lip and recovered his military decorum. 'Come on my dear, we are late. We had better go in.'

Felicity followed her husband marvelling, not for the first time, at his ability to revert to normal when his professional image was at stake.

Now Simon, still feeling hurt and hard done by, surveyed the wreckage in the High Commission reception room. He had not seen such carnage since his spells in the Falklands and in Northern Ireland. One thing was certain, the IRA had struck again, and it was up to the professional soldier to take command. He also needed to take action to catch the Irish terrorist who had driven straight at him when he arrived. It was now crystal clear that the terrorist, on seeing a military uniform, had deliberately tried to kill him.

'Quiet everyone, may I have your attention please. There is no need to panic, but there could be other explosive devices in the vicinity. I would like everyone to file calmly into the garden. I will then call the police and the bomb squad. Nobody is to leave; the police will want to take statements and we cannot rule out the terrorists still having accomplices among us. Alan…' continued the Colonel, spotting his Ministry of Defence (Naval Command) Clerk, Alan Withers. 'Alan get me the number of the bomb squad pronto.'

'It's alright Simon,' said Peter now on his feet. 'It was only a domestic incident. If everyone would give us a few minutes to clean up the mess the party can continue.'

'Call an ambulance immediately,' said Annabelle. 'Mr Bloggs may have suffered a heart attack.'

Anthony, having assisted the High Commissioner, was now kneeling down next to Angus. The Deputy High Commissioner was clutching an official brown envelope. Andrew glanced at the name on it and put it in his pocket. It did not take him long to assess Angus' condition.

'Annabelle, you'd better come and have a look at Angus here. Not that you can do much, he's dead.'

Stefan viewed the scene with mixed feelings. Apart from Nicu, he was probably the only person present who had any idea about what had happened. He had not been certain that Nicu had tampered with his drink, but it had seemed odd that his adversary had offered to fetch him one. Nicu could easily have summoned a passing waiter, but instead chose to go to the bar himself. Nicu's actions, after he discovered that Stefan had changed his drink, only confirmed his suspicions that the drink had been spiked. He now watched as Annabelle and Anthony examined the two fallen Foreign Office men. Whatever had been put in the drink must have been pretty potent to have killed the Deputy High Commissioner outright. What did puzzle him, was how one drink could knock out two people. Whatever the reason, he was grateful that he had passed the drink on. He felt no guilt that indirectly he was responsible for at least one death. After all life was a lottery, and you just had to make sure that you took precautions and that your chances of survival were better than the other fellow's. The next problem was what to do about Nicu. He had watched the Romanian make his escape. He had thought about following, but realised that he might bring suspicion on himself if he left the scene. He wondered whether there was any way that he might ensure that the authorities knew where to put the blame, but once again he decided that it was better to keep a low profile and pretend total ignorance. He had not been able to tell Nicu that his insurance policy was in place again, but even that seemed little protection against such a ruthless opponent. Nicu might even now be waiting in the bushes, outside the Residence, waiting for Stefan to appear and ready to put a bullet in his head. Stefan had strong nerves, but he did not like the feeling of constant danger. The only solution was positive action; he would find Nicu tonight and kill him first.

One of the strengths of Her Majesty's Diplomatic Service is the ability to handle a crisis and put some order back into the situation. And so it proved that night at the British High Commissioner's Residence. Peter and his team set about resolving the crisis; Peter even found five minutes to change his suit and shirt and to remove pieces of shrimp and devilled chicken from his hair. The ambulance took David Bloggs off to hospital accompanied by Annabelle and the Management Officer. The reception was moved out onto the terrace and overflowed into the garden under the supervision of Andrew and Fred Forbes, the Commercial Secretary. Mavis went up to see the Princess and to try to prevent calamitous fallout from London and the Palace. Anthony stayed to deal with the main outstanding problem, Angus' corpse. The Police had arrived, and an inspector began his investigation.

'Now Sir, perhaps you could tell me exactly what happened.' The inspector took out his notebook and, as he had seen on foreign movies, licked the tip of his pencil.

'It's a little difficult to be precise,' Anthony began. 'It seems that one of the guests pushed a young waitress. She was inexperienced and slipped, dropping her tray. The drinks waiter was also knocked into and collided with the High Commissioner and some of his guests.' Anthony decided not to mention the Princess, who would certainly not welcome requests by the Police to interview her.

'So, all that happened was that a couple of trays were dropped, and we are left with one, possibly two dead people,' the Inspector looked at Anthony sceptically.

'Well I can only tell you what happened. It seems likely that the temporary excitement of the incident caused two middle-aged gentlemen to suffer heart attacks.'

'One, yes I could certainly see that, but two. Are you really telling me that two people suffered heart attacks simultaneously?'

'Coincidences do happen. We do not of course know for certain, that they had heart attacks.'

'In my business coincidences are usually man-made. I have called for forensics to look at the body. He will of course have to stay here until enquiries are complete.'

'How long will that take?'

'No more than a day or two.'

'*A day or two*. That's out of the question. The High Commissioner is hosting an important reception. May I remind you that these are diplomatic premises and he,' Anthony waved at Angus. 'is a British diplomat.'

'Was,' corrected the Inspector.

'OK,' Anthony decided it was time to be conciliatory. 'I appreciate that you have a job to do, but we… that is the High Commissioner and the British Government would greatly appreciate it if we could move our Deputy High Commissioner into the study. He can then stay on the desk there until your forensic experts have had a look at him. I hope you will agree to the Deputy High Commissioner then being taken to the morgue.'

'Well it is a bit irregular; we do have to follow procedures.'

'Would you like me to go and ask the Chief of Police if it is alright? I believe he is in the garden talking to one of your Ministers.'

'Err… no… As this is a diplomatic residence, I will agree to your request on this one occasion.'

'Thank you very much,' said Anthony, wondering how many occasions in the future the inspector expected to find dead bodies in the British High Commissioner's Residence.

Anthony summoned a couple of members of the High Commission cricket team to help him move Angus to the study. It was no easy task as Angus was quite heavy and seemed to sag in the middle. Finally, with much effort and direction-giving the task was achieved and Angus was nicely laid out on Peter's desk with a clean white tablecloth over him.

Anthony was just about to thank the Inspector once again, and return to the Reception, when he was interrupted by a voice.

'Excuse me, I believe you have some of my property.'

Anthony turned to find Geoff Forrest striding towards him. The Inspector pricked up his ears at the promise of yet another serious crime.

'What is that?' asked Anthony.

'I saw you remove a brown envelope addressed to me from Angus' body.'

'Really, and what makes you think it was addressed to you?'

'Angus told me he was bringing it. Please hand it over.'

'I'm sorry,' said Anthony. 'I'm afraid any items in official envelopes are the property of Her Majesty's Government. We have no way of knowing whether it would in fact have been given to you.'

'But it is addressed to me. I really must insist.'

'Perhaps I could have a look at this envelope to ascertain its true owner,' suggested the Inspector helpfully.

'No, I am not permitted to release it on grounds of national security. If you would like me to ask the Chief Constable his view, I am happy to do so.'

'There is nothing I can do,' said the Inspector to Geoff, unwilling to test his superior's patience on behalf of a foreign journalist.

'I shall write to my MP,' hissed Geoff, and he turned on his heel and walked off towards the front door.

'Strange business this all round, I must say' commented the Inspector.

It had been an exhausting evening. The High Commission staff stayed on well after the guests had departed, partly out of shared grief, or perhaps more precisely shared disbelief, and partly out of loyalty to Peter and Mavis. The police, and their forensic team, had finally gone with a promise that they would be back the next day. They had finally conceded that Angus had probably died of natural causes; but had warned darkly that there would have to be a post-mortem. The Management Section were busy trying to contact Angus' next of kin through the Foreign Office. Everyone felt a bit ashamed at how little they knew about Angus' private life. According to the Diplomatic Service List, a shiny green volume that gives a potted biography of all serving officers, Angus had been married and divorced. He listed one son, who must now be in his twenties. Everyone was now trying to think of Angus' good points. It was true that he had smoked like a chimney and drunk like a fish and so thoroughly deserved his fate, but somewhere beneath the unattractive façade must have been the real man. A man who had once loved and been loved, a man who had ambitions before they were thwarted and turned to bitterness.

Daniella, whose acquaintanceship with Angus was rather shorter than that of the others, had no such benign feelings. However hard she tried, Daniella could only think of the sexual predator who had tried to attack her. She did her best to rid herself of the thought that she was glad that he was dead.

Annabelle was still at the hospital, but had telephoned to say that David Bloggs was weak, but out of danger. What had hit him had been a mystery as initial tests on his heart showed that it was basically strong. They were going to do more tests tomorrow, but suspected that he had been attacked by a mysterious virus, which was unlikely to be identified. Peter took Daniella and Anthony to one side and invited them to lunch the next day. It was time, he explained, for the whole family to talk things over. He was sure that the twins would relish having a new sister, but he was less sure about Annabelle.

Finally, at eleven o'clock they left the Residence, tired and emotionally drained.

'Can I stay with you tonight?' Daniella asked, as she and Anthony walked to his car.

'Of course,' he replied, giving her hand an almost imperceptible squeeze.

Chapter 19

Stefan opened the front door without difficulty. He was rather surprised that the High Commission did not provide their staff with better security locks. It was true that the crime rate in Barbados was relatively low, but burglary was certainly not unknown. Stefan was grateful for the High Commission's laxity; a more complicated lock might have resulted in damage, which might have alerted the occupants to the break-in. Stefan had a broad plan in mind, but he accepted that the plan had to be flexible enough to deal with the circumstances. As Nicu had left the party early, Stefan reasoned that he had probably gone back to Daniella's flat. Ideally Stefan would be able to deal with Nicu before Daniella returned. He had taken his gun and knife from their hiding place, in the boot of the mini-moke, and strapped them on his person. He had also equipped himself with a small bottle of chloroform and a soft cloth.

As he slid the front door open, everything was in darkness. It seemed probable that the flat was empty. Nevertheless, he painstakingly examined each room to make sure that nobody was in. He hoped that Nicu would return before the girl, as he had no stomach for hurting young women. Still whatever had to be done had to be done. He looked around for suitable hiding places and finally decided to position himself on a chair just behind the front door.

'Would you mind passing by my flat? I would like to pick up some clean clothes for the morning.'

'Fine,' replied Anthony. 'Will your Uncle be in?'

'No, he flew out earlier this evening. I think he had an urgent business call.'

Anthony looked at her quizzically. He thought back to the reception, Nicu had certainly been involved in the incident and it seemed unlikely that he could have suddenly been called away and been able to get a flight out. Daniella was looking straight ahead and half biting her lip. Anthony decided to let the matter pass, perhaps later he could press her for a little more information. 'Do you want me to come in with you? If so, I had better park the car inside the compound.'

'No, don't bother. You stay here in the car. I will only be a few minutes.'

'OK, but keep to your word, if you are more than five minutes I shall come up after you.'

'Don't worry,' said Daniella, bending over and kissing him on the lips.

Anthony lay back against the seat and waited. Her flat was on the first floor, and he glanced up as the light went on. Two minutes later it went off again, Daniella should be on her way down. But she did not appear, and the light stayed off. Anthony got out of the car and entered the block of flats. He went silently up the stairs, all the time expecting to meet her on the way down.

Stefan heard the car pull up and the front door of the block of flats open. He quickly took a soft cloth out of his pocket and put a few drops of the colourless viscous liquid on it. The footsteps coming up the stairs were certainly not Nicu's. He waited to see if the footsteps continued up the next flight of stairs, but they stopped, and he heard a key being put in the lock. The door opened and the flat was bathed in light as the new arrival switched on the light. Blinking slightly, Stefan moved quickly from behind the door, one arm went around her neck whilst he pressed the cloth against her mouth with the other hand. She gasped and struggled briefly as the irritating fumes hit her throat, quickly it was over, and she slumped on the floor. Stefan immediately turned off the light and pushed the door to. He stood waiting, silently, for more than a minute, listening for any sound. He was about to drag Daniella into the bedroom where he would be able to tie her up, when he heard something. Something very faint, but very clear. Someone else was coming up the stairs.

Anthony paused as he reached the door; a distinct pungent odour hit his nostrils. Something was wrong. He assessed the situation quickly. Every muscle in his body tense and prepared he gently pushed against the front door. It swung easily open about a foot. Looking through the gap, his body tensed with a mixture of suppressed energy and dread. There was no doubt that the body slumped on the floor was Daniella. He wanted to rush forward, to kneel down beside her and check for signs of life, but he knew that the perpetrator must still be there and that would be exactly what would be expected of him. He had no weapon and whoever it was, was almost certainly armed. He had to move quickly, and he had to check on Daniella's condition. He had to take a risk. With every ounce of strength in his body he flung himself at the door throwing it back on its hinges. The loud grunt, followed by something clattering to the ground, proved his supposition correct. Someone had been waiting for him behind the door. In an instant Anthony was inside, he saw the hand reach down to the ground for the fallen gun. Anthony stamped hard on the hand and had the pleasure of hearing bones crack before the sound was muted by the howl of pain. Anthony picked up the gun, and recovered his balance in time to side-step a flashing blade. He brought the gun down hard on the temple of his attacker who crashed to the ground. He closed the door of the flat. Holding the gun pointed in the direction of his fallen adversary he knelt down beside Daniella. He felt a surge of relief on finding that she was still breathing. Her pulse was a little slow, but still strong. He turned his attention back to Stefan who was beginning to stir.

'Mr Teduscu, I don't know what you are doing here, but let me warn you, I know exactly how to use this thing and I will have no compunction about doing so if you do not follow my instructions exactly.'

Stefan nodded his agreement. The counterattack he had suffered left him in no doubt that the man meant what he was saying.

'First of all, what did you do to Daniella? How much chloroform did you use?'

'Only a little, just enough to give me time to tie her up. She will be alright; you can take my word for that.' Daniella stirred slightly as if to confirm his contention.

'OK, what are you doing here? I advise you to tell me the truth, if I decide to kill you it will be accepted as self-defence.'

'Who the fuck do you think you are? 007 with a licence to kill?' Anthony did not reply but calmly kicked Stefan in the ribs.

'Now,' he repeated. 'Why are you here?'

'I came to get her uncle. You might not have noticed, but he tried to kill me this evening by putting something in my drink. Unfortunately for him someone else drank it, your Deputy High Commissioner or that chap from London. I don't know.'

'Nicu has already left the island, which is more than you are going to do. I imagine you will spend the next twenty years in prison here, if you live that long.'

'Look,' Stefan was beginning to plead. 'I meant the girl no harm and I had every right to protect myself.'

'You could have gone to the authorities. Anyway, I shall ring them in a moment and you will be able to explain everything to them yourself.'

'Call them by all means, but just remember that your girlfriend here is likely to suffer if I do tell my story.' Stefan flinched as he saw Anthony's foot twitch. He knew he must watch his language, or the boot would be used again.

'Explain.'

'First of all, there are papers in London that will go to the Press and the Foreign Office, if I don't collect them personally within the next ten days. The papers prove that the girl is the illegitimate daughter of the High Commissioner.'

'That is unlikely to be a problem. I think the High Commissioner is about to reveal that to the world himself.'

'Secondly,' continued Stefan. 'Everyone will know that her uncle is a member of one of Colombia's biggest drug syndicates. Not only is she fond of her uncle, but I doubt if her employers would appreciate her having harboured him in an official property. Furthermore, he will probably be sought for the murder of your Deputy High Commissioner, once I have told the police what I know. The press will have a field day.'

Anthony came to a quick decision. 'OK, this is what I am going to do. Tonight, you will go back to your hotel. You will speak to no one. Tomorrow you will take the first plane out of here. If you come back or cross our paths in any way, you can rest assured that you will pay a heavy price. Understood?'

'Yes, thank you. I think you have made a wise decision.'

'Don't bother to thank me. If I had my way you, and scum like you, would be locked away forever. Now stand up, keep your legs wide apart and put your hands behind your head. Stefan did as he was bid, facing away from Anthony.

'Now turn around to face me, keeping your hands behind your head and your legs wide apart.' Stefan was not prepared for Anthony's next move, but it was a memory that stayed with him for the rest of his life. Anthony raised his foot and with cool deliberation kicked him hard in the testicles. 'That,' said Anthony quietly. 'Is for what you did to Daniella.'

As soon as Stefan had left, looking pale and still rubbing his injured groin with his one uninjured hand, Anthony devoted his full attention to Daniella. He fed her small quantities of coffee and whisky and tucked her up in her bed. He then rang one of the High Commission panel doctors and persuaded him to pay a house call. By the time he arrived Daniella was sitting up in bed and breathing normally. The doctor examined her and pronounced her none the worse for her experience apart from a headache, which should go away with a good night's rest. Anthony thanked him and went to show him out.

'Have you reported the attack to the Police?' asked the doctor.

'Not yet, but I shall probably do so in the morning.'

'I think you should.'

'I will,' said Anthony.

'I would prefer that you did so tonight. We cannot have maniacs breaking into houses and chloroforming people. Daniella was lucky, but chloroform is a poison and can cause serious liver and kidney damage. I really ought to make a report myself.'

'I would prefer to leave it for the moment. What Daniella needs now is rest, I don't want her subjected to lots of questioning tonight, however well-intentioned.'

The doctor looked thoughtful. 'OK,' he said at last. 'But I have to say I'm not completely happy. I must trust you to do the right thing and report the matter to the police first thing in the morning.'

'Don't worry. I will. Thank you again doctor' and he ushered the doctor out closing the door behind him.

Anthony spent the night sitting beside Daniella's bed, periodically checking that she was all right and dozing briefly in-between. The next morning, she was fully recovered and her appetite outstripped Anthony's, as she feasted on the scrambled eggs and toast and marmalade, he had prepared for her. He gave her a sanitised version of his conversation with Stefan, preferring not to burden her with the claim that her uncle was a drug dealer and a murderer. Daniella was puzzled at why Anthony had allowed Stefan to go without calling the police, but she too felt that there were some things best left unsaid for the time being.

Peter's first task before going to the office was to visit David Bloggs in hospital. The Inspector was propped up in bed looking pale but contented, as a young nurse fussed over him.

'How are you?' Peter asked.

'Feeling much better thank you. The doctor thinks it is all right for me to fly back to London tomorrow as planned.'

'That's good… I mean it's good that you are well enough to travel.'

David Bloggs smiled. 'I know exactly what you mean.'

'Do they know what the problem was?'

'They are not quite sure. They are almost certain it was not a heart attack, that is not a normal attack. It might have been a virus or even a toxic substance that affected the functioning of the heart.'

'Toxic substance? Does that mean I have to sack the cook?' said Peter, only half joking.

'I don't think so. If it was the food at the reception more people would have probably been affected. There was Angus of course, but I gather his was a real heart attack.'

'That's the preliminary view, and given what we know about his drinking and smoking it's hardly surprising. But your case is even more worrying. If it was not the food how could a poison have got into your system?'

'I've been giving that some thought,' replied the Inspector. 'I had not eaten anything for several hours before the reception. One possibility could be that someone may have put something in my drink. I do remember only sipping a little from a new drink just before I collapsed, and I seem to have a nagging feeling that it tasted a bit odd.'

'But who could possibly want to harm you?'

'Lots of people in the Foreign Office have it in for the Inspectorate,' said David laughing. 'That gives us some 4000 suspects. We don't of course know that it was the drink, it may have been just a bug.'

'Are they doing any more tests?'

'They've done all they can here. I think they are going to send blood and urine samples to Miami, but they won't know the results for at least a week.'

'Have you finished your work here?'

'Yes, I think so. Although it's a terrible thing to say, in a way Angus' death has removed the main problem. But you should know that I'm going to have to say that Angus was not the only problem. There have been too many incidents since you took over, including last night. Now I'm not saying it's your fault only that your reign has been accident-prone.'

'I've been giving the matter some thought too.' Peter went on to explain to the Inspector what he had in mind.

'Well I must say that that would provide some sort of acceptable outcome. Oh, and one more thing, your daughter Annabelle was wonderful. She did all the right things and the doctors here think she may well have saved my life. I owe her a very deep debt of gratitude.'

Daniella and Anthony arrived at the Residence for lunch straight from the police station. Unfortunately, on hearing that they were from the British High Commission, the desk Sergeant called for the same Inspector who he had seen the previous evening.

'Ah Sir, we meet again. What can I do for you?'

'We would like to report an attempted burglary at the flat of Miss Briggs here,' said Anthony.

'And a physical attack on my person,' added Daniella.

The Inspector sighed. 'You had better come into my office,' he said. He listened in silence as Daniella described how she had returned to her flat after the reception and had been attacked by a stranger from behind.

'Did you see him?' asked the Inspector.

'No, he came behind me and stuffed a rag with chloroform on in my mouth. The next thing I knew was when Anthony here revived me.'

'And you Sir, did you see him?'

'Not really, I came up to the flat and he rushed past me before I could stop him. It was dark on the landing.'

The Inspector raised his eyebrows. 'I trust you called the police immediately? Funny, I don't remember seeing anything about it in the duty Sergeant's hand-over report.'

'No, well actually I thought it better to attend to Miss Briggs and report the matter in the morning.'

'*You thought it better to wait until the morning.* If you don't mind me saying Sir, I do find that a little odd.'

'Yes, with hindsight, I was probably wrong. It's just that I was so concerned for Miss Briggs, that I didn't think it through.'

'But didn't you seek medical attention for her?'

'Yes, our doctor was kind enough to visit and said that she would be all right.'

'Well Sir,' began the Inspector slowly. 'You no doubt have your reasons for acting as you did. I personally find the whole thing very strange, just as the incident at the High Commissioner's was strange. I must remind you that we do rely on the co-operation of members of the public in dealing with crime. I do hope that your High Commission is not involved in clandestine activities on another State's territory. I will now ask you to make full written statements. I should perhaps inform you that I will be submitting a full copy of my report to the Foreign Ministry.'

Daniella and Anthony spent the best part of an hour making detailed statements, waiting for them to be typed up and signing them. Finally, they were able to leave.

'You told them a rather different story from what actually happened,' said Daniella, as they walked to his car.

'As the Inspector observed, I had my reasons.'

Daniella said nothing, but she did wonder how much she really knew about the man she was going to marry.

Peter sat at the head of the large polished dining room table. An informal buffet of salads and fish was set out in the centre so that everyone could help themselves. Mavis sat at the other end of the table with Anthony on her right and Jack on her left. Jack's twin Becky sat next to him. Annabelle was on Peter's right next to Becky and Daniella on his left next to Anthony. Daniella was pleased to be seated next to Anthony at a meal that might yet prove to be an ordeal. She wondered if Peter had planned to have his three established children on his right and his newly discovered one with her boyfriend on his left. It was almost as if the two sides of the family were already set in opposition. Peter had informed Annabelle and the twins that they had a half-sister that morning at breakfast, so the news had had time to sink on. When Daniella had arrived, she was greeted by an ebullient Becky who was ecstatic about her new acquisition and lost no time in telling Daniella that she hoped that *she* would not prove to be as mean a sister as Annabelle. Jack regarded the news with bored indifference as he did with anything that was not full of computer chips. Annabelle was polite but cool. She did not exactly ignore Daniella; but did not make any attempt to draw her into the conversation.

Peter waited until the group had been served coffee before tapping his spoon against his wine glass.

'Could I have everyone's attention please,' he began.

'I hope you are not about to embark on a diplomatic speech Daddy. We all know why we are here, and we all know the score' cut in Annabelle.

'That will do Annabelle,' said Mavis sharply. 'Please listen in silence to what your father has to say.'

'*Very democratic,* I must say.'

'Please Annabelle,' Peter looked at his daughter, pleading with her to co-operate.

Annabelle shrugged, but said nothing more, leaving Peter to continue.

'You all now know that Daniella is my daughter from a relationship I had just before I met your mother. I am truly sorry that it has taken so long for me to acknowledge this, but I hope you will believe me when I say I was not totally aware of the situation myself.'

'We do believe you Daddy,' said Becky helpfully.

Annabelle opened her mouth to speak, then thought better about it and shut it again.

'I hope that all of you will be grown up about the situation. I am not expecting you to fall into each other's arms but do, at least, be friendly to each other and try, in time, to get to know each other.'

'We will,' said Becky, ignoring a hostile glare from Annabelle.

'Now for the second piece of news,' all eyes were suddenly on him as Peter continued. 'Your mother… that is Mavis and I have…'

'*My* Mother,' said Annabelle pointedly.

'We have decided that I will take early retirement from the Foreign Office and return to the UK. I envisage that this will take about six months to allow Angus' replacement to settle in and a new High Commissioner to be appointed. We are taking this decision partly in view of the various incidents that have occurred since my appointment, but also because we feel it the right thing to do both for the Foreign Office and ourselves.'

'You are throwing away your career because of this… this.'

'No Annabelle,' Peter turned to his daughter and spoke with unaccustomed sharpness. 'We are not throwing anything away. We have decided to take early retirement and that is the end of the matter.'

Chapter 20

London: 3 months later

'How did the exams go?'

'Pretty well considering. Anyway, I'm sure I've qualified.'

'That's good. It's been a pretty hectic time for all of us. By the way Anthony got his promotion. It looks as if we are off to Washington after the wedding.'

'That's great. I'm really pleased for both of you,' said Annabelle. 'It's really quite nice all being a family now.'

Daniella picked up her fork and dug it into a large succulent prawn. 'I'm glad you and I finally became friends. Being an only child, I always missed having brothers or sisters.' She put the prawn into her mouth and chewed it contentedly.

'Well I've only got the horrible twins, or should I say the horrible little Becky and the incommunicable Jack.'

'Oh, they're not that bad. Becky is quite sweet really.'

'Maybe if you don't have to live with her. No, what I really mean is it is nice to have someone you can have a proper conversation with.'

'Funny really how we met at the airport and fell out straight away.'

Annabelle grimaced. 'It wasn't so funny at the time. I'd had a terrible time getting to the airport, the cabby ripped me off and then I got stuck in the automatic door and, to cap it all, this snooty dark-haired girl prances through and travels out on business class.'

'Careful, less of the snooty,' said Daniella, laughing.

'Well *you were*. And then there was Andrew, I saw from the beginning you were after him.'

'Well, you got him.'

'Maybe; but not for long.'

'Have you heard how he is doing?'

'Yes, Daddy says that he's hoping his Japanese girlfriend will come back from Tokyo.'

'Ah well,' said Daniella. 'Win some, lose some.'

'Oh, I minded a bit at the time, but I don't think he was really my type. Bit too much the up and coming young diplomat, couldn't get him to relax.'

'Yes, I know what you mean. Are you seeing anyone at the moment?'

Annabelle leant forward conspiratorially. 'Actually, yes. But don't tell Daddy, he probably wouldn't approve.'

'Who? Come on, tell.'

'David Bloggs.'

'*David Bloggs?* You mean the insp...'

'Yes, one and the same. He rang me up a couple of weeks after I got back to medical school. Invited me to dinner, said he wanted to thank me for saving his life. Well I couldn't really refuse, could I?'

'And how was it?'

'Fun, we've been seeing each other ever since.'

'I hope you're not going to upstage my wedding by getting married first.'

'No,' Annabelle laughed. 'We're not like you and Anthony, all starry-eyed and in love on your first date.'

'Pig, now I know what Becky meant when she said you were mean.'

'Well you deserve it. Seriously though I did want to ask you if you would mind me bringing him to the wedding.'

'Of course. We'd love him to come. I'll send an invitation for you to give him.'

'Thanks Daniella, I really appreciate it. I expect I will have to let Daddy know in advance, otherwise it might be too much of a shock.'

'But he did like David, didn't he?'

'Yes, I think so, but he might think he is a bit old for me.' The sisters looked at each other, as the same thought struck them. 'Then again, he didn't mind you and Anthony so he shouldn't mind me and David.'

'He might see it a little differently with you,' said Daniella, a little sorrowfully.

'I don't think so. Come on let's have some dessert. They do the most scrumptious tiramisu here.'

'Yes,' said Daniella, brightening. 'I'll go for that, and one of their coffees with cognac and cream.'

Barbados

'Thank you, Andrew, for all your support. I've appreciated it and it's good of you to take the trouble to see us off.' Peter held out is hand for Andrew to shake.

'It's a pleasure High Commissioner. I have enjoyed working with you. I just wish that circumstances had been different and that we could have worked together for longer.'

'Me too, but it was not to be.'

'Bye Andy we'll miss you,' Becky jumped forward and, standing on tiptoe, kissed him on the cheek.

'I'll miss you too Becky, life just won't be the same without you.'

'Oh,' squealed Becky, 'You don't really mean that. You always said I was a ton of trouble.'

'Exactly. Life will just not be the same.'

'Now you're being rotten. I'm not sure I like you anymore.'

'Don't be stupid Becks,' said Jack. 'Can't you see he is winding you up?' Jack held out his hand to Andrew. 'Take no notice of her Andrew, thanks for everything.'

'And from me too,' said Mavis, kissing him on both cheeks. 'You've been a brick.'

'Give my love to Daniella, I hope the wedding goes well; and to Annabelle too.'

Peter and his family waved goodbye as they walked through the barrier.

Andrew walked slowly back to his car, he felt slightly despondent at the departure of the Parker family; he had grown quite fond of them. A thought struck him as he remembered the letter, he had received the previous week. His mood brightened and he quickened his pace. The letter had been from Meriko, she might, it was not yet definite, but there was a very strong chance that she would return to Barbados sometime in the next few weeks.

The following day Andrew was back at the airport, this time he was not alone. He was accompanying the new Deputy High Commissioner, Janice West, and the Defence Attaché, Simon Perrigrew to meet the new High Commissioner. Simon was very quiet having found that the new Deputy High Commissioner was no pushover and cut him short as soon as he started developing one of his misunderstandings. They watched through the window of the VIP lounge as the British Airways jet taxied to a stop.

Following a nod from the Chief of Protocol, the small group walked out onto the tarmac and positioned themselves at the bottom of the steps. Huw Davy the new High Commissioner was first down the steps followed by his wife. Andrew looked up to the open door of the aircraft and watched as a slim girl with short-cropped blond hair emerged and came down the steps. Her skirt was billowing in the fresh breeze and Andrew looked away quickly. One glimpse of her legs was sufficient to let him know that this meant trouble.

Huw Davy introduced his wife to his staff and then, turning towards the blond girl, said 'And this is my daughter Erica.'

Erica looked Andrew up and down and held out her hand. 'Nice to meet you Andrew,' she said.

Caracas: Venezuela

Stefan leant back in his chair, and took a long drink of his beer. It was refreshingly cool. Sitting out in the sun in pavement cafés had become one of Stefan's favourite pastimes. The experience was made more pleasant by the constant stream of dark-haired girls in short skirts who passed by, usually in pairs, chattering and soaking up the sun. Life was good. Stefan had succeeded in transferring all his funds out of the Caribbean banks and had set up new accounts in Brazil and Argentina. Soon he would move to Buenos Aires and begin life afresh, far away from the people who would still like to see him dead. He would then be able to bring Rodica and the children over from England and repay them for all the hardship they had endured on his behalf. He caught the eye of a girl sitting at a nearby table and smiled. She smiled back. Perhaps he might take her response as an invitation; perhaps he would go over and join her.

Nicu looked through the sight of the high-powered rifle. He was savouring the moment, something he had been waiting to do for months. Like a cat playing with its victim he moved the cross wires of the sight onto Stefan's head, almost squeezed the trigger, and then moved it onto the heart. His finger pulsed on the trigger enjoying the pleasure of almost completing the action, maybe he should shoot off Stefan's testicles first. He moved the rifle down, re-focussed, smiled and then moved it back to the head. The game was almost reaching its end. Suddenly Stefan stood up and went to go to a neighbouring table. Cursing, Nicu focussed quickly and pressed the trigger.

Acknowledgements

With warm thanks to my five children for their practical help and unstinted support.

About the Author

George Edmonds-Brown retired at 60 from the Foreign & Commonwealth Office, having served for 38 years as a British Diplomat in nine countries. He worked for the Canada-UK Council organising high level international conferences for 16 years and for Parish Councils in Oxfordshire for 12 years. Now, at the relatively tender age of 80, he is working on his fourth career as a writer.

He has five children, two of whom are Anglo-Japanese, which has sparked his interest in Japan. He lives in Oxfordshire with his wife, Teiko.

In December 2019, his first book 'Diplomats, Spies and Assassins' was published' This is now being followed by his first novel 'Oh Dear Me'. Both books reflect his life travelling around the world in the Foreign Office. Both books develop rapidly from the factual environment of life in British Missions overseas into a fictional world of espionage, crime and treachery, laced with a dash of humour, romance and emotion.

Born and educated in Newcastle upon Tyne, he still values his Geordie roots. By no means a football fan, he still has to suffer, along with other Geordies, when Newcastle United are on the pitch. Apart from writing, his interests include politics, cricket, art, table tennis and healthy eating.

Available worldwide from

Amazon and all good bookstores

―――――――――

www.mtp.agency

www.facebook.com/mtp.agency

@mtp_agency

www.ingramcontent.com/pod-product-compliance
Lightning Source LLC
LaVergne TN
LVHW041633060526
838200LV00040B/1560